Indra Bahadur Rai (1927-2018), one of the most acclaimed writers in the Nepali language, was the author of thirteen books—apart from the novel *Aaja Ramita Chha*—spanning the genres of short fiction, memoir, literary criticism and drama. He is credited with bringing fresh modernist aesthetics, as theory and in practice, to Nepali literature, and also played a major role in having the Nepali language officially recognized by the Indian Constitution. He was the recipient of the Sahitya Akademi Award, the Jagadamba Shree Puraskar and the Agam Singh Giri Smriti Puraskar.

Manjushree Thapa is the author of three novels: *All of Us in Our Own Lives*, *Seasons of Flight* and *The Tutor of History*; a collection of short stories: *Tilled Earth*; and four books of non-fiction: *The Lives We Have Lost: Essays and Opinions on Nepal*, *Forget Kathmandu: An Elegy for Democracy*, *A Boy from Siklis: The Life and Times of Chandra Gurung and Mustang Bhot in Fragments*. She has also compiled and translated *The Country Is Yours*, a collection of stories and poems by forty-nine Nepali writers.

There's a Carnival Today

Indra Bahadur Rai

Translated from the Nepali by

MANJUSHREE THAPA

SPEAKING
TIGER

Speaking Tiger Books LLP.

125/A, Ground Floor, Shahpur Jat,
Near Siri Fort
New Delhi 110049

First published by Speaking Tiger in paperback 2017

Translated with the support of the Banff International Literary Translation Centre at The Banff Centre, Alberta, Canada, and a PEN/Heim Translation Fund Grant from PEN America.

ISBN: 978-93-86702-31-9
eISBN: 978-93-86702-32-6

10 9 8 7 6 5 4 3

Typeset in Arno Pro by SŪRYA, New Delhi
Printed at Sapra Brothers, Noida

IN THIS NOVEL

Writing a novel requires a pen and paper, and it requires some knowledge of life. Knowledge of life consists of three measures of experience and one measure of imagination. As age and experience teach us about life, our view of life and the land starts to form. It is this view that spurs the writing of novels. If a single story about similar characters is written from five different perspectives, what results are five different novels; but if written from a single perspective, a hundred volumes merely amount to different aspects of one novel. What I think of life due to my experience differs from what others think of it. Therefore not everyone has an identical, uniform perspective on how to write a novel. Through our experience and our contemplation of it, or what is in brief called consciousness, each writer must gradually discover a perspective of his own and bring it to the fore. A literary effort that lacks consciousness is but a pretence, an act.

I saw that life was moving forward, but not in an organized manner, with everything falling into place. I've disarranged this novel in a similar way. I didn't see life as a singularity, or as the chemical purity and unhindered progress of a single subjectivity. Love is the mother of all emotions: Touch it, and all of our other emotions awaken and writhe. Yet even someone pursuing love undertakes many other tasks along the way, which are just as important for understanding life. If that's how it is in life, it shouldn't be otherwise in literature. It is said that a novel ought not to contain unnecessary characters, but this novel contains such characters, though they serve no purpose in the story, because the world I've seen doesn't contain only necessary people. If someone lives near us for all of our lives and has no impact on us, that is also a story: It is a fascinating story of what didn't happen. Literature mimics life and the land; yet such is the philosophy found in refined books about mimicry. There's a rage against that philosophy in this novel. A realistic mimicry of life and the land can consist of no foolishness or crudeness. There is no literature greater than reality. Simply living for three hours contains far more literature than spending three hours plunged into the world's highest artifice. There is no literature greater than existence. A novel about love can contain a story about the absence of love. The threads of a story can be every bit as indiscernible as the future.

It took me many months to create my main characters—Janak, Bhudev, MK, Ravi. To make Janak, I calculated the greatest common denominator of the good and bad qualities of many people I know. I had to fuse together three people to create MK. I met "Khagprasad" on a winter's day in 1954, at a Chainpure tailor's shop in Damak bazaar, beyond Jhapa. He had come to get a bag repaired before returning to Dhankuta that day, and I'd lost all my clothes on the trip, and had come in to have a shirt sewn. We were both in a hurry, but the tailor was toothless and his machine old: When he sped it up, the machine's needle would race ahead without placing a stitch. We were forced to wait around all day, chatting. A writer must know more about his characters than what he writes; only then can he write convincingly, even when using few words.

And another thing: it seems to be possible to write only about people you like.

Darjeeling INDRA BAHADUR RAI

18 February 1958

There's a Carnival Today

Gleaming black from the rains, the Cart Road knocks against many cliffs, bluffs and sloping hills, joining Lebong, that flat patch of land in the north, to dusty, clangourous Silgadi bazaar. Cart Road. This artery that makes life flow through the mountain districts. Landslides tug at it for four months in the monsoon; its mud top tumbles and it is buried; ancient sal trees lay their bodies across the road in an act of civil disobedience. The mountain-dwellers then set out to fulfill their duty, securing the walls, clearing the soil, hacking off the male pride of the trees. Countless ox-carts, train trolleys, Jeeps, buses, cars and trucks are this road's daily passengers. A train vanishes at each turn in the forested density of Sukna, playing hide-and-seek, like an unsightly lover, with a Jeep. The Jeep leaves it behind and speeds on, as though it were the truth of the world. When, trailing behind at a feeble pace, and pausing, the train climbs the Bataase hill and can't see "him", she emits a deep, smoky exhalation, shrieks, soaks the ground with hot tears. It must be masculine pity that compels the Jeep—which, like a bumblebee, goes anywhere—to love the train, a woman who must follow a fixed route. When, at some point, the two are able to meet as in the aligning of two planets, a truck transporting loads of coal, potatoes, tin and cigarettes views them with a split personality—one eye blazing red with desire, the other soulless with fear.

With a honk of warning, the truck descends from the road carved into the chest of Giddhe Pahara. Seen from above, the truck looks like a burgeoning emotive life-force as it speeds single-mindedly through the endless, lonely turns below Kharsang. During the monsoon months of Asar and Saun, the fogs eradicate the division between night and day from Panchan to Ghoom, evoking the earth's ancient past. The driver must wipe away the trickles of moisture that form on the window, and ascend each slope with supreme patience. The truck is the labourer of society; it is half of its driver's soul. For its owner, it is a small factory that earns him a living. The truck has no home, nor has it a place to rest and close its eyes. It spends the night on the roadside, occasionally sheltering in someone's courtyard. A single tent guards its life on a dark, terrifying night of slanting rain. Tomorrow, once again, it must sustain society and civilization by transporting a one-ton load one hundred kilometres away. Each paisa multiplies tenfold every time each of the truck's four wheels turn, touching the ground. It is a slave bought for ten thousand.

The red truck approaching Kagjhoda, No. 3761, is Janak's.

"If you don't sell it, it'll provide for you," Janak's father had told him. The old man had just bought a car that year, an Austin of an old model that seated four people. The car used to ply between the bazaar and Ghoom.

The old man had a teashop near the train station. Janak's mother would sit in that shop with potatoes, boiled soybeans, beaten rice, sweet puffed-rice balls, buns and paan. Drivers would come there at nighttime to drink. They played cards. The old man would collect money to keep the lights on.

Massive brawls would erupt from time to time; the drivers would end up in blows—some would go to the hospital with cracked heads, or to the police station for doing the cracking. "My house isn't for hooking in gamblers, no more cards from today!" the old man would fume. The card games would resume gradually, four or five days later. The old woman held on tightly to money. Other than the flat gold jewellery on her ears, the old couple made no display of their wealth.

When Janak passed the matriculation exam, many people offered to help enlist him as a constable in the police department, but the old man shook his head in refusal. The British bank manager had raised the hope of finding work right here—he'd already told him, in broken Hindi, "We see, achha!" Dressed in a red felt cap and a white shirt done all the way up with hooked buttons, the old man would boast, "It's because of what the Sahib said that Janak is studying in Calcutta."

Janak received news of his father's death in Calcutta, in his second year of studying banking. The colleges had been closed, since the day before, to celebrate CV Raman's Nobel Prize victory. Janak put off a plan to visit Dandi, the site of Gandhi's Salt March, and returned to Darjeeling to support his grieving mother. Her composed bearing and serene countenance took him aback.

The Ghewa-Sange mourning rituals took place. After everyone, including the lamas, had left, Janak's mother called him over and said, "How many more months of study do you have? Even as he died, your father told me to educate you, he said: Make that one pass, do so for certain… So go, go and pass quickly, and come back. There's so much work to do after that…"

Upon saying this, his mother wept that night, when no one else was at home.

Janak couldn't even recognize his mother when he returned home eight months later. Thin, sickly, elderly. What had happened to her girth? It alarmed Janak. But there was the same serenity on her face. She sat at her accustomed spot in the teashop till Sita arrived.

Now, after accounting for every last paisa at the bank, Janak would come home exhausted at seven or eight in the evening, yet he would still tell his mother about the commotion and uproar taking place outside.

Draped in a chequered red Highlander shawl, his mother would say, "How could the British ever quit a Raj so grand? That's just people talking. Would they really quit a Raj that they made their own through so much warfare, intelligence and effort, just because people demand it? The British made all these cities, roads, buildings; how could they just stop caring and leave?"

Displaying great tenderness towards his mother, Janak would try to explain. "Our country is our home. You tell me, Aama, what would you do if a thief were to enter our home?"

"Me? What would I do? You're the one who wouldn't beat him up and chase him away: what could I do?"

"No, you mustn't beat anyone, Aama. Non-violence…" Janak would tell his mother about Gandhi. "You must have faith in humanity and love everyone, even a foe, understand, Aama? You must lovingly conduct a satyagraha and make him realize his mistake. Do you know, Aama, that demands grounded in the truth have the power to bring about a complete transformation in the heart of a guilty man? And even if by chance he becomes harsher or more oppressive or cruel, we must observe the vow of civil disobedience, and not be enraged or seek revenge. Do you understand now, Aama?"

"I don't understand. I don't understand a thing."

One day, fifteen or sixteen summers later, after a huge struggle, India became independent. Its liberated moments began ticking away from midnight onwards, when half the world was hushed and asleep. Millions of joyful banners were going to flutter from each house all over India the following day.

"Janak, is our country really free, then?"

"That's what they say." Janak had changed.

"Thank the Lord! My life has proven meaningful," his mother said.

From the names and dates scrawled on the novels and other books that Janak was reading at the time, it can be discerned that he saw Sita on his final return to Darjeeling.

No one can be found to expound on the subject of the introduction, progress and love between the two, and one mustn't write an entire story concocted from the imagination. What this demonstrates clearly is how closely Janak and Sita—the "father and daughter" of the *Ramayana*—guarded the secret of their "sinful" love, the precious truth that only they knew. Janak's confidant Sumshere knew only this much: Sita had come here from Nepal to study. She was probably a Pradhan by caste. Because on Sundays she came shopping with a Pradhan family who lived in Haridas Hatta below the court.

One day, when their novelistic love-drama had passed the halfway chapter, Janak read Sumshere a passage from a short letter that Sita had sent him: "Your soul is a thousand times more precious to me than my own."

To Janak this single passage seemed to contain all of the world's literature and devotion.

"One thing," Sumshere said excitably to Janak that day. "Have you noticed? The second toes on both of Sita's feet are long. This alone makes her seem to be of good birth!"

Pathetic Janak must have had nothing better to do than to blab about this to Sita. From the next day onwards, whenever Sita and Sumshere crossed paths, she glared at him like a black serpent.

Some people from Sita's home arrived with porters and took her back for the winter holiday. Like others in that situation, Janak spent all night writing Sita an especially literary "letter of solace". Without so much as changing out of his dirty shirt, he folded up his handiwork to hide most of it and showed Sumshere a relevant passage:

isn't either. To be locked in embrace
staring at each other's face isn't love, Sita.
To face in the same direction while standing apart
and keeping the same goal, that's love. Today my

Janak sent off the letter after placing it in a blue envelope (one with a picture of a flying bird with a letter in its beak).

Sita began to live in Janak's house from that winter on.

It was only twenty or so days after Gandhi's re-arrest. From the mouths of all the wedding guests emerged debate and disagreement about the banning of the Congress. News of the arrest of four members of the Nepali Congress in Kharsang had spread even more sensationally through the bazaar.

Janak quit his bank job and his monthly salary of

Rs 173 on the same month that Mussolini's Fascists invaded Greece. Not because he heard the call of human rights, or because he felt a grave responsibility towards his nation or his peoples, but to do business. First the Tommies, then the Yankees, came and danced all night, and also threw up, in the dining room of his hotel, Beechwood. The Goans played jazz; Gurkha "Johnnies" fed them chowmein and millet beer. Janak's tables and chairs splintered many a time. Plates would go sailing out of the window, yet the bond and trust between Janak and the bank only grew. Friends who had invested in the bank were dazzled by bright visions.

In the week that Hyderabad joined the Indian union, Janak began to run a government ration-control shop. His behaviour towards everyone was friendly. He didn't grease up anyone, nor did he spit on anyone. Equanimity was his supreme policy. In the dark of the night, sack upon sack of high-quality rice would disappear. People would consider themselves lucky if they could buy sugar, wheat flour, flour, kerosene, matches, soap easily, at double or triple price. During this spell of shortages, many families were safe islands in an ocean of rationing. Janak's was as well.

The three or four years between the Second World War and India's Independence swept Janak along, as if on ocean currents and waves, to the meeting points of different situations, different nations and eras. Though it was no longer possible to keep advancing in the same way, he tried to remain in commensurate circumstances.

A lot of time had passed since his father's death—a lot of water had flown under the bridge. Among the Nepalis of Darjeeling, Janak was respected for many reasons, including for having transformed his father's Austin into a truck. If it were true that only those Nepalis known to and respected by the local Marwaris and Bengalis were human, and the rest were rubbish, then the name Mr Janakman Yonzon would appear at the very top rank.

If it were true that all voting citizens and their sons and daughters were human, then, in the recent election, Janak's name came out at roll number 4897 at an address in a bazaar ward, where he, Sita, and their son Ravi and daughter Divya lived as a family in three rented rooms. There was also a boy, Birman, to do the housework.

On clear evenings, Sita would go to stroll through Mall Road, taking along her neighbour Babuni for company. She once saw an Anglo-Indian woman with a ponytail and easy, loose-fitting knee-length pants photographing a Sherpa child, who was carrying her brothers and sisters against the backdrop of a fiery sunset. Sita only wore saris made of cotton or voile. Extremely fair, with a round face, she would comb her hair tidily in the Ilam style, and place blood-red vermilion powder in the parting; this gave her an allure that perhaps no make-up could. The vermilion powder was from her wedding. It was the vermilion powder that had been placed in the parting on her bowed head at the wedding with the approval of all members of society.

Sita always looked at the statue of the poet Bhanubhakta erected on the expanse of Chowrasta. She lingered, looking at the children of all caste and kind swinging on the metal chains which surrounded the statue. Released from thirty or more years spent bent over an office desk, old men warmed their frail bodies in the sun, talking about sin and dharma, the British and the Congress, and revealing the history and past glory of Darjeeling. Sita would tell Janak about all of this at night.

A little ways down the way from Chowrasta was a large picture studio. Its shop windows were decorated with many beautiful images. In one window hung a huge photo of a man's face in a fake leather frame. Fine, coiffed hair, full lips. A slanting scar on the forehead, with smudges on the photo betraying a subtle attempt to erase it. That square face, those eyebrows displaying a clear resolve, and those exceptionally attractive eyes—these were a prize, a gift, that Janak had also received. Nowadays there were black-and-red pouches under Janak's eyes.

We can see a copy of this very photo in the outer room of Janak's home. Four other copies of it are at the following locations:

1. At the house of Daniel S. Pradhan at 31-A, Wellesley Road, Calcutta. In the guest room. The photo graces a pale blue wall.
2. In Gairigaun, Dhankuta bazaar, in a house visible from as far away as Lamidanda, which till recently used to be the only flint-roofed house there, the house of Janak's in-law, His Royalest Highness Dharmaprasad Shrestha. It is not possible to say how it's displayed there. It may well be stashed away in a chest for fear of smoke.
3. Right in Gangtok bazaar, in the house of Da' Namgyal, with whose help Janak is trying to procure some

contracting work in Sikkim. It was he who repaired the road to Lacha Lachung and further beyond, to Rangang River, last year.

4. Placed second from the right in a row of three or four photos in Janak's party office.

This photo reached Dhankuta on the very year of the wedding. Janak, Sita and their relatives from this side travelled to Nepal with Janak's brother-in-law and other people who had come over from there. Dharmaprasad came down to Rangeli bazaar to stay with the family at his farmhouse. A simple exchange of teekas took place. Relatives from the maternal line in Madhumalla, a day's walk away, didn't even bother to come to offer their blessings.

Janak and his relatives, who were Indian, were thrilled to be stepping on Nepali soil for the first time. Brimming with the anticipation of the folksong—"What has the mailman brought over the hills of Dhankuta?"—the hills seemed to vanish into the clouds high up in the sky as the haze lifted in the evening.

With childish enthusiasm, Janak asked, "Which direction is our own Sailung in?"

"Sailung's off to the west—who knows where!"

Janak had seen pictures of Sailung's pastures and the misty villages below, pictures brought back by those who had been there. He believed that he'd also go there some day and meet blood relations and see the ancestral homeland of the Yonzons. It will be frigid in the pastures, but the sun will come out in the afternoon, and—Janak fantasized—he'll carry a gauzy umbrella that lets in the warmth, one with a curved bamboo handle. The top of the umbrella is torn, and he'll mend it with the leaf of a taro plant. Janak will sing a selo song, flirting with the Himalaya's pure Tamang women who come by to graze goats.

It can be any selo, because many songs came to mind with each of Janak's fantasies about Sailung.

The pastures of Sailung are forlorn, where out on the rolling hills a few solitary trees might bend, swaying in a furious gale, and where, on another day, the black shadow of a cloud might race in and then, under the bright sun, race away. The foresakenness and loneliness of those pastures is once again boundless. This echoed through Janak's subconscious all the time. Perhaps this was why, every so often, he heard tunes in the concave of his ears. It was, maybe, the unfulfilled desire to go there that gave Janak's life such delicious dissatisfaction. It was quite possible that all of his ambitions were but the disguised apparitions of many such yearnings.

Dharmaprasad-jyu had been transferred from Dhankuta to the Madhes-based courthouse in Jhapa district twenty-two years ago, during the season of gales and windstorms in the hills. Before that, while Nala Sumshere Badahakim was still living, he had worked right in the Dhankuta office in the post of Subba. An annual salary of 400 Company rupees. Other than going to Kathmandu with office papers, and once, during an office break, visiting Olangchung Gola near the Tibet border, Dharmaprasad-jyu had not travelled anywhere.

The story of the progress he made after moving to Jhapa was the story of almost everyone with large landholdings in neighbouring Morang district.

He obtained some cultivated land by registering three or four names in the properties awarded to the elder Queen Mother. He settled ten or fifteen Sattar and Dhimal families who cut down the trees, cleared the jungles, ploughed the fields and dug the irrigation canals. After a year of hard labour, Dharmaprasad Shrestha owned about sixty-five acres of fertile farmland. All he had to do for the workers was to store some rice in a granary, and have new clothes tailored for their weddings; those who didn't work, or who sought too large a share or created trouble, were easily seen off. When asked, Dharmaprasad-jyu would simply say, "They ran away."

"These folks aren't like us," Dharmaprasad would declare. "They're not at all concerned about the future. They die of joy at the very mention of fishing. They head out for three or four days, and return with a fish the size of your pinkie finger. What can you say?…Ey, Shuniya, are you going to go fishing again?"

Sitting in the sun eating puffed rice—freshly prepared in earthen pot and mixed with spicy oil—dark-skinned Shuniya would flash his white teeth and grin as if to say, "We didn't catch any fish this time. But next time… Our master just doesn't have faith."

After looking around to see who owned large, productive plots of land, people would start cases against those Rajbanshi, Sattar or Dhimal families and take over the plots for themselves. The history of Morang's indigenous peoples carried the ancient curse of the court cases and offices of Gorkha's rule. Although the saying went "Go to Gorkha if you want justice", the indigenous peoples' experience taught them, "Yet live on in the Gorkha kingdom if you don't". They would flee overnight, abandoning their homes and fields, their wives and sons and daughters. The day after they fled, their land would become the property of some brave Gorkhali victor. In those days, when day and night were equally murky in Morang, the Gorkhalis committed daylight robbery, looting wealth and life and dignity.

Dharmaprasad-jyu quit his job after the political change and disorder of 1950.

He now owned 250 acres of farmland in Damak bazaar, and together with the 110 in Rangeli and the settled and forested plots in Bhadrapur, had a total of 570 acres of land. As a landlord, he had a separate plot for his own use. His fields in the hills produced eighty or ninety sacks of fine Bayerni rice.

Sita's biological mother still lived in Dhankuta. She had visited Darjeeling twice. Sita's brother lived in the Madhes and helped out with their father's work. Dharmaprasad's younger wife lived with him in the Madhes. She wouldn't leave her husband's side for even a moment. There were no children on the younger wife's side. She had a dark, wiry body wasted by malaria, and throughout the winter she offered meals and hospitality to countless guests who came down from the hills, as well as to passing strangers. She spent her busy days shouting out orders amid the grumbling of servants, offering uncooked rice to flocks of Bahuns from the west who insisted on cooking their own food, and performing endless other services and rituals. In the hills, stray travellers could always find blankets, but no food; whereas there was no question of not finding food in the Madhes, but there were no blankets here. Inconsiderate visitors drove her mad. At winter's end, in the month of Chait, when the heat started to rise along with malaria in the Madhes, all the guests and their new servants would return to the hills, but she remained in the Madhes with Dharmaprasad and their Madhesi servants.

"It was about two years after I moved to the Madhes from Dhankuta," Janak's father-in-law said to him one day. "The deer would run in herds all over the dense, sweltering forests of Morang, in heat that could boil you alive. You'd get dizzy from the flowering of the sal trees. It felt as though all the mosquitoes of Birgunj town had swarmed here. You couldn't see things ten feet away through the haze. The Limbu people would come down from the hills and spend all night dancing in circles around blazing bonfires, one girl to one boy—later on, you'd see those who had broken out in a fever lying all over the road, as if to die. Even then, I never heard, back in the hills, of a single Limbu's daughter having being ruined."

After the conversation veered off course, Dharmaprasad gradually said, "My life was like that of a prisoner's in these long, hollow, depressing gravel pits furrowed by cart wheels, it passed like the life of a man ostracized by society, whose loved ones in the hills had perhaps passed him a death sentence. My heart just wouldn't permit me to bring my daughter and her mother to the wastelands of Morang—so I had to marry a second wife."

That day, Janak learned from his father-in-law that a considerable part of a man's love consisted of pity: he had married, and also abandoned his first wife, out of pity.

On the return from Rangeli, a small incident took place on the India–Nepal border, in Jogbani:

India's territory started as soon as you passed through Nepal's sal forests in the Terai. Janak and Sita were walking ahead, leaving the elders behind. The porters were trailing even further back. A male peacock, its golden tail fanned out, was strutting ahead of everyone, as though showing the way. Even fifteen kilometres on, it wouldn't leave the trail and go back into the jungle. Janak picked up a fallen branch from the trail and made as if to strike it. It didn't run away. That peacock was unafraid of travellers; it was perhaps accustomed to the affections of exhausted journeymen. They all crossed over to Indian soil.

Then, all of a sudden, Janak bolted ahead. Sita was startled. He disappeared as she watched on.

Everyone who had trailed behind caught up to her. Someone said, "The rule of Nepal is behind us. He's run off to catch the peacock because no one will arrest him now."

Janak returned after a long time, panting. There was no peacock in sight.

Everyone turned to him with questioning eyes.

"Did you see that, what a wicked peacock!" Janak cried in a rage. "We are compelled to leave our homeland, but that peacock also wanted to go to the land of the Mughals, just like us! I chased him right around! I saw to it that he went back to Nepal. I left him with a stern warning: 'We humans, we have to move abroad, but if the flora and fauna of the forest also start going abroad, how long can Nepal last?'"

This was the first act of public service of Janak's life.

"You returned from Calcutta only yesterday, so I didn't say anything..." Birman said to Janak, who was sitting on a chair.

"Then tell me today."

"These dreams..." Birman Budathoki shifted even lower than the wooden slat he was perched on, and said, "I only ever see terrible dreams. I went to the temple on Mahakal hill the other day. My dreams still haven't improved. This has never happened to me before, Hajoor! I even had a chart drawn in the bazaar."

"Lies!"

"How is that a lie, Hajoor? I'd sooner eat cow's meat than lie!"

"Me, I'd happily eat the meat of a cow or a bull or any other animal—it's just that Bhauju won't allow me to bring it into the house, that's all. What you're saying is a lie because fortune-tellers don't draw charts on the ground nowadays. They draw them with pencils in notebooks. I've seen it. If anyone tears up the cement and asphalt that the municipal office has laid down in the bazaar to draw a chart, the police will arrest him."

"It's exactly the same thing, even if it's written in a notebook," Birman said with a laugh, and mustered up the courage to confide even more in his master. "I've been needing to buy a set of clothes, including for myself, Hajoor. And saris are cheaper on this side."

"What's this one saying?" Janak spun around in his chair, and said, glaring at Birman, "Are you planning to get married?"

"Not at all, Hajoor. Why would a tramp like me put on a show and get married? I've been trying to say this from the day before yesterday, I just couldn't speak."

Janak lost patience. "Just say what you mean!"

His rebuke caused Birman's speech to dry up like a rivulet

in the wintertime. Birman became so confused that for a few minutes he was afraid to even breathe. Only when he saw Janak get up to leave did he squeak, "I also told Didi this morning."

"What did you tell her?" Janak hurled an insult: "I'll have your head!"

No reply. He was stunned, his head bowed.

"You need money?"

Birman only fidgeted.

"You want to go home?"

Silence.

That morning, after fetching water from the spring, Birman had spoken to Sita about going home.

"Don't say that, Birman!" Sita had scolded him. "I can't fetch the water myself when it's this cold."

"It's only for ten or twelve days, Didi. I'll be right back."

"You think I'm dumb?" Sita had raged. "You think I'm from these parts? Go, go and tell Divya's father! Don't talk to me."

Pushpa's mother was cradling her younger daughter and listening in on the quarrel from the window next door.

Sita turned to her for support and said, "Listen to what this Birman's saying, Bahini. He says he wants to go home!" To Birman, she said, "Aren't you the one who was counting the days to the Sankranti festival just yesterday? Who'll prepare the goat if you go?"

Sita found her point of view perfectly reasonable.

Pushpa's mother Babuni offered a formula for compromise: "Why not go after celebrating Sankranti? Now that Didi's said as much…" Just recently, when she'd asked Birman to perform a small errand and sent him out to buy four paisa's worth of sugar, Sita and she hadn't spoken for days. They'd both forgotten about that by now.

Dark, lustrous Birman slipped a small green comb out of his pocket, and tidying up his hair, said, "After all, I also love my home, Bhauju. The way our Dai keeps coming back out of love for his home."

Somewhere inside, this touched Babuni and she blushed. "You're such a dandy, how will you ever last in the hills!" she said.

"Birman's probably going to the hills to get married. Keep watching: we women are always correct!"

"May Bhauju's blessings come true. Thenkyu."

Upon coming here from the hills, Birman had learned to stop calling people by their caste name and to address them politely as family relations. The second thing he'd learned was to say thank you in English. "So even though I weigh fifty kilogrammes, I still weigh a hundred pounds, thenkyu!" "I may be dark but it suits me, doesn't it? Thenkyu!"

Three years ago, Birman's father had sent him to the temple in Teenkanya to make a religious pledge and release a pair of pigeons. A journey of thirteen kilometres. Birman set out, and fifteen days later showed up out of nowhere in Jhapa bazaar. By dawn he was sitting on a long wooden bench in a shop in a small tent, having downed a cup of black tea. To those on the way who asked, he'd say, "I'm going to Assam." On the afternoon of the seventeenth day, after travelling for a day on foot and for an additional night on a Sattar man's ox-cart, Birman crossed the border at the Mechi River, into freedom.

He spent two months in Bagdogra. Making bricks.

He spent nine months in a Sikh hotel in Silgadi. Washing plates.

He pulled a rickshaw for twenty days.

He was laid flat by malaria for four months.

On the day he showed up at Janak's, he looked like a man from the Madhes wearing a hill man's daura-sural.

Within six months, the air and water of Darjeeling restored him to the old Birman. He would never again revert to being unkempt. Janak wouldn't allow it.

Janak, who was himself not given to dressing up, often said, "Everyone is forced to be well groomed in Darjeeling—for as long as its roads are paved with asphalt and its air and water stay clean."

So deeply did Birman internalize his master's statement, he began to wash the clothes of all of the building's residents to earn a little "cigarette" money on the side. Janak found out and beat him. Mrs Das from the neighbouring house wept openly.

"Look, Bhauju, there's only one whorl, see?" Birman spread his fingers in the afternoon sun to show Babuni his fingerprints.

"A man like that will be either a king or a hermit," Sita said, interpreting this sign.

"I don't want to be a hermit and can't be a king!"

"I mean equivalent to a king: who said you'd actually become a king?"

"Well, I'm already like a hermit."

Both Sita and Babuni laughed. One even choked.

"You left-handed scoundrel, even your conversations stray leftward! Don't go to Nepal anymore! The king will see that single whorl and cut you to pieces."

"If he captures me, I'll tell him I'll become a hermit!"

Ajoy Das had once told Birman that left-handed people gave birth to twins. Birman, who believed that Bengalis knew everything because they were educated, had taken this deeply to heart.

When silver airplanes occasionally roared in the skies above Darjeeling, Birman, who was given to dancing all over the streets in the Saraswati Puja procession, would scramble up to the rooftop from wherever he was. And turning up to the sky he would yell at the airplane. He would tell a joke that, given his experience and intellect, struck him as very poignant.

"Oh, airplane! Why would you ever look at me, your father-in-law! See here, I'm going to kill you, I'm going to shoot you down from the sky, look out!" He'd pretend to be holding a gun, and place a finger on the trigger, and close one eye and aim, hitting the flying airplane with a cry: "Pwak!"

Struck on the wing by the bullet, the airplane would blaze up with fire and smoke and tumble down in pieces in Birman's imagination.

During his two months in Bagdogra, Birman used to stare like a mesmerized deer at the revolving lights at the airport at night. In the evenings, he'd go with a friend to a field where the airplanes sat around as though chatting among friends. He'd circle them, look at them, and when no one was looking, touch them. He and his friend had even chosen two airplanes, one each, to scratch their names on.

Three days later, Janak was asking Birman, "When you go, you take the road through Gorkhey, don't you?"

"No, Hajoor, the lower road is better in the wintertime," Birman said. Then, with some pride, he said, "They've improved our roads nowadays. They're saying cars will go all the way one day. I'll go to Fikkal today, I have relatives there—I'll spend the night."

Janak had never ventured past the bifurcation to Pashupati. Around last year, on the way to a fete in Mirik, he'd seen the road to Pashupati bazaar from the car, and he'd also seen a few tiny old teashops and houses by the roadside. All he could say now was, "Have a good journey. Be careful."

Birman's vision blurred. In preparation for the arduous undertaking that lay ahead, he began to dwell on the ups and downs of the journey. In his mind he saw the morningtime view from somewhere high up in the sky along the border between Darjeeling and Ilam. Having spread light over the Majhkirant homeland, the rising sun was bringing daylight to the houses on the Namsaling hills and to the headwaters of the Yogmai River. Birman moved on, examining the sprawl of Beni Bazaar, where he had for eternity fallen in love with Anamika Sainli. There were three more hours left for the sunlight to reach the Tilkeni hill.

"I'll have to wake up at night and start walking at three o'clock," Birman said as a warning to himself. "I'll have to reach Ilam bazaar well before this hour." He wanted to spend a day in Ilam bazaar and go to the office above, to see if anyone from his village had come there.

"So you'll be home day after tomorrow!"

"No, Hajoor, it's a five-day journey from Ilam; our home is in Mulpani!" Birman pointed at the Falelung hills, which were visible through the windows from where they were sitting. "There: I have to cross ten or twelve peaks like that one."

Janak got cross and said, "Don't go." Inwardly, his two hands were applauding the audacity of humankind's two feet. "Don't go," he said. "You have neither sons or daughters nor a mother. Why kill yourself travelling all the way to visit a so-called father who's brought home three wives?" It wasn't pain but anger that flashed over Janak's face when he thought about the polygamy of the Nepalis over there.

"I can't not go, Hajoor!" Birman kept insisting. Then he lied outright: "My Ba says he's also coming to the Jogmai temple to make an offering for the Sankranti festival. If I run into him there, I'll turn back immediately. And there's a business matter in the tea plantations in Ilam. I can talk to some people if you know anyone. You can buy stacks of carpets cheaply in the fete in Beni. If I could buy them and bring them over here, it would amount to a lot of money..."

The tinkling of bangles made Birman stop talking.

Sita came from inside and stuffed some rupee notes into Janak's hands.

"Bring it all. He has a long way to go."

"It's all there," Sita said.

The grand "Janak Clothes Store" had opened in Daroga bazaar. Those who wanted to buy suits and saris of the latest designs at the "right" price, in styles no one had worn before, flocked there.

"We shouldn't look to profit for a year or two," Janak had told Sumshere. Sumshere sat in the store dressed in a black sherwani over a white cotton shirt and trousers. He worked very hard. The thin black moustache on his dark face gave him a certain easygoing, inoffensive and almost non-existent personality. He was the sort of person from whom customers thought nothing of asking for a discount, or for credit.

"We mustn't displease even those customers who make

us take out a stack of clothes, and then leave without buying anything," Janak told Sumshere.

"Is that all?" Sumshere said with a smile. "Do you want me to share some tricks for attracting female customers?"

"Don't tell me; show me by doing it," Janak said.

Those who had suits tailored without paying the instalments, and those from the hills, who took away sack upon sack of clothing on credit and then never returned, had made a mess of the shop's accounts.

Furrowing his brows, Bhudev quipped, "How shrewd of Janak-babu to turn so many customers into shareholders."

"We must make Nepalis buy at Nepali shops," Yashraj added.

"The sales have been great so far," said Deobahadur, who worked in the store as a clerk.

There was endless whispering among the Marwari traders. They too had started to sell clothes to customers on credit, using only bills and invoices.

Janak and Sumshere would laugh, but both of them were unsure about who would have the last laugh. After adding up the shop's rent, the salary of the employees, the cost of travelling to Calcutta and Bombay and the income tax, Janak, Sumshere and Jayabilas, all three, would place their heads in their hands. The debts to the commission agents alone were getting quite steep.

"There'll be no loss if we can raise all the credit," Janak said.

He had printed up colourful flyers and distributed them in the schools, in the offices, and everywhere in Chowrasta bazaar. There were even flyers glued to paan shops and electric poles.

A copy of the flyer:

Towels—Two rupees for the large ones, one rupee for the small ones. There's no smaller price than this because there's no smaller towel than this. Obviously, it looks terrific when new. Although after one wash—don't even talk about it. You won't miss it if you leave it behind at your in-laws'. Your sister-in-law won't have to wash it and return it to you. If your respected husband's gaze wanders to your unmarried sister, you'll want to go over to bless her after her buying this towel. There's danger, Sir, in towels of higher quality.

Socks—We have around thirty pairs that no one has bought since our grandfathers' time. If you're willing to mend them for your own use, they're thirty-two paisa a pair. We won't, ourselves, be wearing them.

Shirts—If your husband-god or your husband-demon should grumble, have a shirt tailored for that worthless man. Price: 8/- rupees.

Suit pieces—Attractive new designs that no one has ever worn which, upon donning, will make you yearn to rove around aimlessly, till you risk losing your job or destroying your family. This suit will resurrect your departed youth, and if it has merely fallen asleep, it'll wake it up.

Saris—For wives, the value of a sari is in its price. If you come to us in advance, we can ask for 53 instead of 35 when you come back with her later to buy it. We have a variety of saris. We have saris that cling tightly to beautiful bodies, and saris that refuse to come off, which after a while, alarm even those wearing them. We also have saris in colours we dislike, but which someone else might like. It must be because some people like such colours that such saris are made.

"Etcetera, etcetera," Yashraj said, reading the flyer out loud.

Janak dreamed of building a house, a house of his own. To rent out four or five suites and live in the rest. This was Sita's wish. Janak's promise. Janak harboured the following life ambitions: to be the father of exactly two children; to write a book; to build a house of his own. His self-styled philosophy was: wealth is greater than or equal to knowledge. Only if it's specialized knowledge can knowledge be power. Only if it's a liquid asset can thieves steal an asset. A frozen asset like a house is a thousand times greater than ten stacks of tattered knowledge. If he doesn't forget everything, Janak's knowledge will serve him through his lifetime, but a house will serve his family till the end of time.

And yet, not long ago, Janak moved into someone else's house. After the small wooden structure that used to stand here collapsed in the earthquake of 1934, Ramnath Jain had bought the land from Prabhunarayan Bahun for four hundred rupees and erected this building. Harshadhan Subba had since bought it with his earnings from the army. There were six rooms on the upper storey, but they weren't very spacious, so Janak had rented three side rooms to live in. It was his policy to live as comfortably as he could afford to. He would greet visitors in the room at the top of the stairs and host them there, offering them tea and biscuits. In the centre of that room were cane benches and a round teak table. His books were in a low cupboard near the window—two of "Nehru's", all of "Shah's". Janak's favourite playwright was "Balkrishna". On a wall above the cupboard, on the January page of a calendar that the wind kept trying to flip, was a picture of Khilji Alauddin who, by means of a mirror, was imbibing the image of a beautiful woman standing beyond a railing. There was a radio in the middle room. Two other pictures hung in this room, and they shed further light on Janak's character. In one picture, a wounded deer had got separated from its distant herd and was waiting despondently for death. In the other picture, a mother and son had come to the door to welcome an indisposed father returning from abroad; a young daughter watched on, forgetting to eat her meal.

"This composition," Janak had said fondly, hanging up the picture one evening during the Tihar festival, "doesn't it illustrate the difference between the world of animals and the world of men, Sita?"

MK lived in a room next door. One room over lived Ajoy Dasgupta, who worked at the court. Both clerks had a wife and family. MK had been transferred to the post office in Pedong. Demonstrating a number of reasons, and without failing to furnish doctors' certificates as well as letters of recommendation from prominent people, MK was lobbying relentlessly to have himself transferred back to the Darjeeling post office. First he submitted a petition claiming that the cost of travelling back and forth from Pedong, and the expense of food and shelter in both places, were too high; after that, he submitted a second petition, turning his dead mother gravely ill. They didn't succeed. He also submitted a third petition claiming that his health didn't allow him to live in Pedong. MK would get drunk, he would get very badly drunk. He had two daughters, Pushpa and Amrita, who were studying in Class 2 and kindergarten respectively. Babuni gave Sita company to go to the bazaar and Mall Road, and to the cinema on Mondays. Mrs Dasgupta was never to be seen, except when she came to put the laundry out to dry. Since she was dusky, and since the beauty of her face came from the cut of her bones, she was bound to remain attractive in old age.

"You—go and eat fish-bone sauce. What do you know, you Bengali who sleeps in a skirt?"

"You—go and eat stale rice. What do you know, you hill man who sleeps in a sack?"

MK and Ajoy addressed each other in the most informal of terms. If MK took Ajoy to an English film, Ajoy would feed MK some letikeli afterwards, explaining that Lady Canning used to love these sweets so much that its name was changed to letikeli.

Ajoy would break out in praise of Bengal: "Ah, Bengali sweets…"

"You're number-one slaves," MK would say when the sweetness began to fade from his lips. "You buttered up the British by naming your sweets after a chief sahib's madam."

In response, Ajoy would turn to the shopkeeper and call out in Bengali-inflected Nepali: "Look, Bhai-ji! He's insulting Bengali sweets. I'm not going to pay for him."

"Then why did you go and see the film earlier?" MK would cry. "Forget everything. Forget it."

Ajoy Dasgupta was a person born and raised in Darjeeling. MK's birth had taken place in the army cantonment of Kuita, in the plains. While it may be true that God had created MK's body out of soil, MK had created his own life out of the ordinary grammar of nouns and verbs—to wake up in the morning, eat a meal, go to the office, come home, eat, sleep, get drunk. When enraged, the clerk-babu would yell, "I'm the grandson of Batas Munshee! Batas Munshee was my grandfather! I'm not the son of some aloo-dum vendor at the train station!" Batas Munshee used to be a trusted employee of the tea plantation in Singtam back when Dalbahadur Giri spread Gandhi's "word" in the plantation. Munshee went on to lead the Congress Party's volunteers, who set themselves apart by wearing tricolour bands. The plantation's sahibs had the guards destroy his ripe rice fields, and expelled him from the settlement. After working for many years in the bazaar, Batas Munshee died exactly a month after returning to the plantation with his family.

Some days, one clerk would tease the other, asking him, "Why do you-all take such big bribes at the court, huh? Why don't you do what you're supposed to do without taking bribes?"

Ajoy used to say, and still said, "People are terrible. They just give you money. I'm so used to it now that I feel bad, I feel hurt, if I don't get money. Not everyone's an important man or politician. Not everyone's a leader. People have to offer bribes to get their work done. And as for our Darjeeling politicians—oof!" Ajoy stuck out his tongue after saying this.

"They need to be kicked," MK blurted out.

"That's easy to say, but what to do..."

"What? If you keep saying it, you might actually do it at some point."

They both laughed. They were targetting Janak. Their laughter carried the pleasure of retaliation.

"I'm new at all of this. Weren't others before me taking bribes at the court?"

"They were." MK laughed again, still savouring the earlier point.

"You should come to work at the court," Ajoy said. "What do you post-office clerks ever see? How can you possibly hear as much as I do at the court, Bhai?"

"True, we don't see any robbery, rape, cheating," MK said. "But we see all of Darjeeling's innards from the counter. For the Marwari, the post office is a place to dispatch money. For the Bengali, the post office is a place to send telegrams. For the Nepali, the post office is strictly for sending letters. 'One stamped envelope,' the Nepali will say as he comes in. 'I've arrived safely, all is well.' The Bengali comes to send telegrams. And your father comes to buy insurance for a thousand rupees."

"No, *your* father comes!"

Fakruddin Ahmad, the owner of the roti shop at the junction near the temple, lived in two ground-floor rooms directly below Ajoy. He had a Nepali wife. Fat, of flabby build. Janak had read somewhere that women could walk around wearing thin, fluttery blouses because the layer of fat on their bodies was thick. It puzzled him to see Fakruddin's wife wearing a ladies' coat in the wintertime and monsoon alike. She would gather the children of the settlement and make them sing new songs and dance all day long. She hosted feasts for everyone in the neighbourhood on Shab-e-Barat, Eid and Bakr Eid. Sita never went to them. No one in the area could match Fakruddin's wife in one matter, which was in arguing—except for Ratan, who wore a round knitted cap that covered only the back of his head, and who lived in a small house across the building next door. Made up and decked out in a theatre-dancer's costume, Ratan would gaze admiringly at himself in the mirror and say, "Tchee, why aren't I a woman!"

Not even Fakruddin's wife could argue with this Ratan.

On the ground floor, a garage had been fashioned out of extra tin sheets, and next to it stood a paan shop. Kisanram, whose photograph hung in the paan shop, had moved to Darjeeling twenty-one years ago from Araila neighbourhood, Jagdishpur post office, Ara district. If there were no customers in his shop, Kisanram would immediately take out a hand mirror and a comb and start tidying up his hair, grooming his moustache and massaging his neck. This Madhesi was talkative. He also sold songbooks from films and photos of film stars in his shop. Schoolgirls would stand outside his shop, staring at the pictures pinned up in the front.

One of the girls would inevitably ask, "Who do you like, huh? Tell me."

Shyly, another would say, "That one. I like him."

"Correct!" Kisanram would say, pointing at a picture of himself holding a flower, his eyes wide and his hair styled with a downward parting. "He's the best—he's really handsome, isn't he?"

The girls would shout, "Tchee! Madhise lowlife!" and leave.

"Tell your father at home that you like me, all right? Buy it and take it with you—not the picture, the person," Kisanram would call out with a laugh.

The girls would bicker and yell vociferously as they left.

Two boys wearing black monogrammed coats passed by on that road one day. "This is how the cinemas have ruined our girls," one declared.

"That's all right..." said the other.

Sita had a habit, brought with her from Nepal, of chewing a slice of betel nut after a meal. Janak never chewed betel nuts. He tried many times to break this "bad habit" of Sita's. "You must adopt good habits," Janak would say. "Good habits are as useful as Bihari servants; bad habits are as evil as Bengali masters."

On the rest of the lower floor was Pasang-la's shop—"Fresh, warm pork momo, thukpa, chowmein are available here." Pasang-la's brew of chhyang was renowned. The clerk, the schoolmaster, the police, the driver all sent their representatives to his shop. The atmosphere they created there, and the chatter-assembly they held at night, were truly worth witnessing. A few partitions had been slapped up to create small rooms in the shop. On each room's wall hung a flowery red curtain which served as a door, a veil for hiding or escaping, and also, on occasion, a towel for wiping the hands and face. Doma and Kanchhi would walk back and forth in the shop a hundred times, their yellow wooden sandals clacking against the floor.

The old priest Shukanath snuck in here regularly. Sharma-jyu had a thesis: people didn't simply become what they ate, their faces also resembled the animals whose flesh they consumed. Chinese faces resembled those of pigs, Chhetris and Bahuns had the faces of goats, Bengalis looked like fish. Himself exactly like a goat, old Shukanath would come into the shop, and, taking great delight in breaking all the taboos about caste and food, cry out, "Bring me samosas, and also an order of sauce!"

Everyone acquainted with his ways would laugh. After

gobbling up everything in a millisecond, Shukanath would cry out, "Never mind, I won't eat it, you're too late. I'm going. I'm gone. I'll never come back here again!"

Accepting the claps and murmurs of appreciation of the audience, old Shukanath would lower the door's curtain and leave like a comedian exiting a stage, followed out by laughter.

Those working as politicians came at night with Triple X rum. When they were drunk, they'd get up to such shenanigans that all the other customers had to flee. The MLA Yashraj had put on a new kind of show here only a week before. "This is how people should actually walk," he'd said, and got down on all fours on the wood-plank floor. He'd walked quite a ways, and back, in this manner. Friends had clapped and jumped around, laughing and enjoying themselves.

Janak invited Sumshere to his house one evening, and opening a bottle of rum, said, "The shop's not doing so well."

"There'll be no loss if we can raise all the credit," boasted Sumshere, who was managing the shop.

Janak was worried. "The interest on the fifteen thousand from Jayabilas is really growing."

"The letters from the commission agents have also arrived."

"Even the sly Marwaris are selling clothes on credit now, using invoices," Janak said.

A certain unpleasantness arose in an otherwise pleasant evening. The sun was no longer visible, but its red-and-yellow hues were spread out over the valley of Pulbazar and the hills of Sikkim. It was growing dark nearby, but it was still light elsewhere, farther away. The bazaar's shops and houses were preparing for the transition. The spirit of eveningtime was spreading everywhere.

Abruptly, Janak asked, "Is there anyone in the world who's happy?"

Babuni took a kilo of rice out of a storage bin and placed it in a bamboo tray, then picked up a little bit from the tray and put it back into the bin.

The pages of many a day turned on this twice-a-day routine, adding up to annual compendiums spanning eight or ten years. It is said that there's no such thing as time, there's only work. If time truly doesn't exist, then for the sake of measurement alone, we can say that the tender shoots had become trees and spread out through these into branches.

MK returned home from Silgadi in time for the Holi holidays. He was sitting outside in the sun, chatting loudly with Ajoy, who had only just been promoted after all these years at his job.

"There's no one in the world quite like Bihari porters!"

"Bihari people are very bad," Ajoy agreed.

When MK had gone to watch the festivities and the bonfire last night, a Madhesi stoner high on bhang-laced sweets had come up to MK's ear and hollered, "Wow-mister-wow!" MK had been cross ever since. He grew even crosser now seeing Madhesis, and even hill Nepalis, splashed in red dye and covered with mud and dung, roving around with buckets of water, looking for a chance to pounce on others.

The thoughts of these two friends quickly transformed into two manmade satellites spinning in the emptiness of space, from where the hillsides of character, the peaks and crannies of desire, the cliffs and bluffs of pride and the rivers and marshes of love and compassion all looked like a flat wormhole.

There was no one as dirty as Biharis. Their grams-and-rice and fried pulses were going to spread cholera in the Madhes and tuberculosis in the hills.

"Those gram-flour eaters are such a torture in Sakliya Ghat!" MK went on. "You have to change trains there because of Pakistan. Those thieves approach from far away, dressed in black shirts. They climb right up and talk so assertively! Me, I've fallen asleep on the train because I've been up all night—my body aches. They come over and, like police inspectors, demand in Hindi, 'Whose suitcase is this?'

"We have to say, 'It's mine, Babu-ji,' sitting off in a corner, like this (MK folded his arms and sat meekly.)

"'How much will you pay? Can I carry it?'

"'How much are you asking?'

"The rate for coolies—twenty-four paisa—is marked plainly on the noticeboard. But the black shirt says, 'I want five rupees.'

"'Only five rupees?' You have to laugh as though astonished, and say, 'One coolie asked for fifteen rupees, another for twenty-five rupees. You're saying only five rupees? Carry it, then, carry all of it.'

"For a while, the black shirt stands there mistrustfully, but then decides, from our broken Hindi, that we're honest people, and he lifts the suitcase onto his head.

"Once he carries the suitcase to the steamer, though"—MK puffed up his chest—"the rate is twenty-four paisa, so we start by giving him eight paisa. He's shocked!" (MK laughed.) "He gets angry, he's seething with rage. He says he'll call the police, he gathers his friends, he tries everything. We mustn't argue with him, we mustn't say a word. We have to act as though he's talking to someone else, and just sit there quietly."

(MK did so for a moment.) "Later on, we take a little bit out of our pocket and toss it to him. 'Here.' He picks it up, examines it, and comes over to put all sixteen paisa back in our hands. Now, again, it's our turn to stay quiet. There's no one around observing this quarrel. The steamer is filled with exactly the same quarrel. In the end it's twenty-four paisa according to the rate, with four paisa as a tip, and then it's…" MK was going to say "done", or "fixed", but only shook his head at the end.

To this, Ajoy added, "The red shirts at Sealdah Station are even worse! If you don't ask for a ticket beforehand, they'll steal your suitcase and mattress! Bihari people are really bad."

"If people hear you talking like this…" MK pretended to be nervous, "they'll get upset."

"Who'll get upset?" Ajoy said loudly.

"Shhh!" MK yelled. "Janak-babu will get upset!"

Just as loudly came the question: "Why will he get upset?"

"Why, now? He's a man who understands psychology."

This time, Ajoy mimicked MK and spoke more softly: "What kind of psychology?"

"Communal hatred," MK explained. "How pointless is that?"

"What is it?"

Switching to English, MK said, "Persecution mania, he says. Isn't that absurd?"

Ajoy also replied in English: "Of course!"

A misinterpretation of Nietzsche's philosophy, "Live with suffering," had started applying to MK's character. An ungrounded fear of losing his job defeated him in the way a decimal point defeats a weak student. It felled him for no reason. For him, the safest place in the world was either in bed at home or at the post office counter. MK treated those who came to the post office as if they were, themselves, deliveries.

MK had wedded pretty Babuni within caste, in an arranged marriage.

His mother was a hothead. When she got angry, she'd either not speak at all to anyone at home, or else she'd explode like a volcano, without warning. Babuni had learned from her mother-in-law that those capable of losing their temper could also love very fiercely. She wondered whether people who were incapable of love ended up hating others simply because they couldn't lose their temper. It wasn't that MK didn't love Babuni, but rather that other emotions took precedence in his pysche. I might lose my job, I might fall ill, I might lose money, someone might shout at me, etcetera—innumerable such anxieties and terrors found shelter in his mind. He'd start fearing those he borrowed from from the very next day onwards. He got upset with both types of clerks—those who arrived at the office before him in the morning, and those who arrived afterwards. When he returned home happily without getting drunk in the evening, he would read every signboard, not skipping a single one—not even he could understand why. His hair was cut high, he was skinny but not dark—there was some discolouration in the white of one eye, and his lower row of teeth looked nice, like a child's teeth, when he smiled. It wasn't that MK lacked imagination or zest—he had collected phrases such as silent night, moonbeam, gentle breeze, blue sky, the strings of the heart instrument, twig huts, water from the eyes, evening pyre, etcetera, and had even used them to compose a few poems. He'd also written stories in which a man visited the gravestone of his lover and committed suicide, or if not that, then scattered two handfuls of flowers. In another story titled "Reunion", MK's ragged, hungry pauper was run over by a fat, rich merchant, and his blood trickled down the street to form the word, "revolution".

On this visit home, in order to wear a new blue suit that he'd had tailored for eighty-seven rupees, MK bathed early in the morning of the previous day and put great effort into polishing his pointy black shoes. He ate quickly, and washed every part of his shirt, even the buttonholes, then hung it out in the sun to dry. After dressing up, he left the house and walked so rapidly through the bazaar that he came back home within twenty minutes. Then he took off his clothes and spent the entire day in bed, like a cat.

That evening, he set out wearing a fuzzy cap, and returned home drunk.

He got into a shouting match with Kisanram without even coming face to face with him. The small radio in the paan shop wasn't playing any songs that he knew, so MK picked a fight, saying it was a cheap radio. By the time people gathered around, he was insulting the government, and Nehru, and all the MLAs. Only when Janak yelled from above, admonishing him, did the scene come to an end.

Babuni begged and pleaded: "Don't get so drunk. We'll run out of money. We haven't even bought books for Pushpa's new class, and the fees also have to be paid…"

MK defended his actions saying, "Men have three faults: gambling, whoring and taking intoxicants. Each man has one or the other of these three vices, he must have at least one.

Otherwise he's either a god or a eunuch, not a man! Now, I don't play cards or gamble, and I'm not a womanizer…"

"You drink alcohol."

"I don't drink alcohol," MK cried excitably. "I drink wine!"

"Don't drink wine-swine or anything else; can't you do that?" his wife pleaded.

"I'll drink wine. Men who don't drink wine, like Janak, kiss the wives of other men!"

MK's assumption—that Janak didn't drink—wasn't accurate. Janak was one of those people who was abandoned once by sleep at exactly four every morning, but who could then fall back to sleep; he felt no craving for tea after about one in the afternoon.

"Alcohol makes people lose their health and wealth, that's why you mustn't drink alcohol," Janak would say. "But wine allows you to acquaint yourself and attain equality with important people. Large trade agreements and important decisions are formed at the wine table, you can't wait for them at the door."

When the time came for MK to return to work, he had no money for the fare.

"You don't want to go back to work, so you cause us trouble," Babuni cried, growing despondent. "You should have saved enough for the fare."

MK was sitting on a chair, having given up on his legs and mental faculties. He was sure that Babuni had money, though how she'd have money he didn't know. He was like a child who had placed all his hopes on his mother.

Though Babuni shouted at him for a long time, MK didn't reply, so Babuni finally asked, "Is ten rupees enough?"

"It'll get me there."

Babuni got up. Headed out.

"Where are you going?" MK asked, tugging at her from behind.

"To look for some money. I'll ask Sita-didi from next door."

"Don't do that."

"It's our own money, we need it back."

"I said, don't do that."

(This, a form of rivalry. The pride is wounded when we thrust out our hands before acquaintances of our own caste. Pride is inextricably woven into the soul, and when that is wounded, we die a little. While self-respect may well be rust on the soul, when we pick it off and discard it, a part of the soul also breaks away and vanishes.)

Babuni wasn't beautiful in a dazzling way, but in the way of a soft light. A slim body, with skin on her face that was also fine. Due to poor health, dark spots had formed on the bridge of her nose and below her eyelids. She always wore a traditional gunyu-cholo with a white woollen shawl. She wore her hair long. Only a few years ago, many men had emptied and tossed away many a cigarette case on the road to the hospital, waiting around to catch a glimpse of her in her pure white nurse's uniform, and to talk to her.

As for Sita's life, it was cleaved into two chapters: from before marriage and from afterwards. The threshold of Janak's home was the dividing line, and once she crossed over it, she didn't feel any need to keep turning back to look at her old life. Sita had a home now, she had children. She forgot about everything else that had interested her as a young woman and set her mind to new subjects. From this it was easy to surmise how happy her married life was. The same thing didn't happen in Babuni's life. The dreams and desires she had harboured back when she was known as Chandra, and worked as a nurse, were probably still with her, sad and suppressed in the darkness in her heart. Thus, the difference between these two women wasn't merely about one having a pierced nose and the other an unpierced one, but, at a psychological level, akin to the difference between light and dark.

After she returned from even the Das home without procuring a loan, Pushpa put out a jug for MK to wash his hands before the meal.

They discussed how to take MK's boxes and bedding to the motor stand once he returned from the court. Babuni was going to find a coolie boy in the meantime.

But even after Babuni found a coolie and waited around till one in the afternoon, MK didn't come home. The coolie boy began to grumble about losing a full day's wage.

The Women's Association was hosting a party that day. Babuni scrounged up ten rupees from somewhere and left it in Pushpa's hands, and went out with Sita at three o'clock.

Janak was spending time at home because his father-in-law Dharmaprasad was visiting. Many years had passed since his last visit. Only occasionally, when the price of rice crossed eight rupees per thirty-seven kilogrammes in Bhadrapur, would Dharmaprasad cross the Mechi River. It never even occurred to Sita and Janak to go over from this side. Both sides would exchange, "We are pleased to learn that you are well," through letters—and this sufficed. With her father around, Sita reverted to being the proper miss that she used to be. A regimen of purity fell over the house. Daily ablutions, regular prayers. These were good days for their copper, metal and brassware, which finally got their turn. The house rang with the polishing and clinking of old pitchers, jugs and bronze plates. Unadulterated ghee came into use. All of this made Janakman Yonzon feel like a stranger in his own home. As it was, quite a few novelties had come into the Yonzon household upon his marriage to a Newar woman. Flower patterns were drawn onto the ground on the day of teeka during the Dashain festival; a feast was held on the third lunar day in springtime, Akshaya Tritiya. Janak found all of this extremely endearing, and for his part, had surprised Sita-from-Nepal by introducing her to Darjeeling's Saraswati Puja and the animal sacrifices that took place during Dashain and Tihar in Dali. Now Sita was staging a week-long Nepali-culture show in his home in order to make Dharmaprasad feel welcome.

After eating several servings of fresh, fine rice and an array of vegetable dishes on a large, low-trimmed plate, Dharmaprasad mixed one more handful of rice with ghee and a ripe banana and some sugar, and ate that too.

"This is the Nepali form of Aryan food. The pudding that the British eat at the end, the rasgolla that the Bengalis eat—this is that," Dharmaprasad declared.

When she was little, Sita used to stand by her father, waiting for a taste of that sweet mixture of ghee-and-rice.

"You can't expect that anymore," Dharmaprasad had said to her at the end of the previous day's meal. "You're grown up now. Why, you're already a mother."

Sita had smiled abashedly. The love between the father and daughter had only deepened.

"Jwai-saheb!" Dharmaprasad asked, addressing Janak. "How's the shop doing?"

"There was a loss, but we're still making an effort."

"Why make an effort at something that won't succeed?"

Janak fell silent. Many people had asked him this question, and he'd offered them a variety of answers.

"You have a truck, don't you?"

"I have a truck."

"And you have land?"

"I do."

"Those of you on this side can't really come over to the other side and make a go of it anymore. And out here—I don't know—I don't see any prospects."

"There's plenty to eat. The children are studying," Janak replied.

At age sixty, Dharmaprasad-jyu was a formidable, hardy old man. A body packed with muscles, as big as a barrel. Sixty-six inches tall, with thick black hair on the ears, on the arms, and all over the chest. Exceedingly hale and fair. Even now he would challenge rough, brawny cowherds in the hills to wrestling matches, sustaining bruises all over. He believed that scrapes healed quicker by themselves, without Dettol. A battery-powered Philips radio at home kept Dharmaprasad informed about the state of the world. Dharmaprasad's pastime, his "hobby", was: counting and sorting out money. He passed his free time turning over bank bills, examining them, and arranging them into tidy piles tied with rubber bands, piles of one hundred Re 1 bills, two hundred Rs 2 bills, five hundred Rs 5 bills, and one thousand Rs 10 bills. Most of his transactions took place with numbered bills.

Sitting stuffed on a comfortable chair, Dharmaprasad called over his granddaughter Divya and said, "You're a girl, why aren't you wearing a gunyu-cholo?"

"I'll wear it tomorrow."

Dressed in a sky-blue kurta-pyjama, Divya stared down at her toes, which were peeking out of her sandals.

"I see that your brother is also wearing clothes from overseas."

Ravi was leaning against a nearby table, dressed in a yellow woollen crewneck pullover and faded red worsted trousers. He had a somewhat dusky face and short, cropped hair.

Receiving no reply, the old man took in a deep breath.

"Eighty per cent of the world's diseases today are of the stomach and chest," Dharmaprasad declared. "By offering double the cover, the traditional daura protects the stomach and chest..."

Ravi gradually began to pay attention to what his grandfather was saying.

At night, after the meal, the three of them had another talk. Even after the rest went to sleep, Dharmaprasad kept telling Ravi and Divya about things they wanted to know.

Divya and Ravi heard about how Prithvi Narayan Shah conquered Nepal, but how there had been a constant threat from foreigners—the British and others as well. How, in that era, he had sought the help of the ascetics who roamed at night blowing trumpets carved from thighbones.

They heard about how the Kusule caste used to subsist on government donations till the reign of a certain Newar king. How they fell behind due to mistrust after Alauddin's conquest in Nepal.

How Mahatma Gyandeel started a new Nepali religion of the "Yashmani sect". And why he did so. Dharmaprasad explained everything.

"Grandfather's really scary, isn't he?" Divya asked Ravi after they went to bed.

"That's how men are!" Ravi said.

"Disgusting too!" said Divya. "Why is the nail on his right pinkie finger so long?"

Ravi got irritated. "Let me tell you something, Divya."

"What?"

"Don't talk like that about Grandfather."

Yet it puzzled Ravi as well. And Divya didn't see that she'd said anything wrong.

"We young people receiving advice must have only ears and a mouth—to listen to our elders and to tell them that we'll obey them," Ravi said. "If you have eyes, you'll see other peoples' flaws, and their advice won't enter your heart."

Divya suspected that there were many ways to counter her brother's argument, but found no immediate reply. Still young enough to hanker after the crust at the bottom of the rice pot, she was impressionable to advice.

"That's why…" Ravi went on, "that's why devotees shut their eyes before the deities. That's why God remains invisible, and conveys messages through the sky without ever revealing himself."

"Really?"

After Ravi and Divya fell asleep, at around twelve or one at night, there was a loud banging at the door, and the sound of quarrelling. Dharmaprasad, Janak and everyone else got up.

MK had come home drunk. He was shouting out slogans:

"Wake up, ladies and gentlewomen! Don't sleep anymore, get up! Open the door and serve the meal! Awaken!"

It was drizzling. The women were picking clothes off the rooftops. The clouds above the Mahakal hill were lighter and brighter than usual, but those higher up had solidified into a dirty, black, unmoving cluster. Three or four sparrows came fluttering by in a panic, alighted on the branch of an alder tree, and instantly fluttered off somewhere else.

Ravi had put on a brown suit and got ready quite a while back. The day outside disheartened him, he felt irritable. His youthfulness inclined him to gaze upon the atmosphere, to ponder the strength and weakness of the sun's rays. He had planned to go out and take a stroll around the cinema hall. There was likely to be a line-up for ladies' class tickets; his friends, and maybe even Parthiv, would probably be at the hall; and this upset Ravi. The idea of strolling around the hall aimlessly struck him as distasteful, even embarrassing, today. Though untested youth may have rendered Ravi restless and impatient, the relentless urges that coursed through him also made him feel purer and higher than anyone else.

A burst of laughter from the kitchen interrupted Ravi's thoughts. Sita and Babuni were talking about a Japanese film that had recently stopped screening in Darjeeling. Babuni was in the habit of coming over often to chat for an hour or so. If Babuni didn't come, then Sita went over to her place.

Ravi stood up and started pacing. When he glanced out, the day seemed to be improving. He couldn't go where he wanted to go. Having got dressed up, he remained a prisoner in his own room. It felt as though his desire, too, was cramped up in a cave in his mind.

The door slammed open, and it sounded to Ravi as though many women had entered the house.

Janak had come home. Behind him was Divya, returning from college. Ravi stood by, staring on blankly.

Divya turned around, and called out from the door, "Do come, why are you lingering downstairs? Do come up."

Janak also said, in English, "Arre, why now, please come. I'm telling you, Daniel, come up. And, Daughter, come along with your father."

Daniel-babu and his daughter Isabel. Isabel!

Out of sheer nervousness, Ravi grew alert and circumspect; he tried to become so. He stood by, trying to recognize the footsteps on the stairway's eleven wooden steps.

Daniel Pradhan came into the house. Though not far from her father, Isabel entered after a long gap.

Ravi had yet to recover from this unexpected turn of events when Isabel greeted him with a namaskar.

Dumbstruck, he returned the greeting by cupping his splayed hands as if to hold something round, and then, drained, he dropped them halfway. He stole a glance at Janak.

Sita also came from inside, and they all went into the house amid an exchange of namaskars. At the centre of them all was Divya, chirping like a happy baby bird.

Daniel-babu, who was only as tall as Janak but quite a bit fairer, lived in a flat on Wellesley Road in Calcutta. He worked at a British firm. Though he was always clean-shaven, a black shadow was visible along the sideburns on both sides of his pale face, below the thick chin and all the way to the lips. The hair behind both ears was beginning to grey. His pate was bald when he took off his hat. Because his eyes were large, they seemed to pop out a little. He didn't blink very often.

The father and daughter had returned from a visit to the mother at the Kharsang TB Hospital. The mother had been ailing for four or five years.

In 1940, Daniel-babu had left his one-year-old daughter and her mother to enlist in the Gorkha Rifles as an officer in the Royal Indian Army Service Corps. After completing his training in Pachmarhi in the Central Provinces, Daniel was dispatched to Jhelum, Damdil and Gardai Razmak in the Punjab. Three years later he went to Bannu, the capital of Waziristan. He lived a unique sort of mountain life on those far hills, subsisting on nothing but dried fruit on the banks of the Tochi River. During his month there, a soldier from Ipi Faqir's battalion, which had come from Mirali, almost succeeded in making Daniel Pradhan's body stay there permanently by using a locally built rifle that went "tak-dhung!" when fired. By the time Daniel-babu returned to Damdil, the Second World War had ended in Europe. He was then placed in the 14th Battalion and sent to Burma, but he didn't have to go beyond Shillong. Japan was losing. After fifteen days in Shillong, the battalion heard news of Japan's unconditional surrender just as they were boarding the train in Amingaun. When Daniel returned to Darjeeling on a month's furlough in 1945, his wife was somewhat unwell. One Sunday, Daniel put his wife and school-age daughter Isabel on a rickshaw and arrived at church at eleven o'clock. Standing alongside everyone in the church to sing a hymn that he'd learned as a boy, S. Daniel, the son of the headmaster of the Primary Mission School in the Milling Tea Estate, couldn't help but feel his eyes well up with tears.

"In the beginning was God
Who created the sea and the earth..."

What Daniel witnessed when he went back in 1946 wasn't pretty. Communal violence and murder.

It was August 16. The Eid moon had risen in the sky around four in the afternoon, and the Muslims' Ramzan had ended. The excessive daytime heat had begun to ease. Daniel was in Fort William with friends. Afterwards... He never wanted to think back to the rioting and killing that took place. He found some consolation, and a little peace of mind, remembering the aid he was able to offer in Bhawanipur, Park Circus, Hazara, Alipur, where there were many Nepalis...

Ravi cut off his own endless internal debate and went in.

Aside from Sita and Divya, everyone was seated in chairs around the warm heater.

"Namaskar," Ravi said to Daniel-babu.

"Oh, finally," Divya teased him.

Everyone laughed. Ravi blushed, and found himself in a muddle, but Isabel alone didn't laugh.

"Does not matter!" Daniel-babu said in English, patting Ravi on the back. "Namaskar, namaskar!"

Sita brought out a plate of fritters and samosas that Rambahadur had delivered. Daniel only had tea. Isabel picked up a samosa but just held it, and sat there without even trying it.

"Why don't you put it on a small plate," Divya said.

Isabel did so compliantly.

Janak was telling everyone about Namgyal. Dressed in a soft grey scarf and a chequered three-button tweed coat, Janak began talking like a trained TB specialist, expounding on the best method for examining X-ray plates, on the superiority of dry powder treatments and on the drawbacks of streptomycin. He also told the story of a patient who died while the doctors at the General Hospital and Chest Clinic bickered, unable to decide whether it was hepatitis in the liver or tuberculosis in the lungs, and whether the sputum was positive or negative. Daniel-babu listened patiently to all of this. Now and again he even spurred Janak on with expressions of agreement and admiration.

Ravi noticed that Isabel was listening to Janak's lecture very closely. Yet she didn't reply with a single word. He turned his eyes into a cine-camera and used the technique of the "close-up" to study Isabel. An elongated face, bright, large eyes with thick lashes, a soft but high, proud nose. A pale, full, extended neck, like proof of good health. Lots of hair piled into curls at the nape. It felt to Ravi as though he were seeing something forbidden. Isabel's peacock-green Kashmiri-silk sari and pitch-black ladies' coat gave her the gravitas of a woman far more mature than her years. If Isabel had folded her hair back and put it up in a net instead of braiding it and leaving it loose, without ribbons, Ravi would have been daunted; all his hopes would have withered away.

Isabel had taken the school-leaving exam last year. She'd failed after breaking out in a fever halfway through the exam. She was going to stay with her mother's elder sister in Rockville and retake the exam after five months. Her father wanted her to study science and take up medicine after she passed. The daughter had internalized the father's decision, accepting it as her own.

Daniel-babu and she left…

Stunned, Ravi sat by himself in his room. He felt enlivened and exhilarated. He got up and lifted the curtain, and peered out with the window still closed. There was no one outside. Then he saw Janak returning from having escorted away the guests, and he slipped into the kitchen.

Sita and Babuni and Divya—and everyone—was in the kitchen, but they fell silent when Ravi came in. So he went back out.

A little later, Parthiv dropped by.

Ravi told him, in a single breath, that Isabel had come to this very house with her father.

"Your fortunes are good," Parthiv said breezily, examining Ravi's forehead. "Buy a basket in the bazaar this Sunday, and use it instead of a bucket to milk a cow. You'll succeed even at that."

Though he tried to caution himself, Ravi was thrilled. "What a dazzling face! She's so fair!" he murmured to himself.

"Keep in mind," Parthiv said, "that skin that looks fair tends to feel rough, for some reason. It's yellowish skin that tends to be soft."

"So?" Ravi said.

"So you're bound to suffer a certain amount of disappointment when you feel her."

This only made Ravi more gleeful. "Such large eyes," he said.

"In addition to eyes like those being extremely useful for expressing feelings in drama, it's also fun to taunt someone with such eyes, and to watch them cry." Parthiv was enjoying himself.

"Look, Parthiv, Isabel really is beautiful."

"I'm not saying she isn't," Parthiv said. "She's beautiful. If you were to cut out a round piece of paper and place it on her head like one of those battery-powered halos, she'd make a fine Saraswati statue."

Ravi stared at Parthiv.

Parthiv stared at Ravi.

They both grinned after a while.

"She won't be like a Saraswati statue," Ravi said. "No matter how pretty those statues are, they always look sad. Isabel isn't sad."

"I see!" Parthiv said in English. "You're really in love."

Also speaking English, Ravi responded with a question: "Now, do you advise me to..."

"To what?"

"To write her a letter?"

"Most definitely not!"

Sitting Ravi down on a chair, tall, fit, strapping Parthiv brought his flushed face right next to his and, gripping his shoulders with both hands, said, "People's collarbones are so weak. Look at the way they move when I do this."

Irritated, Ravi rearranged his coat's shoulder pads. "Is that all you have to say?"

"No." Pacing the room, Parthiv said, "We're already in the second half of the twentieth century. It was our grandfathers' custom to have arranged marriages. Back then, they'd marry off boys and girls without even asking them. In those days, there was no meeting of four eyes, and especially not of hearts shaped like paan leaves. Fate and life were intertwined back then. Then came our fathers' custom of love marriage. This business of writing love letters is the by-product of love marriage. You want to follow that old path now?"

Ravi, who saw himself as a youth of new thinking, felt lost in this unfamiliar terrain.

"We're in an age of direct negotiation today," Parthiv

said. "The era of sending love letters through brothers and sisters, friend and servants, is over—just as, instead of sending diplomatic staff or ambassadors, they've invented a whole new method of holding summit discussions in politics. It's time for us to be able to present ourselves directly, like the heroes of English films and novels, and say, in English, 'Honey, I love you.' And our heroines, too, should say, 'Oh, but this… Just so sudden.'" Parthiv burst out laughing.

Ravi couldn't help but laugh as well. "Is that what you're going to do?" he asked at the end.

"Me?" Parthiv said, pointing at himself. "It's different for me."

Ravi didn't ask about this.

Parthiv stood at his full height, took on a grave expression and looked sharply at Ravi, who was still seated. "I worship the ancient ways," Parthiv said. "My father will find a girl for me—taking all aspects into consideration, making sure the match will endure. The girl must be of the right caste and kind. My caste is Rai, my clan is Chamling, my father's lineage is Wa-Bhuchha, my mother's lineage is Wa-Buli Kurepa. I must preserve all this and also ensure that no incest is committed when I marry. We pure Rais don't observe the clause on Degrees of Prohibited Relationships in the Hindu Marriage Act. You may think that flat-nosed, sloe-eyed girls aren't pretty, or aren't stylish, and claim that no Rai woman has ever been a heroine in Bombay. That's all propaganda. You have to habituate your eyes to the principles of Mongolian beauty. You must train them."

Ravi couldn't tell whether Parthiv was saying what he truly felt, or making things up for no reason. The truth often got lost amid all of his half-truths. To this day, Ravi had never checked to see whether the influence of the ultranationalist Bhudev had fallen on the better or worse side of his son. Parthiv had the ability to say the world's most ridiculous things without smiling at all, in such a convincing manner that for a while even he would believe himself.

Bhudev the ultranationalist! Bhudev had travelled to every part of Darjeeling, Sikkim, Bhutan and Assam that was inhabited by Nepalis. He'd also been to "Pakistan", though that was before India's partition. Though his gaze had never once fallen on the vision of Nepal's hills and mountains, that country was extremely dear to him.

"Forget about the people," Bhudev would say. "Why, there's even a difference in the flies! India's flies eat dirt and spread germs, but the flies from our homeland eat milk and yogurt from the mountains, and aren't like that at all."

You're suppposed to sympathize with someone when you see your own flaws in him, and yet wittingly or unwittingly, from deep in your heart, you feel an aversion instead. If, however, a flaw that you don't have shows up in someone else, you feel pity—such is the human heart. Ravi loved Parthiv because he saw in him some good traits that they both shared; he also loved and respected Bhudev because he saw in him some good traits that he himself lacked. If Ravi were to change, and if his views on character were to alter, then from tomorrow on his feelings towards these two individuals would also change.

All of these thoughts came rushing all at once into Ravi's mind. They rendered him speechless. Finally, because he had to say something, he asked, "Why won't you fall in love?"

"Did you watch that film?" Parthiv said. "The director

showed the predicament of an old man who had married a young woman. I want to be like that old man."

"All right, all right."

"I'm going to marry when I'm fifty-six years old, which means that my bride will appear in this earthly realm only when I'm forty. There's a lot of time left."

"You sinner! You utter sinner!"

Parthiv wouldn't back down. Like a brave soldier who kept advancing despite being bashed up and bloodied, Parthiv spoke in an unwavering tone, as though compelled to announce an important decree or express some great truth. "Don't you know, Ravi, that there are no rights without duties?"

"This 'question' also came up in the exam the other day."

Assenting gravely, Parthiv said, "A month from now, one evening—since the first encounter of true love always takes place at eveningtime—you'll stand quietly with Isabel in a pergola by the side of a deserted road. You'll both be afraid to speak. The light brown hair above Isabel's ears will be tousled. The poor thing will want to tuck back her hair, but she'll be too shy to even lift a hand in your presence. What will your duty be at that moment? Your duty will be to fearlessly tuck back her hair. Once you fulfill that duty, you'll obtain the right to kiss Isabel."

They both began to laugh.

"Had you been born in Austria, there would have been many more additions to Freudian philosophy," Ravi said. This was the kind of thing he understood.

Bowing ostentatiously in the Muslim fashion, Parthiv accepted his praise and said, "Now let us conclude today's vulgar literary program." Then he said, "I have to go home. I can't come by tomorrow. There's an exhibition match at Melatar in Kalimpong. Lama from Jalpaiguri will be playing defence for the other side. But if I can get around him a little, just a little…" With a wink, Parthiv bent his strong, muscular leg.

The two of them finally noticed the heavy drumming of rain on the roof. Though they couldn't see it in the darkness, the surging waterfall of Rajbari was probably muddying the water below the bridge and turning it yellow. The electric dam in Sidrabung would finally receive adequate water. The employees would be on alert all night. All night long, water would gush through the flumeline over the high bridge in Barbot.

Ravi went in to get some tea and samosas, then asked Parthiv, "I wonder what's on Isabel's mind. Do you think I'll win her love?"

"I don't want tea. There are no vitamins in tea," Parthiv said.

"Tell me, do you think I'll win her love?"

Parthiv opened up a Bible.

"Why are you reading that now? Tell me if I'm going to win her love!"

In a voice loud and clear enough to cut through the drumming of the rain, Parthiv read aloud from the Bible: "Nine. I say to you, ask and it shall be given to you; seek and you shall find; knock and it shall be opened unto you.

"Ten. For he who asks is given, he who seeks finds, and he who knocks, it opens for him…"

"Isabel must have read that for sure," Ravi said.

Four or five men who were standing around and chatting by the paan shop greeted Bhudev with a namaskar as he came down the road. Bhudev slapped his hands together and returned the namaskar, smiling politely. After he passed, one of the men spat paan-stained saliva into a can beside the shop. When he was done spitting, he spoke, trying to extract shards of betel nut from his mouth with his tongue:

"This time…in the elections…even this scoundrel's trying to become an MLA. I'm sure he'll go to Chowringhee in Calcutta like the rest, and capture the moths trapped in the lights."

"All the scoundrels have gathered. They're all the same. If you were to put them on a scale, no one would weigh any less," said a teacher in a dark black suit, who'd come there after finishing up at school.

A clerk beside him said even more vexedly, "Men who rove drunk through Bahunbasti on Saturday lecture us as politicians on Sunday; how will Darjeeling ever progress?"

"These people have no scruples."

"That's true," the bespectacled teacher agreed.

"Scruples are exactly what's needed," said another tall, stout gentleman with a reddish complexion, who was a contractor, and moderately successful.

"But Bhudev's not like that."

"No, no, Bhudev's not like that," the contractor said. "That man's gusty, even feisty. He's not afraid to speak up in front of anyone."

The clerk-babu turned away to spit in the can, but before spitting, said, "Don't lie to me! Ask me where he was last night, and what he got up to!"

The rest huddled in, forming an image of those who enjoyed hearing only of the failings of others.

Bhudev was heading to the party office. He made sure to go there daily—not to work day and night, but to be seen. Workers who had beaten up the managers of their tea plantations, or who had been denied bonuses, would wait for him there. Villagers who looked like simpletons, but who, in fact, were quite shrewd, also dropped by. Townspeople, especially those in government employment, met Bhudev outside the office. The people of the plantations came running to one party to solve every kind of problem. The townspeople chose different parties, depending on the nature of the problem. This party for a job, that party for a shortage of rice or coal.

Rumour had it that the party was about to launch a movement. This was the topic of today's meeting.

Bhudev's ability to extemporize was masterful. Adlibs shot out of his mouth like cannonballs; by comparison to Janak's meek, gentle responses, his retorts were ballistic missiles that could seek out their targets. Bhudev's replies at a speech in Melatar, in Kalimpong, had become legendary.

When debating equality, Bhudev would say, "In my sense of justice, it's extremely unfair to make everyone equal. We've experienced Congress's equality of self-rule, and we've witnessed the equality of the communists—in Russia, in Eastern Europe." Bhudev would hold up Djilas's new book, *The New Class,* before the crowd.

To those who argued that if we were to look closely—very closely—we'd see that there was no God, Bhudev would reply, "Don't look so closely. If you look at your own father too closely, he'll start to seem like another man—and then will you say there's no father?"

Deploying such bullying tactics, Bhudev was progressing along in life, in the world and in Darjeeling.

The boys who volunteered at the party adored Bhudev because he had all the traits required to be a dictator.

Even Janak admired Bhudev for his honesty and courage.

Janak would never forget a gathering from one Sunday many years back. Addressing public gatherings at Chowkbazaar, greasy politicians always tried to ingratiate themselves by flattering people as respectable citizens, or as people's power, or as human deities, etcetera, but Bhudev wagged his finger, saying, "It's not only Darjeeling's politicians, you people are also opportunists! I know what you want. You want a few of us to always yell at the government, to constantly voice our opposition. You figure that you'll stay safe this way: your sons can still find employment. That's your self-serving interest. Then, at voting time, you say you're going to vote for us without showing us who you're actually supporting: Isn't that what all that sacrifice, your bravery, amounts to? I despise you…!"

The chairman had grabbed Bhudev by the coat and dragged him away.

The people of Pankhabari, Ambate and Kumain had first run across lanky, vigorous, prematurely greying Bhudev in 1944—he had come to solicit votes for Dambarsingh Gurung. His party had ensured the victory of their "Vote-babu" candidate by crossing the narrow bridge over the Relli River and climbing the hill at Lole to canvass in Gitdabling, Biyong and Pemling. Many nights later, far past the Geeta River, on the descent to Gorubathan, Bhudev had stood on the edge of a field and shared his political philosophy with Yashraj: "Desire is the seed of rebirth. Any desire lodged in the mind at the moment of death doesn't go to waste. That desire is reborn, and is most definitely fulfilled, the way the seed of a banyan tree grows by sending its roots into the soil and gathering all the fluids it needs. Only a saint feels no desire at the moment of death, and thereby liberates himself from rebirth; and only a genuinely brave man can hold some great ambition in mind at his moment of death. Desire is the seed. Desire is more powerful than prayer. Prayers are a form of dependence on God; desire is self-reliance. The world can live by the desire of a single individual, and furthermore, if many individuals are unified by the same desire all day and night, this can make God—not to mention the nation's capital!—bow down. But false fancies mustn't be mistaken for desire. It's necessary to have true desire. Consciously or otherwise, for many aeons we have felt the need for a powerful political Great Man to lead our peoples forward; we kept hoping to find him. He, who is born out of a communal need, is our Dream Man. If his success proves to be short-lived, or if he can't be as powerful as we want, we must accept that it's simply because there's not enough force or urgency in our desire…"

In his heart, Bhudev harboured this staunch vision of a Man of the Age as he went about his duties.

Impressed by Bhudev's thoughts, Yashraj had tried to find something to say, and had finally said, "Politicians need to be selfless."

At this, Bhudev had hurtled from the thought-sky down to earth, reverting back into his usual self. "That's not at all necessary!" he had yelled. "Even self-serving men can make great politicians! The reason we're suffering a blight of leadership is that our people trust politicians who don't take a single paisa, and fritter away everything they've got, and fail. The only thing a politician needs is a large vision! When two long lines meet, the angle they form is wider than most because their breadth of vision is wider—do you understand?"

Janak couldn't attend today's meeting because of a task at home. He had brought Da' Namgyal from Gangtok and placed him in a private room in the hospital. The doctors still couldn't ascertain whether it was a disease of the liver or the lungs. Unable to discover anything from the blood from Namgyal's mouth, the doctors were testing his saliva. Namgyal's wife, who came with him, was staying at Janak's. Janak often stayed with them when he was in Gangtok. They had a two-storey wooden house with a green roof just above Gangtok bazaar. A new cement addition was under construction. The house had many suitably large windows facing the street, though they were never seen to be open at the same time. A photo of Janak hung in the ground-floor room.

"You're even better looking in person than in photos," Namgyal's wife said to Janak.

She was Namgyal's younger wife. The elder wife was said to be an officer's daughter from Lhasa. There were two sons on the elder wife's side, and they were studying at Victoria School in Kharsang. Namgyal conducted trade in Tibet. He was a tall, affable Sikkimese gentleman who had studied up to Senior Cambridge. His health had deteriorated in the past two or three years. His younger wife had attended college in Kalimpong, but hadn't passed the Intermediates. Her name was Yamuna.

"Give me a storybook to read, Daju," Yamuna said.

"Choose one for yourself," Ravi said, leaving the room. It simultaneously alarmed, repulsed, embarrassed and thrilled him to be referred to as an older brother by Yamuna, who was more than thirty years old.

That was yesterday.

Yamuna had found a photo album instead of a storybook, and chosen it. She took out the album today, leafing through it while chatting with Sita and Babuni. She compared each face in the album with those of actors and actresses from the cinemas—she knew the names of all the English-film heroes as though they were from her community.

"Didi! You went to Taj Mahal with Janak-bhena! When was that?" Yamuna exclaimed, holding up the photo. Then, without even listening to Sita's answer—"Six or seven years ago"—she said, "I've never been to the south. I really like Madrasis."

Sita glanced at Babuni.

Babuni was downcast. MK had been suspended at work. Babuni and MK had squabbled that morning. "Why are they transferring me so soon?" MK had cried. "I won't go! I'd rather quit a job like this, I'd rather kick this job away."

"What a beauty!" Yamuna exclaimed in awe. "Who is this?"

Sita and Babuni looked over. It was a picture of Isabel.

For some reason, Babuni said, "Some credit should also go to the photography."

Janak, Divya and two of Ravi's friends arrived shortly, and the house filled up.

Yamuna had dressed Babuni's little son in a girl's skirt, and was trying to force him to dance. The child was refusing to do so, and bawling, but Babuni was just sitting by without objecting. When Yamuna thought the child might obey her, she put him down, but he ran straight to Babuni and clung on to her.

Yamuna swooped up the child and whisked him out, kissing him repeatedly.

"Why is she torturing the child?" Ravi said, peeved, to Babuni.

Yamuna returned in a while, clacking her high heels. She turned to Janak and asked, "What English film is playing today? Let's go, all right, Bhena?"

"You're going to the cinema?" Sita asked, surprised and annoyed. "Aren't you going to the hospital, Bahini?"

"There: Didi also wants to come," Yamuna said to Janak.

Sita turned away from Janak and looked down, then glanced over at Babuni. "We don't watch English films," she said. "Only Hindi ones. We don't even understand English."

Janak laughed, and took his wife's side. "I don't understand English films either," he said. "Especially Westerns! They talk in their throats and fight for no reason. I can never figure out why they're fighting—out of what wrath, or to what end."

Yamuna cast a black gaze over everyone.

"We should go to the hospital later," Janak said. "Bhudev's coming over to discuss something." He looked at this watch. "And Ratnabahadur still hasn't come by."

"He should be coming," Ravi murmured.

Yamuna felt spurned by them all. "My poor husband," she said. "He's turned yellow. I have to go now, I'm going. I'll start a big fight if the doctor doesn't let me into his room."

Everyone stared at her.

She opened the zipper of her large, flat, patterned bag, peered in, and closed it again. Then she rushed away clutching the small white handkerchief that she'd taken out.

Yamuna was wearing a long green Tibetan bukhoo and a

yellow sweater, which she hadn't put on fully and had instead slung over her back. She was heading down the street. The sexual longing on her red, lipstick-covered lips was conspicuous and mesmerizing. She stopped at the shops on the street and bought apples and pomegranates for the patient, as well as a novel and some cloth to stitch herself a new blouse.

Alone in his room, Ravi tried, with some difficulty, to compare Yamuna and Isabel. This was difficult, because making such a comparison felt cruel, and to a certain extent, akin to a transgression against Isabel. Though Ravi couldn't delve into the depths of their personalities, there was clear evidence of the differences. Isabel kept her thoughts to herself; Yamuna blurted them out before they even came to mind! This wasn't to do with a difference in age. It was to do with their mental distinctions. Yamuna was still childish; she was the type who always got her heart's desire. Isabel suppressed her inner yearnings and suffered alone in silence.

If you were to ask Yamuna to explain why a certain song was good, she'd go ahead and sing it, but Isabel would deflect the matter with a smile. "It's just a good song, that's why." Yamuna would add her own words to the song to show off her mental prowess and agility, but when Isabel sang the song to herself in secret, she'd sing the correct words while attributing her own meaning to them.

In the time it took for Yamuna to reach the hospital, Janak stood pensively on the verandah outside the room; then he clasped his hands behind his back and started to pace.

Some boys had come down to the paan shop by the garage and were joking around among themselves. One was making the others laugh uproariously. A few of them had slathered white powder onto a carom board and were engaged in a game. Maila was regaling everyone, telling them about how his friends, when drunk, once beat him senseless, and how after they tossed him into the gutter, the sewage had brought him back to his senses. That was all there was to Maila's story, but the way he told it was so enjoyable that it made all the listeners laugh. Without quite realizing it, Janak had at some point taken an interest and started to listen in on their chat. This was because his mind was full of arguments, conflicts and dilemmas: he would start eavesdropping even in the middle of conversations. A round of laughter and clucking arose from the carom players: two nitwits had barely saved themselves from scoring "nil" in the game.

"They'll reap returns by surviving today," Maila commented.

Maila spoke his own kind of Nepali. He would exhort football players to kick the ball with cries of: "Poke it, poke it!" He'd say "carry" instead of "eat". When Kumar married an older woman and brought home all of her children, Maila commented, "He trapped an entire basketful of wild game!"

The thrill of the carom game dissipated when no one could deliver his opponent a "nil" score. The boys marched off to a momo shop, whistling a film tune.

Nowadays Janak felt despondent for no reason. He wanted to do something, and he did a lot too, yet he experienced a certain dissatisfaction no matter what he got up to. He yearned to dedicate his body, mind, soul—and everything he had—to some worthy endeavour. He'd stopped taking on any new tasks as a commissioner in the municipality. He didn't even keep track of the dates of the meetings, and showed up at the chamber only if the other commissioner colleagues reminded him to do so.

Ravi was gazing fondly in the mirror at Janak, who was dressed in a loose, pale blue shirt with fine white stripes.

"Ravi," Janak said, calling him.

"Yes." Ravi went up to his father.

Janak raised his eyes, which were shifting with his thoughts, and examined Ravi. "Are you sure you told Ratnabahadur to come today? He still hasn't shown up."

"He told me, 'I'll come, I'll come with Chhatraman.'"

That was all Janak asked. Ravi just stood by.

Sita called out to them to come and have tea.

Janak went in. Ravi followed him.

"I hear he's been saying that he'll come over only after he sells all his cardamom," Sita said. "Let him do that."

"Cardamom!" Janak was annoyed.

The sum of everything Ratnabahadur had borrowed, little by little, added up to quite a lot by now. He'd placed his home and fields as collateral with Janak. Janak was of a mind to add his own land to it, turn it into a single parcel, and sell it for a high price. This wasn't just an idea: he was under compulsion to sell. Otherwise a warrant would be issued for him.

"How will we go on? I don't see how. I'm lost."

Never before had Ravi seen such despair on Janak's face. The world's practicalities were reacquainting them with each other anew.

Trying to be useful, Ravi said, "I'll go and fetch him, I'll bring him with me this time."

Janak continued to eat. Sita served him more tea. Janak found Sita's tea particularly tasty and delectable. Sita made tart tea for herself using both sugar and salt, but she used only sugar to brew a strong, dark, dense and milky tea for Janak. Imbibing inspiration from the special bowl from Nepal that was reserved for his use alone, Janak said, "You don't have to go, there's no need. I'll do it."

Janak's resolve grew with those last words. Ravi also felt more confident. His confidence was, however, that of a college student, composed of his own innocence and an ignorance of the world, which would not be tested. Whereas Janak's confidence contained a recognition of his own strengths and the world's weaknesses. Ravi was heartened by Janak's resolve, and he felt like everything was lightening up again, as though the problem had been solved.

Just then someone came to the front door, shaking it a little, knocking on it gently.

Ravi got up and went out.

It was MK. "Is your father here?" MK said.

"He is."

MK held out the envelope in his hand, giving it to Ravi. "Give this letter to your father, all right?"

"Whose letter is it? Who sent it?"

"The secretary," MK said.

"Why don't you come in, Uncle?"

MK remained outside the door.

"Do come in."

He came in.

"Sit down."

"I'm fine like this, I'm fine. I'll just meet him and go."

"Arre, do sit down, what's the rush?"

He sat down.

In the letter, Bhudev had informed Janak that the party meeting had gone well, that all of the proposals had passed, and that they should meet soon to consult over other matters.

"Who else was at the meeting?" Janak asked.

MK took a few names. He didn't recognize most of the others.

"Who spoke?"

It turned out that no one had spoken except for Bhudev; the rest had only chatted informally.

There were matters such as employment, trade, the demand on land resources. There was also a proposal on the matter of Nepalis who, year after year, migrated over to settle in Darjeeling and Assam.

Later, Janak heard that Bhudev had said, "The peaceful policies of Panchsheel and co-existence are making us warrior Gorkhalis ineffectual and turning us useless. I've only ever seen one place where tigers, cat, mice, goats, snakes, birds and crocodiles overlook their mutual enmity and live together in harmony. In the zoo below the park."

Ravi, who never went over to MK's room, accompanied him there today. Babuni was chopping up meat. Pushpa was at the stove, lighting a fire to cook the meal.

"I'm not leaving today without eating some meat," Ravi joked.

"Stay," Babuni said readily.

MK took off his shoes and socks and climbed into bed, and sat Ravi down to one side. He said, "I quit my job, Ravi. I didn't like it. I'm going to do business now."

"Or politics? You even went to the party office today."

"I went for a bit," MK said gaily. "But it depressed me. There's going to be, there will have to be, big trouble now."

"What kind of trouble?"

"A movement!" MK took off the striped muffler that was wrapped around his neck and tossed it onto the bed.

"Will that really happen?" Ravi asked.

"It'll definitely happen. To have nothing happen after all this is to die! People are already fired up. You just need a matchstick now, a single matchstick! They'll probably issue a warrant against Janak-babu and others—keep watching, it'll be issued soon. There's a meeting in the bazaar next week, but before that…"

Babuni stood up, having finished chopping the meat. A distinct shadow fell over MK's face, but he kept talking, "Something or the other will happen in the end. I'll be a part of it too."

"You really quit your job so suddenly?" Ravi said.

MK found this question misplaced and jarring, and indicated as much by answering it only after a long pause. "Who wants that useless job?" he said. "Ajoy says there's a job in the office of the district court, but I don't want to work as a clerk anymore. You get sick of copying names all day long. I'm going to go into business now. There's money in business."

Bhudev strolled out by himself that evening and went to the Jalpahad hill. Darjeeling town lay sprawled out before his eyes, not even a half-minute away as the crow flies. He saw the small red-and-green wood houses on the Singmari hill on the way north. Below was the jail, from where the twin wires of the waste disposal system's ropeway rose up. The clock on the four-faced Capital tower showed that it was almost six o'clock. Darjeeling's fashionable homes and offices were in that area. The expanse of Chowrasta was also somewhere around there, but when he sought it out, only the blue rotunda of Rajbhavan came into view. At the centre stood Chowkbazaar, with countless black dots milling around. Furthest away, in the hazy distance, were the Falelung and Sandakaphu mountain ranges. The dazzling Himalayas were even whiter and more attractive in the background. Though the shadow of nighttime was falling here, it was as bright as day up there. Entire new structures seemed to have cropped up on the Himalaya's white expanse and majestic height. That was where the mountainous Teesta and Rangeet rivers originated. As Bhudev looked on, it occurred to him that for his people, the Teesta was even holier and grander than the Ganges.

A flock of birds came hurtling down from the blue of the sky. The birds were small, and more than forty in number. All of the same species, they flew in one flock. None had an identity of its own outside of the flock. Bhudev held his breath in exhilaration and watched the flock's flight and velocity, and the birds' mutual awareness of each other. High up in the emptiness of the sky, where there was no obstacle or barrier or impediment, where there was only limitlessness and liberation, the birds suddenly halted in unison, and then, becoming one, flew off at a great speed in another direction—how did they do it? They flew far away in one indecipherable mass, then, in an instant, dropped like a waterfall, cascading down as though they'd seen some invisible mountain trail in the sky and had started to follow it closely. They skipped along that waterfall with their wings spread out, as though a unified mind, a single soul, inspired and drove them all; their every move, their flight and velocity, were born of a common soul.

The birds landed together on a bare tree, covering its black branches. Then, in a blink of the eye, they were gone.

Bhudev looked for them everywhere.

They weren't visible anywhere.

Over the past week, trouble had begun to spread throughout the bazaar, along with rumours that Bhudev and his ilk were holding meetings.

News of such rumours reached the party office time and again, and it startled Bhudev.

Some boys seemed to have hurled rocks at a large army truck that was driving in from Lebong. One of the boys was even arrested.

The following day, some boys stopped a Land Rover that was coming up from the plains and broke a Bengali man's eyeglasses and threw away his suitcases... Bhudev immediately rushed over, but the only people he saw there were those who had gathered around to discuss the incident.

That evening, again, came news—a few boys had barged into a Marwari trader's shop in Doronga bazaar and hurled rocks, breaking the windows and beating up the shopkeeper as well. A crowd had formed by the time Bhudev got there. All the shops were closed. The police had taken the boys off to the station.

A skinny policeman in plainclothes told Bhudev, "The OC Sahib has asked you to come to the station."

Bhudev understood that once he went to the police station, he wouldn't be let out. But it didn't feel right to run away. The other policemen that he noticed nearby were almost certainly carrying arrest warrants.

Many people began going from the junction to the police station, but just as many people were also coming back from there. A few were claiming that Section 144 had been imposed. The shops at the junction were shuttering up in a hurry.

Posters demanding Bhudev's release were released within half an hour.

Nothing else happened after nightfall.

Janak went to the police station the following day. Policemen who'd come all the way from Dali were lined up along the road to the station. A lot of other people were around. Some college boys were huddled to one side, chanting slogans. There were no girls present.

Janak went straight into the station.

Five or six boys were locked up in a detention room. They perked up when they saw Janak. Only a short while ago, a few of them of had been spiritedly singing film songs, most probably to demonstrate to those on the outside that they weren't scared. It had embarrassed those who'd overheard them. Janak recognized only one of the boys in the lock-up.

The crowd began to thicken. Police officers kept walking to the edge of the crowd, looking around, then walking back. A few men squeezed through the spots that the policemen vacated and peered into the station. A group of thirty or forty gathered at the station door even as everyone watched on.

An inspector came and whispered into the ear of a constable who was lined up on the road. Then all the policemen retreated and went to stand, in pairs, at the door of the police station. After they retreated, the crowd, which continued to swell, began cheering as if victorious, and started to mingle with those at the door. Amid all of this thronging, some people began to chant slogans.

Janak came out shortly. He surveyed the crowd and called a few people he recognized, and took them back in.

A whisper rippled through the crowd: "They're going to let them go now, they're definitely going to let them go." The sloganeering grew louder.

Soon, everyone present heard an iron gate inside the police station squeaking open. Cries of "They've let them out, they've let them out!" rose up from all sides. The crowd's eyes were trained impatiently on the door. Cries of "They're here, they're here!" arose again several times, but no matter how long the crowd looked on, no one appeared at the door. When a fat moustachioed policeman showed up, cries of "Here they are, here they are" rose up again, followed by laughter.

Then, one by one, the boys who had been locked up began to show up for real at the door. They were coming out. With smiling faces, they were waving at people they knew. For some reason, a burst of laughter swept through the crowd. Someone was probably acting a "comic" somewhere. Someone in the crowd yelled, "Move aside, make way, make way!" and a plump woman shoved forward through an opening, carrying a handful of khada scarfs. She placed one on each of the freed boys. The sound of uncontained joy rocked through the crowd.

The crowd then escorted the freed boys, each of them donning a white khada, to the junction.

By the time Janak came out, the policemen were scattered over the lawn in front of the police station, sipping tea from mugs. The crowd had encircled the bazaar, growing in size like a snowball as it moved forward, and had then returned to the junction before scattering.

Bhudev hadn't been in the police station. He'd been taken to the jail the previous day. Janak headed down to the jailhouse with a policeman in tow.

Along the way, an unseemly kind of silence had settled over the Chandmari neighbourhood. Not a single child was to be seen playing on the streets. The short waste disposal ropeway was already carrying away the town's garbage at this hour. Walking on, Janak looked at the eagles, crows and vultures perched on the garbage, being carried along by the ropeway. The Phulbari area, too, was deserted. Janak thought of the many dry, thin leaves that would have fallen in the pond by the office, and how the willow tree on the ridge would be dipping its fine tresses in the water. At each golden dawn and dusk, the ancient trees further beyond would youthfully examine this splendour through the hundred eyes on their trunks.

Janak laughed to himself, recalling an old saying of his—the soul is eternal and indestructible, but the mind never gets old.

It had been years since he'd strolled through Phulbari. This realization silenced him.

Janak couldn't explain to himself why all of these feelings were bubbling up inside him today.

Permitted five minutes to talk to Bhudev, Janak told him to sign a bond, as the others had done, and to come out. Bhudev exploded with anger.

"They wreaked havoc ahead of the appointed time!"

"You call that havoc?"

"Okay, a proper movement…by doing that, they ruined everything," Janak explained. "The people aren't involved, they won't join in. And our friends are content just to fire off telegrams to Delhi and Calcutta. What can we do, what hope can we hold on to?"

Bhudev gave Janak a scathing look. "That I'm in jail is itself an opportunity for you to feel an urge, or find a reason, to do something," he declared.

Janak's face reddened. "Don't act so high and mighty, Bhudev-babu!" he said. "For the sake of party unity, sign the bond and be as humble as the rest."

Bhudev was quick with his final decision, "For the sake of party unity, I must never sign such a document."

Some pamphlets that were printed overnight began circulating through the bazaar the following morning. Ratnabahadur, Waiba and Arjun were going home after having fallen asleep at the restaurant they'd eaten at the previous night. Arjun reached for a pamphlet as they reached Barrick.

Janak's statement was: the party had no links to the mayhem taking place in town. The government had no base for arresting Bhudev, and must immediately grant his unconditional release.

Arjun asked for one more pamphlet, folded both of them and tucked them into a shirt pocket below his pullover.

The light of truth doesn't travel uninterrupted along a straight line. It is obliged to pass through the gravity field of many a prejudice and self-interest, and so must curve and veer a little off course. Janak and Bhudev's paths separated clearly and definitively from that day onwards. Each mulled over this incident neutrally, and each felt that the truth was on his side. What differed was that Janak supported his position with stacks of written rules and laws, while Bhudev with past events, or with events that ought to occur in the future. Janak just couldn't accept the unusual new way in which Bhudev was interpreting established events. The movement cooled down and came to nothing. Bhudev was released about a month later. He began, once again, to go to the party office all the time. To go to the office every day in a small town amounts to engaging in day-to-day politics. Janak and Bhudev were often seen together at the party office, but their relationship now resembled the relationship between pages 1 and 100 of the same book.

Janak never brought external politics into the house, he left it on the street when coming home. He was preoccupied with how to prevent the house walls from collapsing, with how to help the flowerbuds blossom. To claim that he didn't seek some prestige or a legacy is to write an outright lie. On the subject of legacy, Janak always said, "May the name 'Janak' suffice on my memorial, may there be no need to write anything else." On the subject of prestige, he said, "Prestige is like your son or grandson, it looks after your mind and body in old age." Janak's sense of prestige was thus materialistic and bound to his lifetime. His only inner anxiety was—may his position and social standing never diminish. He was worried about rising too high lest his fall be three times as precipitous. Janak sometimes wondered: is this psychological apprehension a result of my increasing age?

But even he knew there was no connection between this apprehension and his age.

Many events, including the Dashain and Tihar festivals, took place over the following months.

Ravi completed most of the fourth year of his BA studies. MK, who was still suspended from his job, finally received a letter of dismissal. Babuni was so distraught she couldn't leave the house for two full days.

That month, a family came and asked for Pushpa's hand in marriage. Though Babuni didn't want this, Pushpa's father agreed. The boy was a sergeant clerk in the Gorkha troops in Malaya. Neither Sita nor Janak nor MK nor anyone else had, till now, so much as imagined Pushpa as a marriageable young woman. Upon hearing that she'd be getting married and leaving home, they were all dumbstruck at first. Then they judged themselves guilty, somehow, of not having paid her adequate attention or given her enough love.

"It's not Pushpa's responsibility to look after Malaya's national independence or the future of the Gorkha troops. All Pushpa has to do with her husband is to look after their own future," Janak said. At the wedding, Sita gifted Pushpa a sari finer than any Pushpa had ever worn at Dashain time. A mic blared out from the rooftop.

Whenever he heard a mic, Janak remembered two things:

Old Ratnabahadur always grew despondent when there was a wedding in the community; he would stuff the fireplace with wood to start warming himself before a fire.

"That's too much," his old woman would say, pulling out a few smoking logs.

When the fire caught and the flames began leaping, Ratnabahadur would move back a little and say, "Tchee, weddings these days—you can't even call them weddings. You stick a mic on a roof for ten rupees and play raucous music all night. You offer plates to those who come, but have nothing by way of food or drink: two paper-thin rotis and some squash roots!"

His argumentative, egoistic old woman agreed: "How could anything these days ever be as good as in the old days?"

The old couple could never forget their own wedding. They'd had an arranged marriage on the sixteenth day of the month of Falgun exactly thirty-one years ago today, with a nine-piece musical band in the wedding procession. Kaase Darzis had blown narsingh trumpets from a platform on the roof, sounding out the auspicious news of the wedding. Lamba Lama, Hukumdas Sardar and Doctor Yuddhabir Rai (the poor men had all since passed away) had danced all night to the sweet melody of the shehnai. Kaji Saheb had taken a photograph when Bagam Kanchha, who was home on holiday from the army, had dressed up as a maruni in women's clothes and danced, spinning a plate in each hand. They'd had to set another pot of rice on the boil after eighty kilogrammes proved insufficient to feed the wedding procession. Nowhere in today's Darjeeling would you see members of a wedding procession sitting in rows to eat in the courtyard while being attacked from all sides by chickens, which, when shooed away, raised clouds of dust with their wings.

As the wedding procession had neared the bride's house, they had recalled that it was inauspicious to approach the bride's house from uphill, and had turned around and come back from downhill. Seeing the women and children from the bride's side waiting to greet them with stitched-leaf bowls of red rice and yogurt, the procession had lit up and started to shout:

What's our groom like?
Like a sack of rice!
He never falls in love,
But when he does, he never stops.
Once he catches you, he'll never let go!

The groom had urged them on: "Say it louder!"

As they were about to return home with the bride in a palanquin, Bhalubabu's youngest had placed two bottles of strained millet beer on a tray and made a ritual offering. Twenty-six-year-old Ratnabahadur had dismounted from the horse and accepted the offering with two of Queen Victoria's silver coins, and then drunk the milky liquid.

The other thing that happened was, Yamuna used to cry. Whenever she heard a mic blaring out from a wedding, Yamuna—a schoolteacher in the old days—used to start bawling in class, in front of the students. Perhaps to give the impression that wedding music evoked a memory of some tragic abandonment, or reminded her of a chapter from an unfulfilled love story. Yamuna was a number-one exhibitionist!

Another event that took place in this period: Ajoy Das moved away from here to someplace near the court. He said his housing allowance hadn't been sufficient to cover his rent!

Yamuna took over Ajoy Das's room before it was even empty. The very next day, she brought a cupboard, a mirror, a table and some chairs, and crammed them all into the room. They moved Namgyal here after his TB diagnosis. Namgyal didn't like either this neighbourhood or this room, but said nothing, since it was only for a few months, for the duration of his treatment. Janak would go over to chat with him. Namgyal would get up to all sorts of pranks, as though he were still in good health. The Hayward bottles to "sip just a little" from soon formed a row. When Yamuna tried to throw them away, Namgyal said, "No, don't discard them. These are the 'cups' that I've won as trophies. We ought to display them properly."

Yamuna was also getting a telephone line installed (so fast) in their room. It's not possible to say a telephone wasn't necessary. Even Namgyal would say, "We may have to call the doctor in a hurry at night. We may have to order some medicine from the shop."

"Everybody's asking my phone number," Yamuna said in English. "And, you see, I feel small without one." In Nepali, she added, "It's getting embarrassing."

The following day, after the workers who had spent a couple of hours setting up the telephone line had left, Janak said, "This telephone line must be inaugurated by Mrs Namgyal."

The proposal delighted both the husband and wife. "Today! Today!" they cried.

From that day on, the telephone became Yamuna's plaything. She marked up the names of everyone she knew in the directory. She placed calls all day long. Even at night, she woke Janak up from sleep to joke around with him. And all day long: "Bhena-jyu, who was that person who came by your place today?" "Bhena-jyu, look down there, on the street, that dolled-up woman going by—whose wife is she?" "Bhena-jyu…"

Babuni and Sita would talk among themselves: "That poor husband, he's a god. She's clearly the one who made him ill. She doesn't look after him, she just roams around. She didn't come home all day yesterday. Their servant boy's exactly the same. He asked to eat chowmein. How would I know how to cook chowmein—it's not as if I've ever had any! That's what I came to tell you about."

"And then, sometimes, she sits on her husband's bed and weeps!" Babuni said. "What's wrong with that woman!"

About two months after Pushpa left home, Babuni told MK something.

MK's entire face crumpled.

MK lost his peace of mind for good from that day forward. Pushpa had got married and gone away; Amrita was already in Class 8. MK thought about his age, and he thought about Babuni's age. Given the circumstances, the birth of a new baby in the house struck him, somehow, as an inauspicious, shameful and extremely uncalled for occurance. Another crisis heaped atop their boundless suffering. The son they'd previously had had died as a toddler.

How thrilled, how excited the husband and wife had been seventeen years ago, when Pushpa had been conceived a few months after their wedding. Babuni was still of a tender age. Overcome with embarrassment, she said she wished she didn't have to go out in public. All night long, MK would insist that it was a boy. He was too ashamed, later, to show his face in front of the mother. After that, when Amrita came, neither of them saw it as anything new. MK was deadened by the prospect of having another baby after all these years. Perhaps he shouldn't have been, but he was.

Not even the thought of a small life growing in the moisture and warmth of his wife's belly ignited MK's enthusiasm.

He finally put forward this brave thought: "God is giving

me this baby to test me, to force me to become a man and confront the world." Inspired by this thought, he showed affection to his sleeping wife as he used to in the past, lovingly stroking her body when the lights were out.

MK laughed a little to himself. Then, even as he tried to figure out why he was laughing, he forgot what he was laughing about. Just as he was blissfully falling asleep, MK remembered Yamuna. Suddenly, he was wide awake.

"Barren, childless woman!" Deploying his fiery rage, MK demolished the vision of Yamuna in his eyes. "She takes phone calls from everyone all day long in her room. She stands up and argues with her sick husband. It would be preferable to die..."

Sorrow and pity for Namgyal flooded MK's mind.

Ravi was looking at himself in the mirror, fixing his hair—he turned sideways to check after tucking his hair behind the ears, then put away the comb. The comb fell to the floor; he picked it up and tossed it onto the bed.

There was no one at home; there was no one in the entire row of homes. Only sickly Namgyal, who, whether asleep or awake, coughed from time to time in the other room.

Ravi was taking Isabel to Sinchel today. So many of the fantasies he'd entertained, the dreams he'd nurtured, were going to be fulfilled...

They're sitting side by side in the front seats of the Jeep... Side by side... There's the fragrance of new clothes in the air. Ravi had lost sleep tonight thinking...I'll look at her when the Jeep turns at the curve in Bataase...

Leaving Jorbangala behind, the Jeep trundles along the

long, empty, pothole-filled forest road. There are two ponds here, one large and one small… A photo from the centre of the road, and then another photo… There are also pergolas; there's a damp, narrow trail around the pond; there are rhododendron trees…

Although there are roads and trees like this everywhere, this particular spot is far away from town, and devoid of people; even ordinary grass and twigs look pretty on that road.

There, I'll tell Isabel about all the love in my heart…

And then, with her permission, just once, on the lower lip…

Picking up his camera, Ravi wondered merrily about what kind of food Isabel might have prepared for the trip. Making sure to place the permit for Sinchel in a novel that he was taking along, Ravi polished his tan shoes and went out to the verandah, shutting the door behind him.

Janak, coming up the stairs, looked at him: "Where are you going?" Yamuna was climbing the stairs too, with her long pale hand in the crook of Janak's left arm.

"We're going to Sinchel," Ravi said. "I'm going with friends. I'm taking a Jeep."

"Come back early," Janak said, heading up. Yamuna went up with him. Then she turned back to look at Ravi through her long, pointy green goggles. He was running off dressed in a brown suit, a camera bag bouncing on his back.

Ravi was walking, then running.

When he checked his watch, he saw that it wasn't even eleven o'clock…

He decided to take the long route so as to arrive at Isabel's house at exactly half-past eleven. The driver would have brought the Jeep to the petrol pump by then.

After walking a while, Ravi realized there wasn't even a single paisa in his pocket.

He stopped in confusion in the middle of the road…

A part of him said: why take any money, you won't need it.

But then another argument came up: what if I do need it?

Even a porter hauling a sack of rice somehow managed to turn around to stare at Ravi, who was standing in the middle of the road. Though perhaps the porter was just looking for the absent owner of the rice.

Nevertheless, this made Ravi stride ahead confidently.

The shops and houses of the area, the drains there, the time and the day, were the same as ever. Some boys, let off for the day after their school won a trophy, had fashioned goalposts out of clods of grass, and were playing an energetic game of football on the broad road, using a large bundle of paper wrapped up in a scarf. The football kept falling apart, scattering white shreds of paper in whichever direction it was kicked in.

Ravi clucked in regret: "I also forgot my scarf…"

He used this excuse to return home.

The first twenty or so steps of the return journey felt arduous; then he got lost, again, in his thoughts and fancies.

He mused over how often, when going to a place he'd never set foot in, he would suddenly feel as though he'd been here before, he'd already come here, everything here was familiar to him…

He began to feel as though all of this had also happened before while going to meet Isabel.

In Sinchel, I'll tell Isabel—I feel, somehow, that the two of us have been here before together. I'm sure that we've been here. Have you forgotten? It's all coming back to me. Look, that's the exact same tree; and that's the same road; and your reflection on the water is also exactly the same…

But Isabel won't believe him…she'll look shyly away at the grass.

Ravi prepared to tell her, "It's a memory from our past lives."

He hoped that Isabel would finally concede: "I'm not sure…"

"I remember everything because my love was so overwhelming," Ravi would say, and then he'd triumph.

The flow of these merry fancies dried up when Ravi noticed that he was almost home. Now he felt sheepish and apprehensive. If only he could fetch what he wanted without anyone seeing him. If his father were to so much as see him and ask, "Why are you back…?" Ravi couldn't bear for this to happen.

The door was slightly ajar.

Ravi snuck up the stairs.

He slipped into his room.

He took out his wallet from below the mattress and put it in an inner pocket. Then he bent down to peek through the keyhole of the closed wooden door between the two rooms.

Yamuna was turned towards the light from the window, dressed in a long pink bukhoo and thin jade silk blouse with white woven high-heel sandals. Her hair was visible, gathered in a bun with a black net. She was looking at a picture in a large English newspaper, saying, "The physique of these people! Look at how nice their bodies are…"

"And isn't yours nice?" Janak said, leaning over, having

taken off his coat and tossed it onto the bed. "What are your measurements?"

Yamuna turned around. Her fine, shiny Tibetan apron came into view. "Mine…? I'm barely… I'm thirty-three, eighteen, twenty-nine!"

"Shall I explain where your beauty lies?" Janak asked, narrowing his eyes.

"Stop, old man," Yamuna said. She lifted her arms and began to arrange the loose sleeves on her blouse, drawing them up in wide folds. Her red nails danced above Janak's forehead.

"I understand it, that's why I can explain…"

"You don't have to, Sir, a four-twenty like you!"

"Me a four-twenty?"

"You, Jasraj and that bearded man—you're all four-twenties. A total of one thousand, two hundred and sixty!"

Janak straightened up, laughing. "Here's where your attraction lies," he said. "From your waist to your feet, that part of you is long and slim and truly becoming. I really like it."

Ravi drew his eye away from the keyhole.

He felt anger, guilt, restlessness, horror. His rising emotions made him feel hot. In his head, in his chest, arose a fear that his heart might burst open and he might scream.

Then he heard, "Let go of me… All of your other habits are all right…"

Ravi left the house and went down to the street. He noticed that there was a chequered scarf in his hands. Without looking back at the house, he crossed the street and took a hillside path where he wouldn't run into anyone.

The father of the house, as well as the son? The father at home…how can I possibly do the same thing outside?

What will my mother and sister say?

Ravi didn't go to the petrol pump. He didn't go to Isabel's house, and he didn't go to Parthiv's house either. He didn't come home till nightfall, after everybody had gone to sleep.

A series of snowstorms had heaped snow on the Himalaya, triggering a massive avalanche. When Ravi noticed this one day, it scared him.

He was furious, and also terrified. He felt disillusioned with life.

He kept looking at his mother and sister. They continued to perform their duties as always. There was a clamouring in his heart. His love and pity for Sita and Divya increased deep within. He tried to remain silent and strong, to be a man of character.

Janak was busy organizing a fete in assistance of elderly veterans. Bitter, resentful lines were hardening on Ravi's face.

This morning, Janak shouted out to him, "Ravi!"

Ravi heard him, but instead of replying, "Hajoor," as readily as always, he just came over and stood by.

Janak, who was scribbling down something, glanced over at him briefly. "What are you doing…are you studying?"

"I was studying."

"Then go and study. I'll assign the task to someone else."

Ravi returned to his room. One by one, he took out his English, history, economics and Nepali books. Sitting in bed under the covers, he formed a table by bracing two pillows against the window, and set to studying. Whenever he looked up from the books and turned towards the window, he would stare for a very long time. His thoughts kept drifting further and further from his studies. Isabel often came to mind. Ravi kept staring. Later, when his legs and back started to ache, he remembered that he was supposed to be studying.

He leafed through the pages of an economics book, looking at the diagrams on some of the pages, but couldn't concentrate.

One day, Sita even asked him, "What's happening to you? Why are you so sluggish?"

"I'm studying, can't you see?" Ravi tried to laugh gaily. "I don't even leave the room."

Sita examined his face. "How many days till the exams?"

"There's still a month and a half left." With another laugh, Ravi asked, "What if I don't pass?"

"As soon as you pass, you need to go and study to become a lawyer. We—your father and I—talk about this all the time."

Ravi fell silent.

"Come, have tea," Sita called out to him, heading to the kitchen.

"No, Aama! I don't want to go away to study any further." Though Ravi tried to sound restrained, controlled and composed, his voice quavered tearfully.

Sita put some gooseberry preserves in a bowl so Ravi could have it with his tea. This seemed to be in preparation for an open, leisurely conversation. She began to recount family stories from long ago to her son. She reminded him how, when Ravi and Divya were small, Janak used to say, "Only on Thursdays will I not beat you. I'll beat you on every other day if you cause mischief." She explained how this rule came to govern their home. Sita wasn't treating Ravi as a grown-up young man studying for a Bachelor's degree. The mother and son chatted for a long time. Never before had Ravi felt so close to his mother.

But none of this could quell his inner frustrations and dilemmas.

Ravi found it very difficult nowadays to venture out of his door and leave the house. Just as hard as leaving was coming back home. Having to have prolonged conversations with acquaintances felt like torture to him. These kinds of thoughts came to him often, and with great force, instead of anything related to his studies. The one-and-a-half months left till exams felt incredibly onerous to him. If a month and a half could pass by in a single day and Ravi could be done with all of his exams, he would, from the next day on, find this earth to be more blissful than heaven. After that, any worries about the results would be his family's—that would no longer be Ravi's concern. He could go anywhere after that—he could even be buried in a ditch somewhere. He found comfort in his own wrath and vindictiveness, and thought: "I'll sink very low. Why not fall? Why not start falling right now? Why hold off on this desire for self-destruction?" There was clearly a reason for it, though he couldn't quite grasp it. Some great power still kept him in check. This wasn't a celestial or divine power, but a worldly one—it was his love for Isabel—but Ravi neither understood it nor tried to do so. He kept telling himself: "I'll go to ruin after the exams."

The unblemished mental innocence of childhood never ends, never disappears, throughout life. With the maturity of age it is displaced into our thoughts as reason or intelligence. That's what idealism is. In the beginning, we believe that idealism resides in individuals. But to believe that idealism resides in individuals is akin to mistaking an idol for God, and praying to it. Right now, Ravi's situation was similar to that of a child standing on a riverbank, watching in dismay as the beautiful idols of the gods were floated away and drowned in a muddy river. His dismay wasn't entirely unreasonable.

Ravi didn't realize that Sita had been scrutinizing him the previous day. The eyes of the mother and son met briefly, then darted away, as though both of them had something to hide. Ravi's heart began to pound against the walls of his ribcage, as if to ask, "Does Aama also know about everything?" Sita looked unnerved to him.

This caused Ravi to feel outraged, but he lacked the gall to take it out on Janak. He had begun to despise Janak, but couldn't cut him off. Ravi found that he couldn't direct his feelings towards their rightful target. He felt that his life had become like a broken watch which, having lost its short needle, could only indicate the hourless minutes with its emphatic ticking. Life had become a watch indicating only the minutes.

Isabel never came over, nor was she likely to ever do so now. Ravi deemed his love weak and insignificant. He couldn't say why, but merely fantasizing about love now felt sinful, polluted and wrong. He didn't notice exactly when this feeling of transgression, of sin, had come into love. Neither was he interested in examining this or in proving it mistaken through analysis, because for him, the feeling had already transformed into a deeply internalized truth.

Ravi ran into Yamuna frequently these days. She hadn't changed. She was as exuberant as ever. She was even more exuberant after buying a new radio. And she spent just as much time as ever gossiping about other people with Sita.

"Watch out, Didi! Bhena might bring home a younger wife!"

"He might," Sita said, smiling wanly.

"I should bring you," Janak said, looking at Yamuna.

At this ruse, the coquettish Yamuna squealed, "This Bhena is really inde-e-e-cent! He's dangerous!"

Ravi left and went over to MK's room.

When he got there, he wished he hadn't come.

MK was sitting in bed. Seeing Ravi, who didn't visit much, he hastily said, "Come, come. Sit here," and sat him down on the bed.

A dark man was seated in the only chair in MK's home, with a teacup resting on the side table.

MK introduced Ravi: "Janak-babu's son Ravi! And this is CS: CS-babu."

Ravi looked over, and the man grinned, stretching his lips, which were covered by a sparse yet unkempt moustache.

"You were discussing something," Ravi said. "I was just dropping by in the middle of my studies."

"Don't study too hard, or you won't remember anything," MK said. "Ravi's taking his BA exams this year."

The dark man grinned again, flashing his yellow teeth. "As for me, I came from Bhadrapur," he said. "To look for a teacher."

"Oh…"

"I'm here to discuss this with him."

MK, going to Nepal to become a teacher? Ravi didn't like this. "Are you leaving?" he asked MK.

For a while, MK didn't reply. Then he said, "What's there for me to do here? I'll be going there with a job, and can do business on the side. It'll also be a pilgrimage, and a service to the motherland."

Babuni was at the stove, preparing tea for Ravi. When she heard MK, she got upset. "He finally agreed to go because I told him to! He was saying, oh, it's a foreign land, people get bitten by mosquitoes out there, letters don't arrive there, money orders don't come through. He quit a job he had right here, one for which he was about to earn a pension!"

"I quit for other reasons," MK shot back.

It turned out that Dharmaprasad had sent Janak a letter from Dhankuta two days back, asking him to send over a schoolteacher for the Nandaprasad Primary School, which he'd recently founded in memory of his father. Janak had told MK that if he wanted to go, he should leave at once. Janak would make provisions to cover his family's monthly household expenses over here. MK had gone along with the suggestion, and had even sent a letter to Dhankuta, but no one knew what had come of it. He hadn't received a reply.

"How promptly do people get their salaries over there?" MK asked eagerly. "How many days after the end of the month are they paid?"

The dark Master-ji only snorted in laughter, "Huh."

"Tell me, how many days after the end of the month are they paid?"

"Five months after the end of the month!" The Master-ji guffawed, and added, "Sometimes they're paid a year later. Though they do stop receiving their salaries when they die."

Even Ravi laughed at this. He took a liking to this dark-skinned man. MK, though, grew despondent.

"You get your salary from the monsoon month of Saun only when the rice fields ripen in the month of Mangsir, or actually, only after the price of rice rises. And even after the price rises, you get your salary only when the contract to sell rice in India opens up. And even that salary you don't receive in full. And on top of that, there are school secretaries who don't share a single paisa of the funds they receive from the office. They use it to tour the Taj Mahal in Agra instead. Thieves!"

There were flashes of genuine anger in the Master-ji's eyes. MK couldn't tell whether the man had come to recruit schoolteachers or to discourage those who had signed up.

"And on this side," the Master-ji added, "the family members of those who go to Nepal to serve the motherland become martyrs!"

Ravi had forgotten the Master-ji's name, so, referring to him as Master-babu, he began to inquire about the education system out there.

"Over there, we have to construct the schools first, and only then can we operate them," he said. "That's not the kind of place, like India, where you can go and teach in a building that someone else has constructed, where you receive your salary in an envelope on the very first day of each month. So it's better for cowards, and those who can't endure hardship, not to go there."

This wounded MK's pride.

"And what about the other customs and practices out there?" Ravi asked.

"What other customs and practices? There are neither customs nor practices out there," the Master-ji said. "Those who have a little education, all they do is write poetry. The rest spend day and night cheating and swindling. The rest of those with an education join the military." After saying this, the Master-ji chuckled for a long time.

Ravi and MK also laughed a little.

"Well, no matter what, you teachers are offering our people something as precious as an education out there, in a blind land," Ravi said, resorting to a wholly bookish rhetoric. "Knowledge is an embellishment, it's a jewel."

"A jewel for sure!" The Master-ji said sardonically. "Nothing is as uncomfortable as wearing that jewel. You can't work as a coolie wearing that jewel, or else you could enjoy that free life, carrying loads without hesitation, without shame. Selling your strength is the most basic hallmark of manhood—but you can't live that life because of this jewel; you must live as though you've shrivelled up and died. Knowledge is definitely a jewel."

Drawn to the Master-ji's words, Ravi laughed. "So let's say education is a poison to destroy our lives," he said, "and schools are factories where we earn iron-jewels of dissatisfaction. Knowing this, why don't you demolish all of those schools?" A textbook answer popped into Ravi's head—the blame lies not with schools, but with the goal of turning schools into places that offer a poor education.

But the dark, shiny Master-ji had a different answer: "The whole world would change today if we were allowed to, or if we could, work according to our convictions. Right now, we must keep our convictions to one side, and our work to the other. This obstructs everything. The only conviction is in having a conviction."

Ravi grew solemn.

MK had grown weary of all of this quite a while back. He motioned for them to be quiet, and said, "I'm not going. I don't think I'll go."

Having received this message, the Master-ji stood, and looking out of the door, said, "People like you shouldn't go."

MK lost his temper. "What kind of person should go, then?" he demanded.

"People like me." The Master-ji lifted his moon-shaped moustache again, and said, "People like me, who don't have children or anyone else to look after. People who, when needed, can cross the Arun, Tamor and Mechi Rivers from one day to the next, and come back here—that's the kind of people who should go. We always talk about Nepal-Nepal, but as for Nepal… You shouldn't go."

After offering a namaskar, the Master-ji left.

"He was fun to talk to. I can't remember his name. What is it?" Ravi asked.

"CS," MK said with distaste.

"His full name?"

"Charcoal Sack."

Today, once again, MK and Ravi sat on stools in the sunshine, chatting. Ravi had started referring to MK as Uncle.

"Uncle, you should look for work soon. You can't sit around idly like this…"

"I'm trying."

The trilling of a phone call sounded out from Namgyal's room. Both of them looked at that room's window. Sickly Namgyal picked up the phone and spoke, then began shouting angrily in Hindi: "Don't know! Don't know!" He hung up, but kept shouting: "Mrs Namgyal, Mrs Namgyal, I'll…!"

MK laughed. Ravi also found the situation amusing.

"You have to look for a job, Uncle!"

As though to himself, MK muttered, "What is this: can't a man live without a job?"

"Try telling my father to look too!"

"I've told him."

The embers of domestic discord sparked up frequently at home these days; Babuni would scream at MK over tiny matters, and argue with him. The dues that he had received upon losing his job didn't last for even ten days. One Marwari trader came right to the house. After that, Babuni paid off their debts to all the other shopkeepers. Even friends and acquaintances began pouring in, as though they'd been waiting to pounce as soon as MK lost his job. The other day, a postal worker made sure to wrest back eight paisa for outstanding tea expenses. There was another reason as well for MK to be angry: he had observed Jayabilas unable to touch a hair on Janak's head, even though Janak owed Jayabilas a huge debt—while the whole world was rushing over to strip MK of all his clothes and possessions.

"It turns out that it's possible to live without money, but you won't feel like living," MK remarked pitiably.

The words, "Tell that to my father!" came to Ravi's mouth, but he stopped himself from uttering them out loud.

MK seemed to overhear his thoughts. "Janak-babu is also quite erratic these days—his thinking is unpredictable," he said.

"Unpredictable in what manner?" Ravi asked.

"He's probably going to quit the party. There's a rumour saying he's quitting, that he's already quit."

"It would be better if he were to quit."

MK looked over at Ravi. Ravi was turned away, his lips pressed tightly together. Examining Ravi's prominent nose and dusky skin, MK felt that Ravi looked even older than he.

In Janak's youth, serving the nation meant that you went to villages to set up schools, and spent your life teaching: a pleasant dream. Janak had himself fallen under the influence of a Congress activist and had, for a couple of Sundays, gathered the children of the villages near Nimkidanda and Dhadgaun in order to educate them. Then it had occurred to him that partaking in politics was itself a service to the nation. By now, Janak had seen a lot. Nowadays, when he heard about serving the nation, he'd laugh but wouldn't say anything.

"Janak has really changed," MK said.

"Let him change," said Ravi.

Instead of growing thinner, MK had got considerably plumper, though not in the body. Only his face had plumped up, and a yellow hue had come over it; his skin had also grown loose and baggy. Perhaps he had some peace of mind: no one ever saw him rushing around to do anything, although it was probably his old habit of curling up in bed that prevented him from rushing around and getting things done. He would scream in anger if his meals were delayed. He was hungry twenty-four hours a day. Babuni would go to Sita's place to ask if she could borrow some food, cooked or otherwise.

"Everyone helps out in times of trouble. They feel important when they do," MK remarked one day. "Who wouldn't perform their religious duties if offered a chance?"

"My children are in this state because of you!" Babuni shouted tearfully, "And yet you say things like this? All right, I won't ask for any more help filling my children's bellies. I won't feed them. Go and get a job and bring back some food. Would we be in this state if you had a job?" She sat down on the floor and cried.

Though the swelling of her belly was beginning to show, MK felt no tenderness towards her. He felt no tenderness, but was afraid of being shamed—afraid that someone upstairs or downstairs might overhear her.

In a muddle, he adopted a meek, innocent tone: "Why this racket now? When everything's just fine."

Babuni had suffered silently through their troubles for all these days. She usually cried only at an enormous crisis or at the faintest glimmer of hope, but today she cried, she cried a lot.

MK suddenly snapped, "Go, go and live at his place from now on. Your Janak-babu! Go right away!"

Babuni was appalled. She gritted her teeth and lunged out to scratch her husband…

MK stood up in bed. He rolled his fists in preparation, but only watched on, trembling with rage, as Babuni sank her teeth into his leg.

The children began wailing all through the house. The horror of their wails became more and more piercing.

After Janak, Ravi and a few other strangers came in and separated them, Sita led Babuni over to her place. MK didn't even look at, or wipe, the bleeding wound on his leg. "Go away, it's nothing, it's just a small thing, go away," he said, desperate for Janak to leave the room.

"Quarrels between husbands and wives are momentary, they're only momentary," said an unknown man who arrived as Janak was leaving—perhaps because he didn't know what else to say. "Everyone knows that quarrels between husbands and wives are like straw-fires."

Someone else—MK couldn't quite recognize him—said,

"Straw-fires catch quickly, blaze up, then go out just as quickly, but they can set off larger fires. If... if they find some dry firewood nearby, then...huh, Sir...that's why we should leave right away."

MK stayed on in a gloom. Evening had fallen. Nighttime had crept in and compressed itself into that cube-shaped room. Now that MK thought about it, he realized that he was alone: everyone, including the children, had left. He didn't turn on the lights. The darkness felt more bearable to him.

Babuni sat with Sita and wept as much as it was possible to weep. Sitting by their mother, the children also sniffled in sympathy over matters they didn't comprehend. Every so often, Sita would say something comforting. In a while, when she was done weeping, Babuni went out to the verandah. The night was pitch black, and the streetlamps shone brilliantly—those lights were so bright that Babuni felt as though the tears must have washed the dirt from her eyes. A cold wind howled, striking her warm forehead. She looked awhile at the long, red streaks of forest fires burning by the faraway settlements of Sikkim.

MK was still sitting in bed in the dark when Ravi came to his door to tell him, "They've asked you to come for a while."

Like a deity in a cave, MK spoke from within the darkness: "Why?"

Before Ravi could answer, sickly Namgyal called out from the next room: "Go, Bhai, go. Go, don't fight. Fighting is no good. Go."

Namgyal's voice was clear and resolute, as though all of his strength had shifted to his voice as his body failed him.

"They're asking for you," Ravi said.

"Send your aunt back. That'll be all. There's no fight. That'll be all," MK said, getting out of bed to turn on the lights.

Ravi went into the room, righted a stool that had toppled over, and sat down, but he didn't have to wait long. MK took a coat out from a chest and put it on, saying, "Let's go."

But when Ravi, leading the way, reached his door and turned around, MK wasn't there. On a hunch, Ravi went down the stairs and out to Pasang-la's shop, and found MK all the way at the back, standing near the stove, drinking a milky homebrew from a glass.

"Arre, Uncle, come along," Ravi said, taking him by the arm. MK's arm was thin enough for Ravi to encircle with his fingers.

"Let's go," MK said again.

This time, Ravi followed MK and made sure he went to their place.

Janak was in the room, fiddling with a needle on the radio, searching for the news. When he saw MK, all he said was "Sit," and after showing him a chair, he continued with his task. Every time the radio's needle slipped even a little to one side or the other, the Chinese would start to shout admonishments, or the Madrasis would curse, or some others would say the unsayable—the way you'd scold someone who had entered your room by mistake. Janak finally grew weary of it and turned off the radio.

Janak felt that simply by coming over upon being asked—that too, to the house of a man he'd maligned—MK had acknowledged his mistake, and it took no time at all for him to grasp that MK found fault in him only because he was unhappy with himself. As for MK, he wanted to ask for forgiveness and forget about everything as quickly as possible. He found it unbearable that this situation should drag on.

Janak talked to MK about many different things, but only regarding other subjects. He told him about the proposals that were coming up in the commission in the upcoming municipal elections; he told him about the job Sumshere had found as a head clerk in the Dooars. He expressed his frustration at having been of help to so few people after joining the party as a politician. Janak brought up many subjects, but never once mentioned this evening's quarrel.

MK tossed a few questions and comments into the waves of the conversation, but they didn't alter their course.

After nearly an hour and a half of this, Divya came from inside to announce that the meal was ready.

"Where's the water for Uncle to wash his hands?" Janak asked his daughter.

"The water's inside."

"Not for me, not for me." MK said.

"Why ever not? You have to eat. Everyone has to eat. That's why we work, that's why we make ration cards," Janak said, standing up. "Get up, Bhai, let's eat."

"Not for me, Daju! Not for me."

"Why don't you take off your coat, Uncle, and come to the kitchen," Divya urged him.

"No need to take off your coat. It's cold," Janak said knowingly, and went to the inner room.

Babuni and the children were scattered all over the kitchen. Sita was perched on a wooden slat near the stove. Divya went to the other side of the stove and began to serve the meal. Ravi wasn't there. MK sat to one side.

Janak began to tell everyone about the way the Bahun women of the hills served food while standing perfectly upright at the side of the cooking platform:

"They drop a pile of rice on our plate from above, as though tossing coins in a game of khoppi!" he said. "We're not even allowed to raise our plates to receive the food. It felt demeaning to me."

"When did you go to the hills?" Sita asked, challenging him.

"Those Bahun women do the same thing in your own Madhes!"

Then, expounding on the expression, "To wait on the kitchen," he went on to prove that there was no such custom in Darjeeling: "It's not 'waiting on the kitchen' to eat your meal and keep a plate warmed up on the coals for those who've gone out to the cinema."

Sita said one or two things as Janak led the conversation; Babuni stayed silent.

Janak and MK got up and went out to wash up as the others continued to eat.

They were in the outer room listening to songs on the radio when Yamuna arrived.

Dressed in a dark yellow sari with a light green sleeveless blouse, Yamuna loosened part of the white woollen shawl that was draped around her body and let it fall, first exposing the full length of her pale, curved, ample arms, which tapered down from her shoulders, and then the three fine golden bangles trembling on her wrist. The scent of perfume wafted off her clothes, and a faint whiff of rum accompanied her voice.

Turning off the radio, she said, "Make a request, Bhenajyu, I'll sing."

"Not now," Janak said in English.

"Why not now?" Yamuna asked. She came right up to him.

Janak scowled, defeated.

Yamuna was about to say something when the phone rang in her room. Obeying its command, she tottered off in a huff on her high heels.

MK took this opportunity to leave. "I'll also go, Daju. This is a domestic quarrel. There's no one at home to do any work, so it happens, it just happens. Don't be upset..."

"That's nothing, it's nothing," Janak said, putting an arm around MK and escorting him to the door.

"It's the same for me," he said. "But Babuni is really suffering, don't yell at her. And Bahini," he said to Babuni, "if you need money, ask for it from Didi, and use that. You've got to feed the children. You can't let them go hungry."

MK and Babuni said nothing. They just listened.

In the emptiness of the night, Janak and Sita, and MK and Babuni, sifted through their joys and sorrows among themselves. The only difference between the two couples was that while one also talked about the outside world, the other talked only of themselves.

After discussing everyone, including Sita's brother and father and mother in the hills, talk of Birman also came up:

"Birman never came back," Janak said. "Do you remember how many years it's been since he left?"

"It's been a long time. He must have got married by now. He'll stay over there, he won't come back."

They were both silent for a while.

Then, with a little laugh, Janak quoted the title of a short story, "Will He Ever Come Back?"

Sita smiled. "You're being literary today," she said to her husband.

They both thought of the protagonist Sani from the story. The road to Chitlang hovered before Sita's eyes—a long, dusty road, the sweltering heat of the day…

"You used to say that you're going to write a novel," she teased him, reminding him of his old dream.

"I'm collecting material for it; I'm examining what I've already collected," Janak said. "I'm close to reaching a conclusion, which is—one lifetime is far too little for one person."

Sita didn't get caught up in Janak's words, and asked another question, "It seems like we're nearing the full-moon time?"

The light of the moon—which itself was blocked by the wall—poured in through the window. From the embrace of her husband's strong arms, Sita stared at it, then said, "Enough! Let's not look at it too long," and turned around to look at Janak's shirt pocket. Janak got up and drew the curtains over the window's cold glass pane. Even then, the moonlight poured in through the ventilation.

"I've looked at, analyzed, and thought about a lot," Janak said after sitting back down. "I feel that we end up wherever the river currents lead. Life is merely a green leaf afloat on the water of a river. You're a leaf, I'm a leaf. What an enormous exigency. We live life, and we make life live in life: this is the only meaning of meaningless life." After a pause, he added, "These are the things I'd write about if I were to write."

Sita didn't understand any of this. She was only just starting to feel an urge to do something, to prove herself by achieving something; she hadn't yet had a chance to look back and evaluate her life.

"Being a writer is terrifying," Janak said. "It's a huge job. Readers of all sorts see all sorts of things in what a writer writes; and all of these things spark fires in the reader's mind, which the writer himself wouldn't have anticipated. The part that the writer leaves unwritten is literature; that's what's terrifying."

Two rooms over, in the same kind of room under the same kind of moonlight, MK was saying, "I just haven't been able to become a man in this lifetime. I grew a little in childhood, and then had to stop; I didn't mature. I was always in need of five rupees or ten rupees, I never got a chance to need a thousand rupees—but we'll also be rich in our next lives. There are so many goods in the shops: I just couldn't become a person who needed them all."

"When I think about all the suffering in this lifetime, I hope there won't be a next one," Babuni said.

Her remark made MK feel that his wife had given up on him, and that, having lost faith in him, and having stopped loving him, didn't want to encounter him in her next life. It felt to him as though even in this life, she had stayed with him only out of necessity.

Observing MK fall silent, Babuni said, "It'll probably be a girl again."

In a sudden rage, MK yelled, "Let it be that, let it be anything! Throw it down a drain!"

This hurt Babuni. MK seemed to be rejecting both her and the baby inside her. She sat up in bed and began to cry.

MK stared; he kept on staring.

The moonlight shifted. Babuni continued to cry.

Then a feeling of pity, and even happiness, began to

fill MK's heart. His wife's crying seemed to him like some proof, or a demonstration, of her love for him; it felt like an acknowledgement that without him she had no foundation or basis. MK slowly drew his wife towards him.

"Pushpa's mother," he said to her.

"Yes."

"What have you stored in my large black tin chest?"

"Nothing…why?"

"When our youngest daughter is born," MK said, weaving a tale, "I'll put her in that chest and set her afloat down the stream. Floating along, the chest will arrive at the confluence of the Rangeet and the Teesta, and it'll continue to float on from there. An old fisherman will see the chest floating downstream, and will capture it in a net and draw it ashore. When he opens it and looks in, he'll see our sleeping daughter, and, not having a daughter of his own, he'll take care of her and raise her with love. One day, a prince will come by on a hunt…"

Even Babuni smiled.

Early the next morning, MK was still asleep and curled up in bed when Yamuna barged in and began shouting, "I only just heard! What a bad man! This man mistrusts his wife with every other man in the building! He says and does whatever he pleases because his wife is so docile. He takes us for the living dead. Won't a man like this give ideas to our husbands? Look at him, a supposedly educated man…"

MK got up and sat listlessly in bed.

"Why did you beat your wife? Aren't you ashamed of yourself for not trusting her? You have such nice daughters:

Look at them. Shouldn't you look for a job so you can raise them? No one calls a man who beats his wife and children brave, do they? No one pins a medal on him."

It bewildered MK.

Amrita brought her father tea in a mug and put it on the chest by his bed.

"Bahini, if anything like this happens again, come to my place," Yamuna told Babuni. "I'm here. To treat you like this because he takes you for a simpleton! I should smack him all over the mouth with a sandal!"

Yamuna's rage kept growing more explosive. Just then, the phone began to ring insistently in her room. As though it were a bell at a debate, reminding her to speak for a set amount of time, Yamuna shut up and went swishing out of the room.

MK had never felt as grateful as on that day for the ringing of a phone.

Shortly afterwards, Ravi came into the room chuckling and looking pleased. Before MK could ask him anything, he said, "I phoned, and she stopped yelling and left."

"You did that?"

Ravi gestured for him to be quiet and, along with MK, listened on—in the other room, Yamuna was screaming at the operator at the telephone exchange.

Within two days of taking the exams, a fog started to swirl through Ravi's thoughts, the way it does through the gorge of Simkuna. He thought about accepting a job and striking out for Nepal; he thought about going to Calcutta to pass the time there till the results came out. Everything felt futile. He wanted to visit his grandfather and look around Dhankuta;

he yearned to gaze upon a terraced field, smooth and levelled, with a heap of threshed straw standing on one part and, in another black lentils sprouting beneath drying, freshly cut paddy. Dreams about things far away struck him as romantic, the way wealth seems romantic to the poor and poverty seems romantic to the wealthy. But he'd never been able to grow close to his grandfather, and their emotional distance didn't make this dream particularly sweet. Ravi wanted to go somewhere for a few days, but couldn't.

One morning, he got up early. He opened the window and looked east, and saw one or two red streaks in the sky. There were small birds fluttering between the houses, staying low, as though afraid of the colder temperatures higher up.

Ravi pulled on an overcoat and went out. He forged onwards, wanting to walk up to Chowrasta. A couple of elderly men and women, some milkmen, and guards who had kept watch over their masters' empty villas all night long, were coughing as they followed their accustomed paths on the road. Their offspring, who were probably already "young men and women", were most likely still asleep in their warm beds. And what was there for them to do but to sleep, Ravi asked himself. The tarred, paved expanse of Chowrasta felt bigger and broader than usual to him. About ten or fifteen cleaners who'd arrived sometime earlier were painstakingly sweeping up last night's litter. Black crows were circling above them, picking up what they needed from the litter, and flying off to the trees to eat it.

Ravi began to climb the Mahakal hill as though drawn by its height. A frigid wind flowed heavily through the expanding streaks of red all around. At the top were tall white Tibetan prayer flags anchored into the hillside, and other white-and-yellow prayer flags strung up on trees, which formed quite a large thicket.

Ravi stopped and looked around at the top of the stairway, which had lost its cement top and consisted of exposed bricks, and was mossy with age. Some clouds were descending and others were rising, bringing the pristine Himalaya into view.

A Bengali couple was taking photos in the dawn light in a small pergola across the way. Two Nepali women were at worship, circumambulating the temple.

A craving to see every part of the Mahakal hill arose in Ravi. He prayed; he rang a bell with large, engraved letters; he didn't have a single paisa in his pocket, so he only bowed to the statue of Mahakal. He even went over to look at the grubby Hanuman statue, which was plastered with vermilion powder, before turning back.

As he descended, he saw an old Tibetan beggar standing in a spot that a patch of sunlight had selected for him. He was holding the railing tightly, having staked his life on the righteousness of strangers on a day as cold as this.

The beggar pleaded with him, "Salaam, Hajoor."

Ravi walked on without looking at him; he simply couldn't look.

Further below was the Mahakal cave. The visible part of the cave had been swept clean, all the way in, where some offerings of flowers and sweets and lit candles lay scattered in front of six rocks slathered with vermilion powder. Some people from the tea plantations, who'd taken off their shoes to enter the cave, were coming out. Though it wasn't a big crowd of worshippers, there was a lot of money near the candles, even this early in the morning.

"The priest is casting a net," Ravi thought to himself. He took off his shoes, slipped in, and scooped up the money that was scattered about the cave. When he came out he had two fistfuls of cash and coins.

That old Tibetan man was still shivering, as before. Ravi put all the money into the beggar's inner pocket.

On his way home, Ravi resolved that from now on, it would be his duty to do the same everywhere else.

Then, out of nowhere, he felt some compassion for Janak.

Last night, after turning off the lights to go to sleep, Ravi's thoughts had curdled so badly that he'd started to examine his own history.

He couldn't remember much from the time before he came into Janak's house. He remembered going back and forth several times with someone to fetch water from a tap, and perhaps to gather grass or firewood from a jungle. He remembered crying while standing on a rock that people used for beating large items of clothing—probably at a spring—and he remembered a large tomato thicket above the spring. Ravi couldn't recall if there were any men in the house. The woman he was with, whoever she was, wasn't his mother. In none of his recollections did he feel any love for or attachment to a mother. Whenever Ravi saw a sleeping man, a fear took hold deep in his heart for reasons he couldn't understand.

Last night, the back of his head had heated up and begun to hurt from overthinking. His eyes had remained wide, staring into the darkness, for a very long time. They were dry. Then a thin trickle had seeped out, stinging his eyes. A cowardly man had entered his thoughts, and in a voice loud enough to echo through the entire room, bellowed, "Mad, you're probably going mad!" In the delirium of half-sleep, Ravi had believed that a finger on one of his hands had enlarged, becoming as vast and spread-out as the sky. He'd finally fallen asleep.

Poisoned memories about Isabel came to Ravi every day now, at the beginning, middle and end of each task. He still felt that to love was to sin. He'd almost taken a vow to never, not even by mistake, go to Isabel's place. Yet he was convinced that Isabel was his, and that she could never be another's.

As if to prove that he was done with college and moving on with life, Ravi had started to make new acquaintances. There was a group that included a doctor, a municipal commissioner, two or three clerks, and a teacher; Ravi and a few other society men mingled with them now and again. It was Hari who introduced Ravi to this new life. When Ravi got to address the doctor as, "Mr Chhetri," or call out to the municipal commissioner with, "Did you hear that, DK-babu?" he felt that this, too, was a life. And though he considered it artificial and depressing, he could no longer be content with his simple life from a few months back. He used these new experiences to create some distance, and to remove himself further and further away from Isabel every day.

Three or four weeks later, early in the morning, Janak called Ravi over and thundered, "When did you begin working at that school?"

"From the day before yesterday."

"Who told you to get a job there? Did you ask any of us?"

Ravi said nothing, but the indignation on his face was plain to see.

"What a terrific job you found! It'll make you so rich!"

Ravi shook his head in anger.

"Do that job all your life! Guru-babu! Sir!"

With such contempt did Janak utter the word "Sir", that it made Ravi's entire being shudder.

Though suffering and ease aren't equal, a teacher will take them as such. He'll also already have been rendered indecisive by the excess of suffering and the dearth of ease in his life.

The fifteen or sixteen teachers at the small school that Ravi had begun to work in represented a variety of mental states and conditions. Mr Chandrabir Pradhan, MA, BT, gave up his entire character and wisdom, as well as all his rights, to please the principal. If the principal noticed a crack in the school's cement wall, Chandrabir would go and stare at it, even if he'd already seen it a hundred times. In doing so, he felt as though he were fulfilling a call to duty. Then there was Mr Jayaprasad Rai—a youthful old man of fifty-three! The boys that he'd beaten and educated were spread out all over Darjeeling and beyond as army majors, head clerks at the bank, policemen, lawyers, waiters, politicians, traders, etcetera. "I meet my boys everywhere, they still love me," he'd say to new teachers like Ravi. There was also LB Sinha—all he did, all day and night, was to study thick, serious books. He despised the cinema, and never wrote anything. There was another teacher, SK Gurung, who was distraught to be approaching the age of twenty-three—not a single month passed in which he didn't run off for a job interview somewhere else. Ravi met no one, except for the principal, who actually wanted to be in the teaching profession. He also didn't meet a single teacher who didn't take much greater pride in another job he was holding outside the school. Ravi met teachers who wrote children's books, and also those who said they'd write children's books but made the mistake of never doing so. He met a Tibetan teacher who would leave home at six in the morning to offer tuition, and return home at eleven at night; there was also a skinny braggart of a teacher who wrote poems, whose debts the Marwari traders would come to school to collect on at the start of each month. It was the birthright of all teachers to claim to be superior to clerks. Ravi also got to know teachers who left for other jobs, or joined the army, and then chose to return to this profession because they preferred it. Someone told him—the job of office clerks made them all similar, but each teacher working in a school was different from the others. Ravi liked this job.

Krishnalal told him, "Your first month's salary will be more than you know what to do with. After the second month's pay, you'll never have enough. You'll really dislike the job by the end."

In Hariprasad, Ravi found a teacher of politics. Though Ravi had already learned a lot about "politics" from Janak, Hari had a different perspective.

Tall, pale-skinned Hari came to school exactly on time and also left exactly on time. On no August 15 did Hari ever show up at school to observe the unfurling of the flag. The other teachers had made Hari the secretary of their union.

Hari hadn't studied anything in his Bachelor's classes, all he'd done was to carry Karl Marx's books around college, and, on hot days, to wear dark goggles in the evening classes and drowse at his desk with his head propped up in his hands. He used to nap in such a way that even friends right beside him didn't notice. The sixty or seventy red, green and yellow saris attending college every day had never attracted Hari; his name alone, "Hari-daju", used to scare them away. Filled to satiation with his mother's love, Hari had not hungered for other forms of love.

One evening, returning from college along the straight road of Singmari, someone in a small group of girls had said, "What kind of people are our brothers! None of them speaks up when that bug-eyed professor belittles us Darjeeling folk. Now, if we were men..."

Hari had overheard them and asked, "Why, Bahini? What did he say?"

Outdoing each other to tattle on the teacher, the girls had said, "He says we're too stylish! He says we...we wear saris and suits! He says we Darjeeling folk have become Christians...we..."

"He said that?" Hari had said.

"He always says that!"

Hari had grown serious. "Achha," he had said. "Tomorrow's Sunday. Doesn't he have a class the following day, on Monday? I'll respond to him day after tomorrow."

That Monday, the class was on. Hari wasn't in the classroom. When the professor was halfway through the lesson, the door had suddenly opened. Hari had come in with a slam, clacking his shoes against the floor.

"Hari! Why are you coming to this class without my permission?" the professor had asked.

"That's the way things are in our Darjeeling," Hari had replied.

The professor had realized that he'd come to cause trouble. Terrified, the other students had neither moved nor made a single noise. The professor had left without ending the lesson.

After failing college one year, then obtaining a BA with Honours the following year, Hari had spent a year working at this school.

He and Ravi were quick to form a friendship. They swapped books to read; in the afternoon, and also after school, the two were always off somewhere by themselves. Hari would sometimes joke around with the other teachers, but never with Ravi. Whether they were coming or going, or simply standing on the street, Ravi listened attentively to Hari, trying to follow what he was saying.

This morning, Hari said, "Want to go to the Tukvar Tea Estate tomorrow?"

Ravi had heard that there was a lot going on there. He couldn't hide his delight at Hari's invitation. "I'll go," he said. "Is it a school holiday?"

"We'll have to take the day off."

"Are you going?" Ravi asked, redundantly.

"I'm going. Bhudev-babu's going. A few other friends are also going."

"Who else?"

"A lot of people."

Ravi gave his word: "I'll go too."

But that afternoon, Ravi received word that Isabel's mother had passed away. A mixture of emotions roiled inside him upon receiving the news. Only after setting off on the road did he realize that he'd taken leave and was running home in a panic. Yet even then, a part of him began to withdraw, and the power that drew him back, trying to prevent him from going to Isabel, grew stronger with each passing moment.

At home, Ravi was about to go upstairs when he saw Janak

rushing downstairs, skipping out to the road and scurrying away without so much as looking around.

"I won't go," Ravi muttered, but felt a jolt in his heart.

He went to his room and lay in bed with his trousers and shoes still on. It dawned on him today that thinking was an unhappy enterprise. If only he could turn himself into an animal with no thoughts in his head…if only he could shut off all of the bodily openings through which thoughts came in. He closed his eyes and took in the pink hue of daylight inside his eyelids. Even as he held on to this vision, a thought popped into his head, and Ravi opened his eyes in alarm. Thoughts kept pouring in even when he stared at the monotonous grey of the ceiling, so he didn't let his gaze rest in one place, shifting it from spot to spot, looking at one thing after another in the house—a coat, some books, a table, a flower vase… Ravi tried to distract himself by training his ears, as well as his attention, on the indistinct noises outside the house. But these sounds disappeared one by one, and were no longer audible.

He'd ask for nothing else right now if he could fall asleep instantly, without thinking at all, and have no dreams.

He remained lying down, trying to keep his mind blank. But his thoughts kept creating a racket; his ear canals echoed like riverside caves.

Ravi shot up and shoved the window open. He returned to bed and lay down as before, staring vacantly at the sky. The black dot of an eagle circled the sky in wide and then even wider gyres and then disappeared behind a roof. It emerged once more and was visible for half a gyre before disappearing again. Ravi waited a full minute, but didn't see the eagle again.

He got up and ran over and looked out, and saw what was perhaps the same eagle—it was flying out to Kalimpong or even further, towards the Pamenchi Monastery in Sikkim…

He grabbed a coat, and without even putting it on properly, headed out to the cinema.

The film had started almost an hour before. At first he had to try to piece together the story, but once he guessed at it, he no longer enjoyed the film. There's always a handsome boy in these films, and a beautiful heroine, and also a "villain" who makes faces, narrowing and widening his eyes, and then there's a friend of both the boy and the girl, who's there to make the audience laugh. That's all there is. Such primitive, childish emotions! Ravi got sick of it. He looked around, and in the light of the screen, which resembled moonlight on a full-moon night, examined the audience that he hadn't noticed when he'd entered in the darkness. He didn't see anyone he knew. At this point, the thoughts he'd earlier tried to shut out began to trick their way into his mind. Everyone laughed. Ravi saw nothing to laugh about.

Interval!

Ravi came out and paced around. He fancied the idea of going to a bar and downing a peg, but didn't dare, since he didn't know the cost of a peg, or the quantity of a peg, or whether a peg was available at all. He saw a couple of pretty girls. He stood staring at them.

"What's happened to you? Didn't you hear what happened?" Someone grabbed him by the shoulder and turned him around. Again, the questioning: "What's happened to you? Didn't you hear what happened?"

"What could I do once I heard about it?"

"What could you do!"

"Yes, what could I do once I heard about it?"

Parthiv examined Ravi closely. Ravi glanced from side to side, afraid to meet Parthiv's eyes. Parthiv said, "What's wrong with you? You have to watch this film today? Can't you watch it tomorrow?"

"I can't. The ticket is for today," Ravi said. "Parthiv! Don't lie to me just because I'm simple…that girl over there, the one who's looking at us, is probably waiting for you. She's pretty. Go, go, don't make the poor thing wait around."

Parthiv was astonished: Ravi had turned into the sort of person who'd say something like this! He hadn't expected this. "Ravi, you have to go," he said.

They both went back into the hall. The doors soon began to close.

After Ravi sat down, Parthiv hovered over him and said, "I went this morning… Isabel, Janak-babu, everyone's gone to Kharsang to bring the body back here. They'll take it away tomorrow. They've wired Calcutta. You should go. You have to go."

"All right, all right!"

When the film ended, Parthiv looked once again for Ravi, but he had already left.

Ravi didn't go home. He wandered around aimlessly, and went back to watch another film later on at night.

He returned home at around one o'clock in the morning. The lights were still blazing at home. Divya got up and asked if he wanted a meal. Ravi couldn't give her a definite answer. Then he said, "Give me a little bit." But his throat felt constricted, and no matter how much of an effort he made, he couldn't swallow a single mouthful; he could only push the food around the plate with his hands as a manifestation of his own mental disarray.

Trying, somehow, to feel better, Ravi said, "How can I eat now, after eating my fill at the wedding! I ate at a wedding. Someone spilled juice all over me, see. It stinks."

"I was wondering what that smell was," Divya said. "Whose wedding was it?"

"Ajit and Radha's."

Puzzled for a while, Divya asked, "Where was it?"

"In the cinema hall. Just now, at around twelve o'clock."

"Tchee! What kind of a person…! I believed you!" Divya said.

Sita, who was still awake, called out from inside: "So that's where you were…didn't you go over to the other place?"

Ravi sobered up. "I'll go."

It was almost two o'clock when Ravi got into bed. Without leaving the bed, he moved the clock hand that usually pointed at six to seven, then turned the clock off altogether and switched off the lights. Janak came home in half an hour. Sita got up. There was the sound of them moving around. Janak said that the hospital had almost refused to let him bring the body, they'd had to stop Isabel from going up to the body, it had been freezing, and Daniel hadn't arrived till eveningtime. Janak heated up some water and bathed that night, and went to sleep only at dawn. Ravi listened in on all of this, and then, afterwards, fell asleep in a blink. When he got up the next morning, Janak had already left.

Ravi opened the tap and stepped into the water without even asking for his usual mug of tea.

Janak returned home at around ten o'clock. Behind him was a coolie carrying a large, circular white wreath. Janak ate a little and hurried off. Divya also went with him.

"You come too, come with your friends. Come to the church," Janak said to Ravi, as his new shoes, made out of soft leather, slapped against the road.

Ravi started to get ready. MK came over, and asked from the door, "Who died?"

"Daniel-babu's wife."

"The poor thing…" MK said, and asked, "When did she die?"

"Yesterday. Yesterday at four in the morning."

"Exactly at four?"

Ravi suddenly lost his temper. "Why do you need to know the time, the moment, and everything? Are human beings clocks that we can say that they stopped at this hour, this minute?"

MK neither replied nor did he go away. He just stood there.

Ravi ran out of the house, feeling that he was already late enough.

The rites had started by the time he reached the church. Everyone had gone in. A couple of people were outside, nailing something onto a hearse. Parked at the door, the black-wheeled hearse was decked with a scattering of yellow alliums and long-stemmed bunched-up blue-and-white flowers.

When he stepped into the church, Ravi's eyes immediately fell on everyone standing in rows along the long benches. A large organ played a heavy, mournful dirge, and it sounded like the thundering of the clouds and oceans. Everyone sang a hymn. Ravi didn't know the hymn. He found an empty spot on the last bench and stood there respectfully. The building was very tall, with elongated stained-glass windows on both sides, and this left Ravi feeling sombre and mystified.

That hymn ended and another one started. Ravi now noticed the women standing in a row to one side. They were singing, their heads covered with scarves. To Ravi, each individual standing and singing there seemed different than usual. They struck him as people who'd grown a head taller than others in the measure of a good human being.

Ravi's eyes were seeking something. They were seeking someone.

The hymn ended. Everyone sat down.

Ravi watched on as a grave, serene-faced pastor in black robes walked up to a podium covered with a red banner. Once again, everyone stood up. Something—he didn't know what—compelled Ravi to stand up as well. Then he saw Janak. Janak was off to one side, one row behind the front bench. Ravi kept looking at him. Tall, ageing, with a growing girth yet still handsome, luminous Janak was standing in a dignified, dutiful posture: it looked like the posture he'd adopt on the day of his final judgment. Before him stood a man with his head bowed down, who someone else was holding up, offering support—Ravi figured that was Daniel.

Children who lose a mother cry a lot on the first day, but the husband endures his grief silently; and yet, from the following day onwards, children start to forget, and smile a little more every day, for all of life lies in front of them, whereas the husband who doesn't cry on the day will remember his dead wife that evening at mealtime; he'll remember her when he's about to sleep; he'll wake up in the morning and immediately remember that she's not there; he'll remember her when he leaves the house to go to work; he'll remember her when he comes back home; he will be bewildered throughout the rest of his life. Even when everyone else has managed to forget, he alone won't have forgotten. His bewilderment will cease only at the end of his days.

Ravi kept looking at Daniel's bald pate.

The gospel of truth was being delivered from the podium in a high, clear, unwavering voice.

"I've come to God's church; I'll listen to this, if only for my own benefit," Ravi told himself.

Reading at the podium, the pastor was emphasizing the full meaning and significance of each word:

"Because death came through man, the resurrection of the dead also came through man.

"Just as everyone died in Adam, so will everyone be saved in Christ.

"For the final enemy to be destroyed is death itself.

"People ask: how are the dead resurrected, in which body will they return?

"But just as bodies are worldly, they are also divine, and they have a separate splendour.

"That's how the reawakening of the dead is; it is sown in disgrace but awakens in splendour, it is sown in weakness but awakens in power. Death is swallowed up in victory!

"O Death! Where is your sting? O grave! Where is your victory? The sting of death is sin, and the strength of the sin…"

Ravi listened closely. Such powerful emotions! How daring, this human challenge to death! Hope and faith always battle against death. If for some reason these two were to give up on the world and go elsewhere, people would still hold on to the hope and faith that they'd return one day.

The immortal lines were being read out:

"Yahweh doesn't treat us differently depending on our sins,
Neither does he punish us for our faithlessness.
Because as high as heaven is from earth,
This is how great his compassion is for those who fear him.
As far as the east is from the west,
That's how far he removes our wrongdoings from us.
Because he knows what we're made of;
He knows that man is but dust.
The life of a man is like that of a blade of grass:
It blooms like the flowers in the garden,
And is destroyed when the wind leaves its being:
And then that garden will never again know those flowers..."

The wind and dust had swirled around the peak of the Calvary hill. And then, according to this faith, the people of earth had had to take the life of a man who had come to save them by sacrificing himself.

Ravi couldn't keep track of how many more hymns were sung, or what else took place. He stood up with everyone else and sat down with everyone else. The pastor descended from the podium. Daniel stood and went up. There, he stepped forward and placed both hands on the black coffin. Across from him, Isabel was bent over, holding the coffin in the same way...

A sudden pain erupted within Ravi. He felt extremely sorry. He saw himself as cruel and hard-hearted. What mistake had Isabel committed? Had she committed a mistake at all? She who had committed no mistake...

The final prayer began: "…Our God, our hope, succour and peace. Blessed be your name. For you sent us your beloved Son to save us. O Merciful God! Bring your grace and come to these people who are grieving for their dead. May they not lose heart. O Father of Peace! Have mercy on those of us who are still alive, awaken us, may we always find relief from the burden of sin and from the fear of death. O Lord, giver of liberation! May the blessedness and splendour of you and the Holy Ghost remain now and forever! Amen!"

"Amen," said a thousand gullets.

They carried out the body. Daniel, who still hadn't cried, went out with the body along with Janak, the pastor and some elders. Ravi stood where he was and waited. The women began to leave. Then everyone mingled in and began pouring out all together. Isabel was also going out with a couple of other women. She was dressed in a white sari that Ravi had seen her in many times. Her face was drawn and yellowish; there were red, puffy circles around both eyes. She caught sight of Ravi from afar and came towards him, looking directly at him. Ravi returned Isabel's gaze till she came right up to him. He wanted to say something, but couldn't speak. Isabel lingered awhile by his side, then walked on.

The black hearse soon sped off, taking away someone who was, beneath all those circular wreaths, half of one person's life and the dearest thing in the world to another person…

Daniel stayed on in Darjeeling for about ten days, then returned to Calcutta.

Isabel continued to live with her aunt, as before.

The father and daughter neither spoke with anyone, nor

cried in front of anyone, and yet, five or six days after the death, they experienced a great void.

All of this had left Ravi earnest and thoughtful.

Parthiv came by yesterday. The two of them went out to Alubari for a stroll.

On their way back, they were caught out by huge raindrops, which came streaming down as though melting in the daytime heat. The potato plants, growing in rows on the steep fields below the road, were already green. The radish plants had sprouted white flowers. Some children let off early from school were helping their mother dig sticks to support the sweetpea creepers.

"Isabel has done quite well in the exams this time," Parthiv said.

"Oh?" Ravi said.

"She's done quite well."

They said nothing for a turn or two on the road. They reached the monastery and turned back.

"Will she study science after passing?" Ravi asked on the way.

"Who?"

Ravi found it hard to say "Isabel", so didn't.

Parthiv figured it out for himself and said, "Oh. Maybe she will." He placed an arm on Ravi's shoulder and said, "You shouldn't do this. You should go. I'll take you to Isabel's. Tell me what happened between you two; tell me—what happened?"

"Nothing happened."

"Then why won't you go?"

"Why should I?"

Ravi and Parthiv locked eyes, but Ravi soon dropped his gaze.

White smoke rose from a field down below in a cold, damp thicket and entered the jungle, disappearing into the pine trees above the road.

After parting from Parthiv on the road, Ravi came home, but stayed for only a little while, then went out again.

Having returned home early, Janak had come to Da' Namgyal's room for a chat. He saw Ravi heading down the stairs, but didn't feel like calling out to him. Carrying on with the topic that they'd been discussing for quite a while, Janak said, "It's become laughable, as it is, for us to claim to do business. The best businesses are in the hands of those of other caste and kind. The petrol pumps, the lumber trade, rice and dal, clothes—these all were snatched up a long time ago by others. What's in our hands, other than vegetables and oranges? To claim that we do business..."

"All the contracting work's been snapped up by the Punjabis," Namgyal said.

"I mean it: Send that letter, will you? I need to go to Gangtok one more time," Janak said before heading back to his own room.

To Janak it felt as though giving up his truck would be akin to losing the plate he ate on, or having his hands broken. It didn't feel proper to him to go to the police station, or the court, for falling into debt. If he were to strip himself of everything he owned and hand it over, he'd be free of debt, but then after that...? To stand up again from bare ground... that would be extremely difficult; thousands never managed to stand up again. Just as the sparse rains of the month of Chait did little but leave the corn looking diseased, Janak's interest payments of five or six hundred rupees had only worn down both the lender and borrower.

Janak was planning to buy and move into an old house on the hillside of Haridas Hatta, below the court. The house was, or it used to be, that of a Gorkha Army Warrant Officer First Class, or perhaps Second Class. The man had bought the house in the year of his retirement, and had also died the same year—that was what had happened to him. His wife had raised and educated their three pretty daughters, all of them now grown up. None had passed their final exams. The eldest ran off with the gatekeeper at the cinema. A clerk at the court took the youngest daughter. The middle daughter was a midwife at the hospital. Janak had got quite a deal, paying thirty-five hundred for a house with such a large yard. The house itself needed thorough repair. The planks had rotted and the ceiling, made of sackcloth, had fallen and was drooping—it had become a breeding place for rats and cats. Sita and Babuni came to walk by and look at the house before the sellers even left. They liked the neighbourhood. The house was a little higher up from, and to the right of, the house they lived in at present—Sita approved of it. Even more than Sita, Babuni began to dream after seeing the house. The house was small, but for Sita's family alone, it was as large as the earth.

"I heard that Didi and Bhena-jyu bought a nice cottage around here?" Yamuna asked Sita. Before Sita could reply, she added, "We should also buy a house in Darjeeling…to stay in when we visit?"

Yamuna had just returned from a week in Calcutta. The new acquaintances that she had brought back often came by to visit Namgyal. Yamuna also went out, frequently changing into new saris and bukhoos. Namgyal could only look on. Then again, on some days she wouldn't go anywhere, and sit beside Namgyal, knitting and making conversation. The son from the first wife came and visited for a few days, leaving behind a servant boy for Namgyal. Yamuna tried to show the boy some affection, but he didn't seem to like it at all. Nowadays Yamuna was mesmerized by, and in love with, the darkness of the cinema hall, the bright white lights of the hotel, the faces she met in the club and by their constant chatter about flowers and dogs.

Janak's lawsuit against Ratnabahadur dragged on; the court had seized Ratnabahadur's land as collateral. Sita kept arguing their side of the dispute. Janak won by saying nothing at all.

Divya was old enough by now to find the sound of her own voice quite sweet.

Yesterday afternoon at around two o'clock, a man dressed in filthy clothes came over, placed a letter in Sita's hands, and left. The letter was for Janak. Sita didn't understand it. Janak saw it at night. His face became frightful with rage, but no one dared to ask him about it. Janak himself tried to suppress his outrage, and making an effort to smile, said, "Now grab my flesh and eat it too."

All the pain and suffering that had been mounting inside Janak finally found an outlet. All of a sudden he began, on this day, to feel deeply sorrowful.

Yes, Janak felt deeply sorrowful today.

He didn't parse through the causes of his sorrow. He was sorrowful; there was an excess of sorrow in his heart—this sufficed for him. Out of a practised self-restraint, or out of some intellectual quirk, a relentless desire to truly experience, and even measure his sorrow, suffering and pain, began to grip him.

The sky was thundering, and it looked like rain. The wind ripped furiously at the fabric of the tall prayer flags outside Pasang-la's shop, while, in the bamboo grove across the way, it left the thin, new-growth bamboo stalks untouched but forced those with old leaves to rustle and bend in its direction. It was as though wintertime had unexpectedly returned for a day, as though a December day had accidentally got mixed up in the month of May. As the day ended and the branches of the trees began to darken, Janak, lethargic and aimless, headed out of Chowkbazaar, towards the train station. The ropeway echoed out its monotonous drilling. A wood-and-iron container left the storehouse and went out along the wire just as Janak reached the bottom of the ropeway building. He didn't wonder about which cliff-top the container would have to spend the black night in when the ropeway halted in an hour and a half. All around him, motorcars came and went, making way for him, but Janak didn't notice. He didn't see that visitors from all over had arrived at the pilgrim's resthouse and were creating a commotion. Across the station, in the ditch of the old road that had been flattened for the construction of the new road, the town's beggars had built shelters with scraps of wood and tin wrapped up in sackcloth. Here, Janak stopped on the road and looked down. Some of the beggars were fetching water in traditional clay vessels—Janak felt an odd sensation at seeing those vessels—and others were lighting fires. This village of beggars was so busy in the evening! The elderly beggars from Chowrasta, the husband-and-wife beggars who wandered from village to village, and the child beggars who stood outside the shops, had all gathered here. Someone had planted mustard in a small patch of land above a stream's embankment, and the withered, stubbly leaves of the plants even looked green. It pleased Janak to see this, and it also made him want to laugh. Here, too, people stole greens, he thought, and thieves had to be fearful. This community looked like the beginning of a land-bound civilization, or the end of a nomadic one. He looked out again, but no longer experienced the same joy.

By now the crows were roosting in the village's bamboo grove, causing the stalks to bend; the cawing of a large flock of crows on a single plant echoed all over. A train pulled into the station and halted. There weren't many travellers. Janak walked on. The electric lights that were on everywhere seemed to shine particularly brightly today.

Several fires were blazing on the courtyard below Khalasi Dhura, resembling red-and-yellow flowers as they rapidly changed colour. Other than a few men burning charcoal, whose faces were as red as their flames, there was no one around. Janak remembered how, as a boy, he'd once hauled a sack of coal from a coal-shop in this area. A little further along, he felt a sharp pain somewhere inside; the breath from his mouth brought something right into his ribcage and made it hurt.

You don't get to see the morning arriving in a big city; and even in a small town, the houses and streetlights, lit in impatience, don't allow you to see the night falling gradually. Janak reached Dali Ground and turned his gaze skyward. A glimmer of daytime still lingered high up in the sky. Without a care as to what people might think, Janak sat on a high ridge by the road, watching the sky till the narrowing stretch of that faint glimmer was completely extinguished... He kept seeing a spot up there for a long time, maybe due to a trick of the mind.

Janak didn't know what time it was when he finally got up and walked on, reaching the Bataase hill; he refused to let himself lift his arm to check his watch. He realized that his legs were sore from all the walking. The cold—a permanent feature of Bataase—blasted against both of his temples. He was glad to suffer physical pain. When he wearied of walking, he stopped and looked out at Darjeeling bazaar. The brilliant electric lights were visible. He remembered how one night, a few years back, he had stood with friends on the expanse of the Chungthung Tea Estate and seen a similar but even more beautiful, grander view.

Janak turned back.

Many of the shops had closed by the time he reached the bazaar. There were still people in the doctor's shop and the paan shops. From Janak's gait it was obvious that his body was exhausted, but his mind was as alert as ever. Why didn't this mind of his ever tire?

He went into a shop that he'd never been to before and ordered a glass of tea. After finishing the tea, when he got up, his legs began to cramp very sharply. The very thought of returning home was distasteful to him. If there's peace anywhere, it's outside the home...

Even at this hour, there was still singing and dancing at the large British restaurant below Chowrasta. Men and women were laughing, and a crowd had formed on the street alongside the shops to gawk at them. Janak stood, allowing his legs a moment's rest.

A woman in a red silken kurtha-garala with white embroidery, and with a light pink dupatta tossed carelessly over the shoulder, tugged at Janak's shirt sleeve. "Where are you going?" she asked.

Janak turned around to look at her.

"Where are you going?" Yamuna asked again, in a drowsy voice.

"Just around here," Janak said. "What time is it?"

"Who cares what time it is!"

She was tipsy. "Come," she said. "A film star…what's his name again? He's here…come."

Janak paid her no heed and left the crowd. Yamuna glared at him, and then, ignoring him, went into the restaurant.

Janak sat alone for a long time on a cold bench in Chowrasta. A swarm of people passed by after midnight, shouting, laughing and creating a ruckus, and then split up along two or three roads, leaving amid a similar din. From their voices and from the way they were walking, Janak recognized former MLA Yashraj; the present MP, K. Lama; two municipal commissioners and other friends and classmates, and also some glass-mates.

When they were gone, Janak took another road down to the bazaar. It occurred to him that nighttime wasn't frightening in the jungle, it was frightening in town. He slipped into a shop that was just closing, paid two rupees extra for a small bottle of Hayward, and drank it without diluting it with soda. He didn't eat anything.

When he stepped out and checked his watch, it was—he couldn't remember what time it was. His eyelids were so heavy that they refused to stay open. When he did manage to force them open, his eyeballs would smart.

A little further along, Janak fell in with a throng of people leaving a night show at the cinema. Everyone in the crowd was walking very fast. The film must have been extremely long. Janak turned his head cautiously to check the yellow face of the Town Hall's clock, but there was no point looking. His vision trembled, his eyes closed on their own. Propelled along by the crowd, he headed downhill…

A waterfall became distinct and visible in the light of the waning moon, which had risen late at night. A hundred thousand fine white lines were coursing down the waterfall…

A bareheaded man in a tweed coat and grey trousers was hunched over, clutching tightly onto the iron railing over the waterfall.

He was weeping.

He wanted very badly to confront everyone who had made him sad, and to talk to them and make them understand. Those who didn't understand him were causing him such pain.

When he was done weeping, he stood up.

He stood up and, as though all his disillusionment were gone, he headed homeward at a resolute pace.

The night was fading. A cold wind began to blow, bearing news that it was morningtime. Streaks of light were emerging in the distance. Many Janaks within Janak began to clamour: I shouldn't be here at this hour, I should be in my own home right now.

Sita heard him climbing up the stairs and opened the door. Janak entered his home with the first faint glimmer of dawn.

Ravi hadn't come home either that night. He used to go from tea plantation to tea plantation, sometimes with Hari and at other times with students living in the plantations. He would spend all evening after work sitting on a bench or at a turn in the road, not even noticing night fall as he examined all the mothers coming home with their bundles of firewood, and the hordes of immature boys and youthful girls, and watchmen, tea-estate workers and labourers. His eyes were full of sentiment: "Don't you know who I am? I've come here from town to serve you." It grieved and worried him when the boys from the tea plantations took cinema songbooks out of their pockets and showed them to him, and then went away singing. When Ravi saw a house with a yard full of ripe maize and dangling cucumbers, and gourd vines that climbed over the long bamboo supports and then drooped back down to the ground, he could tell that the house was rich, yet he tried to convince himself that it was poor. The red-earth hills with heavy-pruned tea plants resembled an old, hard, spiky upside-down brush. The gracefully drawn line of a switchback on a dusty road vanished from side to side as it stretched onwards. Standing at the trunk of the banyan tree that shaded all of Singea bazaar, Ravi looked out at the meeting point of the village and the tea plantation—the village had brought food to sell, and the plantation had brought the week's salary to buy provisions. On the previous Sunday, Ravi had made a speech here over a mic. Ravi had spent the previous night with friends, sleeping on long benches that they joined together in a teashop in Pokhrebung bazaar. He no longer worried that the people from these parts didn't know who he was.

There had been a girl with thick hair, who walked like a duck, in the teashop. Jay, Ravi and the other boys always teased her. As for her, she'd fire off replies as she worked.

"Look at those eyes, they're so pretty," Jay had teased her.

"That's too much!" the girl had said. "I'd better wear a niqab from tomorrow!"

Everyone had laughed merrily.

Ravi had mustered up his courage and said, "And how pretty those lips are."

"And this Daju has such nice ears! They're even pierced!"

Ravi had laughed.

This morning, Ravi reached the school before ten o'clock, but he had come straight over without going home first. As soon as he took in his appearance, Krishnalal asked, "Did you also go to Pokhrebung?"

"Who told you so?"

"You also went to Singla with Hari the other day…"

Ravi had to shut up.

Krishnalal gave him a solemn look. "You must have heard about that matter at Singtam."

"What matter?" Ravi said.

"Didn't Hari mention anything?" Krishnalal said.

"He did."

"What did he say?"

This surprised Ravi: what kind of a man was Krishnalal? Why was he so curious, what was he milking their conversation for?

Noticing Ravi's hesitation, Krishnalal said, "The workers from that plantation gave notice last year, demanding a sixteen-paisa raise in their daily wages, and threatening to go on strike. People say that Chairman Bhudev sided with the plantation owner to prevent the strike. The case even went to the tribunal. The workers didn't trust Bhudev, so they removed him from the post of union chairman. The tribunal recently passed a judgment: they raised the daily wages by only two paisa, which the manager of the plantation had already agreed to the previous year, but hadn't acted on because the workers had demanded even more..."

Ravi listened on.

"Now here's the fun part," Krishnalal said with relish. "If the tribunal had increased the wage in accordance with the demand—or even if they'd raised it by ten or fifteen paisa—Bhudev would have said, 'This case went to the tribunal when I was still the chairman of the union. See what a large raise you got? We proved victorious by taking the case to the tribunal; but my beloved brethren didn't understand, and hurled baseless accusations at me and had me removed.' But now that the wage hasn't increased, Bhudev is sending Hari out. Hari is Bhudev's mic. Hari will say, or actually, he's already saying, 'Our demands weren't met because of the weakness, ignorance and lack of credibility of the union's new chairman. We must sack the new chairman...'" Krishnalal laughed. "So he's called it if the coin falls face-down, and if it falls face-up that's his call as well—and if it stands on its end, he's even called that!"

Ravi tried to, but couldn't, respond. Chatting with Hari later that day, Ravi said, "Listen: I'll tell you what kind of a person Krishnalal is. He never understands anything straight. If you go to him to borrow five rupees, he won't conclude that you're in difficulty; he'll start wondering if you asked for the loan just to test him. If he sees you walking with someone, Krishnalal doesn't conclude that you met on the road and are walking together for a short distance. He'll start to endlessly speculate about whether that person's eyeing your younger sister, or whether you're trying to get something out of that person. If you should forget to call out to him on the street one day..."

"You're telling me not to talk to him..."

Ravi laughed.

Hari also laughed, and passed a final verdict, "People with that kind of character betray you."

Janak lay down on the cane bench waiting for the water to heat up, then took a quick hot-water bath. Only when he was free of inebriation did he go to bed and fall asleep.

It was almost eleven o'clock when he awoke, and Divya had already gone off to college. He felt as though he had a headache, and he was hungry, though he didn't feel like eating. After chewing on a bit of food, Janak changed his clothes and went directly to Bhudev.

Bhudev had just returned home from canvassing for the municipal elections.

"What are your chances?" Janak asked, making the usual conversation.

"Not so bright," Bhudev said in English. "And why did you withdraw?"

"I have too many commitments," Janak said. "Besides, what are my chances now that you've kicked me out of the party?"

Bhudev became grave.

"On what charge are you kicking me out? That's all I've come to ask."

"*I* kicked you out?"

"Yes, one of your people did."

"Are you sure that your understanding is sound?"

"Very much."

Bhudev brought his face right up to Janak's and said, "Well, you should put the question to your own heart. Have you no culpability, no blame? Isn't it inappropriate to inflate your value by associating with the party, and then to trade on that? If that's not an offense, then I'll place you on Vikramaditya's seat of justice!"

"Right now, that seat is reserved for you, and only time will tell about everything else," Janak said. "I know I was kicked out for only one reason—for your own self-interest, to attain sole leadership over the party."

"I won't say that's not true," Bhudev said.

Janak, who had remained unruffled in the face of Bhudev's allegations and arguments, was now stumped by this proud admission of his own selfishness; he felt defeated, and found no logic to hold on to.

"Janak-babu, everyone knows you're changing, or trying to change colours like a chameleon!" Bhudev said. "Shame on you!"

Janak gave a straightforward reply. "I see no sin in a chameleon changing colours. It saves itself from becoming another animal's food: when it's green around, it turns green, and when it's grey, it also turns grey. What crime does the poor chameleon commit by taking this precaution to save its life? It's the same for us. We must change our colours again and again, a hundred times, to save and develop our peoples and our kinsmen. I'm not in favour of going extinct. We change colour not out of self-interest, but for the betterment of our peoples, that's all. You're happy to continue with your wilfulness and let the whole world suffer because of you. I don't care if my personal name is tarnished, I'm happy if my actions make others happy just a little bit quicker."

Bhudev glared at Janak. "How many years did we work together?" he asked.

"I regret admitting that we ever worked together at all," Janak said.

"I'm shocked," Bhudev said. "I'm amazed that I could have worked for all these years with someone of such contrary beliefs."

The cups of coffee brought for them from inside had cooled down, and clots of white cream had formed on top.

"There's something else," Janak said. "Don't ruin Ravi by making him run around from plantation to plantation. Take things out on me directly, don't take this sort of unbefitting revenge by leading an immature boy astray."

"Bhudev doesn't do that."

"Don't do it anymore."

Bhudev ruminated for a while. "I didn't send Ravi. I can't stop him if he comes along on his own. And you think that going to the plantations for work is to be ruined…?"

"Improved, then!"

"No, you're right, ruined is right. Let other people's sons go if necessary, but our own sons mustn't be ruined. Isn't that what you think? How quickly people become so selfish!"

With a laugh, Janak said, "Then why don't you, such a selfless man, send your own son to do all this good work? I'm not embarrassed to put this question to you. Because I know that Parthiv will be capable of doing even more useful work after he returns with a BL. Meanwhile, my Ravi has to run around to the plantations from this age on!"

"Ravi's not your son," Bhudev said abruptly.

Janak became wary at the lowliness of this attack. Displaying no anger, he spoke in a controlled yet cutting voice: "You're correct. This is what you'll comprehend if you're a man. Were Ravi my own son, I'd be able to do as I pleased with him, as though he were my possession. It's exactly because Ravi's not my own son that I must offer him a complete education, and can't let it remain incomplete. I must receive everything he can get, and give him his full share; I can't cut out even a small portion of his share."

Bhudev just sat there with his lips pursed. When he got up, he said, "I'm convinced, now, that the two of us have drifted very far from each other."

Following Janak's visit, Bhudev decided: he'd use a pair of mics while making a speech at the junction on Sunday, otherwise it would be too late. Janak wouldn't counter with a mic of his own. And if the things he said over the mic weren't refuted on the spot, people would, in their final verdict, take them to be true.

Returning home defeated by Bhudev, Janak caught himself directing his rage at Ravi. The colours of love and affection soon arose inside him and altered the red of his rage. When he woke up after a fifteen-minute nap, he slipped back to the day he had brought Ravi home.

It was Losar time. There was going to be a Singi dance that day. A pile of khapsey biscuits and offerings of khadas had been placed in the upstairs prayer room. In each lamp, a wick was ablaze like a torch in a small sea of coconut oil. Outside on the street, Dorje, Nima, Thendup and Kipa, their cheeks as red as apples, were refusing to eat one-paisa apples and throwing them away. It looked like rain, and with each moment the fog swirled and shifted with a new briskness.

Sita woke up at night.

The kettledrum and cymbal were sounding from nearby, from in front of Pasang-la's door. The sound was so piercing that it felt like it might shatter the eardrums. Sita covered her ears, but soon even her covered ears were drawn to the music of the kettledrum and the cymbal. There was a strong beat to the music, there was a power. Janak got up and opened the curtains and looked down from the window. The white light of a mantle-lamp from below illuminated a section of the room. Sita looked at Janak in this combination of light and dark. The sound remained just as loud, and the cacophony of many people's simultaneous laughter floated up and, scattering further afield, launched out, perhaps towards some distant star. The world is beautiful, life is full of suffering. People conjure up community celebrations in an attempt to alter the colour of life. The sombre, thunderous beats of the kettledrum and the cymbal danced on in measured, even steps, like a tireless man and woman.

Jhhain jhham-jhham jhhain jhhain, jhhain jhham-jhham jhhain, jhhain jhham-jhham jhhain jhhain, jhhai jhham-jhham jhhain.

Sita also got up. She went and stood silently behind Janak.

Everything was submerged in the source of the sound.

"Come," Janak said.

Bundled up in a Dhaka-weave shawl, Sita came up to her husband.

The kettledrum and cymbal stopped playing, and the

sweet, lonely melody of a flute started up. A peacock whirled in a dance in the front yard: a peacock of green paper and cloth! If there were any flaw in its mimicry of wildfowl, Sita and Janak didn't notice it from above. The eyes of the paper peacock stared out with a singular stillness. The peacock turned its head from side to side and started spinning—like the vital energy of the eternally spinning wheel of folk art. The musician and his flute weren't visible from above, they were hidden away somewhere. The tune wafting out of the top of the flute sought to ignite a lamp in the heart. Tibet's lonesome roads and desolate, arid hills carried through this sound. The tune evoked the solitary, vulnerable human soul's quest for song, and its desire to banish the terrifying silence by spreading its offspring far and wide. Man found tranquillity and gratification in the unfettered life of a peacock; he saw fulfillment and meaningfulness in it. The relentless winds of the bare plateaus of Tibet called out in that flute, and the sigh of man sounded out; the heartbeat of the love for life called out, and the snow on the mountain peaks tumbled.

"Sita!"

"Yes..."

They both went over to Ravi. It was, perhaps, the same old exhausted human soul that, having got a few days' rest in Ravi, now lay there unmindful of everything else.

The music began to play once again, with the exuberance of a populace that had found a nation.

Jhhain jhham-jhham jhhain jhhain, jhhai jhham-jhham jhhain.

Janak went over to hold Sita, who was quivering with joy.

The horses, yaks, lions, peacocks—all the animals in the jungle—danced in happiness at the happiness of man.

When Janak got home, he saw that Da' Namgyal had come out of his room, having got a coolie to carry away his suitcase. A car was waiting on the road. Dressed properly today in a coat, tie, trousers and everything else, Namgyal climbed down the stairs and came out to the street clutching a tin cigarette-case in his hands. Sita, Babuni, MK and the others had all come out to look.

"Where are you going?" Janak asked, stopping before him.

"I'm going," Namgyal replied curtly, grabbing Janak's hand and shaking it, even though he had the face of an angry man.

"Alone?" Janak asked from behind.

"Alone. I'm leaving that..."

Janak immediately figured out many things. Yamuna wasn't around.

He said, "Look at the state of your health! You mustn't go, Namgyal-babu! That's what women and children are like. I'll talk to Bahini."

Namgyal had already got into the car. "I've had enough. I'm not staying."

The car started up with a rumble. Janak gestured at the driver to wait, and stuck his head into the back window to make a final plea, "If you must go, wait awhile and take Bahini, take her with you. Small arguments can wreck a home."

"That worn-out cunt has already wrecked everything. What's left?"

The car left.

Janak's head spun, and he felt a splitting headache come on. He looked up at Namgyal's room. The door was wide open.

As Janak climbed the stairs, MK began to heatedly defend Namgyal's position:

"How can you roam about day and night, leaving a sick man all by himself? Shouldn't you see whether or not he's eaten?"

"A real whore of a woman…" Babuni added.

"The trilling of her phone all day and night. We were so sick of it…"

Janak went straight to his room.

There was no sign of Yamuna.

The doctor who always came by at six in the evening arrived and asked around. Janak spoke to him and turned him away. The door was still wide open. Janak brought a lock and closed it up. He even disconnected the phone line…

Yamuna didn't return even at night.

Janak informed the police on the following day. He also sent a telegram to Gangtok, but received no reply. The gossip was spreading. Even passers-by walking along the street turned around to look at the locked room.

The following day, as everyone sat outside, Yamuna returned, smiling.

She was wearing the same clothes—a kurtha-garala and dupatta. Somewhat creased and stained. The shine of her hair had faded, but you could see a few glossy, freshly oiled parts.

Janak, Sita, MK, Babuni, Divya: everyone stared at her silently; no one spoke.

Seeing the door closed she tried to open one flap, and when it didn't open, looked with astonishment and alarm at the lock and asked, "What happened? Where did he go?"

MK was so furious that he wanted to say, "He died. He's

dead and we've already come back from taking away his body," but only shouted, "who?"

Before Yamuna could reply, Janak asked, "And where were you for all these days?"

"Me?" Yamuna tittered. "I went to Kurseong."

"Why didn't you call to let him know?"

"Why should I?" Yamuna retorted.

Janak was trying to explain everything gradually, but MK came right out and said, "Your husband left you, he left you. He went to Gangtok. Which husband would tolerate this? He left you and went away..."

"Let him go!" Yamuna immediately shouted.

All the women who were listening on exchanged glances and retreated into their own homes.

"Let him go! What joy have I got from him? I'm blowing my own money..."

The word "blowing" smelled rank to Ravi, who was inside the house.

Janak suggested that Yamuna leave for Gangtok at once. She became inflamed with fury. She dragged Namgyal's empty bed out of the room all by herself, and turned it on its side in a corner of the verandah. She kept the radio on all the time. Sita sent Divya to keep her company overnight.

Yamuna spent Wednesday, Thursday, Friday and Saturday without shedding a single tear.

Even when Sita counselled her on Saturday night, she refused to listen.

"I'll never go to him, not even if I die," Yamuna said.

Early on Sunday morning, Yamuna came to Sita weeping copiously, and asked to be sent to Gangtok.

On the day of departure, Yamuna wept as she got into the vehicle.

Janak had brought a Jeep; all of her belongings went in it. Seated inside, Yamuna pressed her hands together, offering a namaskar to Sita, Babuni, MK, Divya and everyone else who was standing around. Even MK returned the namaskar.

Yamuna, who was silent and subdued up to Ghoom, asked a question when they turned onto the straight road to Simkuna. "You should have brought Didi to Gangtok with us, why didn't you bring her along? Why didn't you?"

The question seemed to signal a change in her mood.

"To cry a little, and not speak for a while; is that all by way of contrition?" Janak asked caustically.

"Contrition, atonement, those are words for those who write stories, not for me. Don't avoid the subject. Tell me why you didn't bring Didi along."

"She has nothing to do in Gangtok; I've got my own errands there; why should I bring her along?" Janak asked.

"Should I believe you?"

"Do."

"I won't."

Yamuna looked out at the retaining walls built out of rocks above the road, at the Jangabir water-spout, at the jungles on the hillsides below the road, and at the sun-drenched villages further below, and asked for the names of all the villages and tea plantations. She saw, and also looked at, Janak's face, hands and fingers, as he drove the Jeep. The sun finally came out when the vehicle reached the small bazaar at Mile Three, where a red flag fluttered atop a tall bamboo pole. A couple of Marwari traders offered namaskars to Yamuna who, in her

Tibetan bukhoo and pangdo, looked very much the wife of a Sikkimese official.

The vehicle kept racing on. It had rained in this area in the morning, and there was no dust. The faraway houses looked so bright, with their white wood walls and red roofs.

Yamuna began to ask for the names of all the trees and plants. Macaranga, cedar, chuletro: she didn't know any of them. Janak began to feel sorry for her.

At the turn at Mile Six, Yamuna slid over on the seat and came right up to Janak. She giggled.

"Again?"

"Again what?"

"Such mischief?"

"What can I do—the seat's like this."

They parked the Jeep to one side of the road and got out to look at the confluence of the Teesta and Rangeet Rivers. White water frothed at the confluence where the dark blue waters of the Rangeet—which meandered down from a great distance, skirting the wooded hills of Sikkim—met the forceful cascades of the Teetsa. The flat riverbank at Triveni was unpeopled and quiet today. There was a hollow silence at the confluence a hundred metres below where they were standing.

From there, the vehicle descended rapidly down to the basin of Teesta bazaar. It was already three o'clock, but the market was still on. There was a crush of buyers and sellers, with shop stalls blocking the entire road. It was torrid… By the time they finally cut across the bazaar and arrived at the bridge, Yamuna felt as though she had been stewed.

A fresh breeze started up as they parked at the bridge and got out by the Teesta River.

Yamuna and Janak walked on either side of the sturdy Teesta bridge, and stopped when they reached the centre. Yamuna looked at Janak, then crossed over to his side.

After gazing again and again at the large, smooth rocks in the middle of the Teesta, all the way across the sandy banks and the ripples of water below the bridge, Yamuna said, "I'll put a one-paisa coin between my lips and drop it in the water below."

Janak looked into Yamuna's eyes. She was allowing her loose hair to sway in the wind, which blew strong enough to tear it all out.

"What are you looking at?"

"Do you have any pledges to make? Of good character, of sound health, of regret or redemption?" Janak said. "Mine's like Lord Ram's: 'I'm taking leave, Goddess Ganga, with only a namaskar.'"

Yamuna didn't smile. "I might have a pledge," she said, and began looking through her bag for a copper coin.

Janak suddenly became afraid that Yamuna might wish for something undesirable…

He brought a notebook out of his pocket. Opened it and ripped off a page. Handed it to Yamuna and said, "Take it, it's got today's date…let it go, let it fly away to the river… it'll be a memento of this day."

Yamuna felt like laughing. She found the idea beautiful, attractive, and also tender and extremely novelistic. Her eyes widened and enlarged with happiness.

"Let's both hold it and let it go!" Yamuna said. She came up to Janak, and leaving some space for his fingers, held the page with two fingers.

They both held it and let it go…

A gust blew the page upwards. They ran to the other side of the bridge. Like a newborn creature, the tiny piece of paper fluttered from side to side as it tumbled down towards the powerful currents of the black-and-blue Teesta. The page was just as likely to fall into the surrounding woods as in the water.

"If the paper falls right into the water, then it means that Bhena-jyu loves me, all right?" Yamuna blurted out.

Janak turned towards Yamuna, his face flushed and swollen from the heat. "Again?"

"Again what? There, look at the paper: did it fall in the water? It fell way over there, in the trees!"

Indeed, the wide Teesta had refused to take that piece of paper into its bosom.

"We've stayed too long, let's go," Janak said.

Yamuna bent down, gluing a cheek to the cold cement railing, and started to stare at a one-storeyed red-roofed bungalow on the postal route which was partially hidden behind the trees.

Helpless, Janak also leaned against the railing. It felt, to him, that the Teesta's waters were flowing very rapidly now.

"No matter where I'm coming from, every time I see that bungalow I feel like spending a night there," Yamuna said, looking into Janak's radiant eyes. "To fall asleep in that bungalow listening to the Teesta flowing by, what sweet dreams; the mind must experience such pleasure, such contentment," she continued. "On a warm night…I'd probably fall asleep only in the morning, as it gets light…" Something glittered in her black eyes. "There's a kind of smell you find in a big old clean house." She was breathing heavily. Then, abruptly, she stood up. "Bring the Jeep over, let's go," she said.

"They say there's a Nepali man in Calcutta..."

"Right..." Ravi said, pretending to be listening to the story.

"They say he couldn't find a job, so his wife works as a nanny, and has supported him for years! That Nepali man just stays at home. He sweeps up. He launders the clothes, cooks and combs and braids his daughters' hair!"

"Tchee!"

"MK is going to be just like that now," Parthiv said.

It was wrong of Parthiv to say so. MK wasn't going to be like that.

These days, when he got completely drunk, MK would say, "I'm going to be a communist!" He would talk about battling against the rich to establish the rule of the poor—but only when drunk. If he were to speak like this when he weren't drunk, he'd be a different man altogether, although speaking like this when drunk was, at least, a sign that he wasn't yet dead.

Worried that he'd get drunk and create a scene in the shop, Pasang-la would often pour millet beer into a mug with handles fashioned out of porridge tins and give it to him for free, just to send him home early:

"Go, go to your own home. Drink in your own home."

"Why you say get out to me, huh?" MK would yell in English, staggering around, his cheeks and forehead glistening. "I am not beggar!" MK always broke out in English when he got angry.

"No get out! No get out!" said Pasang who, with his braided hair, looked like a police officer from Tibet.

At home—

"You always get drunk and say crooked things," Babuni would say.

"I say crooked things? Then who talks straight to you?" He'd pick a fight even when he was slurring.

"Eat your food," Babuni would say to prevent the argument from escalating.

"Food? Whose house did you bring this food from…?"

The very first time MK came home drunk from the office, Babuni had found it funny and had only pretended to be scared. It had been even funnier to talk about it the following day. When he'd first begun to mistrust her, Babuni had argued back, trembling with rage. After that she'd defeated him by saying nothing. Now, when even the smallest scene took place, she'd gather up all her fears and weep.

When he wasn't drunk, MK was extremely anxious. One midnight, during a fit of anxiety, he woke up and opened his eyes. There was rheum in his eyes because of the cold. With great tenderness, he caressed Babuni's hair as she slept beside him…he stroked the few creases on her forehead, her thin eyelashes, the soft nostrils on her high nose, the empty piercings in her earlobes, her dry, slightly parted lips and cool cheeks.

Babuni also awoke at some point that night. MK hadn't been able to fall asleep yet.

"You're still awake?"

They began to talk.

"After I die, find someone rich and go with him, all right?" MK said.

There was neither compassion nor anger nor guilt nor any other emotion in MK's voice. Responses are made to the tone of voice rather than to the meaning of the words uttered. Babuni could find no response.

"Let's sleep," she said. "Only unhappy husbands and wives wake up in the night to talk."

When Janak returned a week later from Gangtok, he brought news of a job that he'd arranged for MK.

With great difficulty, MK said, "That's a big help, Daju."

When Janak glanced over, MK was staring at the floor. He had become thin.

"Don't drink too much."

"I won't, now."

"And don't take too much leave to come back home. You can take your family there later on."

"That's what I'll do," MK said. "When should I set out?"

"First let the letter arrive. It'll come soon. Make your preparations."

Cries of joy spread through the house when MK went over to share the news. Babuni buried her face in her clothes, her eyes brimming with tears. Their lives were completely transformed by the light of an unexpected new sun. Babuni felt her home dear to her once again.

Amrita was the happiest of all. She was so happy that she had to go out, as though her happiness couldn't fit into one small room. Not knowing what to do with so much happiness, she picked up a bucket and ran over to fill it at the water tap.

On her way back, she stopped by Sita's kitchen. "Auntie, our father's going to go to work! He found a job!"

Sita, who was picking through pumpkin greens, put aside her task and matched Amrita's happiness, chatting with her for a while.

That evening, as night fell, Babuni noticed many different shades of red in the redness of the sky.

That night she also noticed the stars, which looked as though they were tangled up in the tree branches.

Then, for the first time, she noticed that everyone in her home had become emaciated.

MK's appointment letter arrived promptly in four days. He had to sign in on the first of the coming month for his new job as a clerk in the chief court.

On the morning after the letter arrived, MK went to Janak and said, "The salary seems a bit low..."

"How much is it?"

MK scanned the letter and read out the basic salary, the annual raise and the compensation for inflation. Then he mentioned how hard it was to find a house in Gangtok, and how costly things were there.

Janak listened to him, and when he was done listening, scolded him, "That's too low a salary? What about those who earn even less? Do you want to starve your wife and family to death...? Who ever has a high enough salary...? But if you have one, at least you can use it to get a loan, and borrow some money to eat... How long have you been jobless?"

"A long time."

"And so?"

"I'll go, of course, why wouldn't I accept the job...it's a job I've got after such a long time," MK said, correcting his mistake.

Janak felt sorry for him. More gently, he counselled him, "People have many routines, just as they have many organs in the body—but if the lung is damaged, we die even if the heart and brain and eyes can last for a few more years. We don't need all of our routines to fail in order to suffer in the same way, and to be destroyed. When one fails, the task is over."

MK kept saying, "True, true…"

Several times a day, MK would count: it was fourteen days till he had to leave, then thirteen, then twelve. A couple of quarrels broke out over what he should pack. There was a nice calendar hanging in the house, but when he said he'd take it with him, Babuni got upset.

Babuni told her husband that the child in her belly was fortunate.

MK laughed. Ironing his black coat, he said, "I've also bought a lottery ticket."

The results of the final exams were splashed all over the newspaper. The schools began to calculate the "percentage" of their success. Although most of the students who had taken the exams privately hadn't fared well, Isabel had passed in the second division.

This time, Ravi went over to congratulate Isabel.

There were other people there, and some girls, and also Parthiv.

Isabel was somewhat leaner than before, and looked considerably more mature. Ravi took her aside and congratulated her.

Isabel didn't say much, and only asked, "Why don't you sit?" and glanced at a chair.

After taking the chair, Ravi noticed that the others had not only congratulated Isabel, they had also brought gifts for her. He felt that his visit had been futile. After chatting awhile with Parthiv, he stepped out and then came straight back home...

The BA results came out immediately afterwards. Ravi had passed. The school closed for a half-day break to celebrate the passing marks that he, LB and three other teachers had scored. Parthiv had passed with honours, and not many students had failed out of the BA this year.

Sita and Divya and everyone else at home were thrilled. Janak was so pleased that he chatted for a long time with Ravi. It struck Ravi that they were the only three people who were truly gladdened by his success.

Among the many things that Janak said, the one Ravi enjoyed most (for some reason) was, "Even after they graduate, can people really find good jobs in Darjeeling any more?" Janak said, "My father used to tell us that in the old days, there were so many jobs in our very own Darjeeling, you couldn't find people to work for you—so dire was the shortage of educated people! They would drag students on their way to school over to the offices and put them to work. Back then, even passing out of high school was a major achievement. The high school exams were held in the court; the magistrate would preside over them and police constables would stand guard; only three or four students would be taking the exam. A huge crowd would gather in the court's front yard just to stare at or peek at those taking the "matric" test. If they passed, they'd put them on rickshaws and cover them with garlands: they'd parade each matriculating student with a five-piece musical band. He'd have to decide which job to accept. The advice not to work in the police—which you still hear sometimes—is an echo of that era, when you could choose from any job. The offices would send peons to the bazaar to look for anyone who had studied up to the fifth or sixth class…"

Ravi enjoyed this a lot, and kept laughing: "They'd parade each matriculating student with a five-piece musical band!"

"Someone really ought to have written a novel about the old Darjeeling," Janak said.

A couple of days later, Krishnalal asked Ravi a question at school: "What do you think of Bhudev?"

Ravi got irritated. "What do *you* think?"

"Don't get angry with me," Krishnalal said hastily. "There are rumours all over the bazaar… Would I ask you something like this for no reason? People say you're opposing your own father."

"Who says I'm opposing him?"

"That's what people are saying."

Ravi fell silent. He wasn't upset about this accusation, but nervous. "I think Bhudev is a gutsy, energetic, courageous man," he said. "He's dedicated to a single task, which makes us also want to take up the same task."

"And what does Janak-babu think of him?"

"On this, well, we're family, there's no disagreement… The thoughts and ideals that we uphold outside bear no relation to our family life."

"That's really how you feel?"

Ravi fell silent again.

"Bhudev is going to pit you against your father, and then, after disgracing both the father and son, he'll toss you aside like a fly in milk."

"Why would he toss me aside?" Ravi asked. "What reason

would Bhudev have to fear me? I stand on my own convictions. I didn't get into this work out of anyone's enmity or anyone's enticement. Today I like Bhudev, I like his work—so I'll praise him. Tomorrow, if necessary, I'll criticize him, I'll expose him…"

"Who'll believe you anymore? Everyone will see a son switching over to his father's side in the end. They'll say you're just obeying your father. Who'll trust you?"

"So people trust me only when I speak out against my father?"

"What else?"

When Ravi finished up at school and went home that evening, he found Kanti waiting for him.

He waved at her with a chalk-stained hand and said, "Where are you coming from, Kanti?"

Kanti stood with her leaf-like hands joined in a namaskar, then dropped her hands and said, with deep embarrassment, "I failed…I have to go back to college. I came to ask for some books…"

"Which books?"

Kanti said nothing.

Ravi found her silence awkward. To end it, he said with forced laughter, "All my textbooks, my entire store of knowledge, are in this cupboard, Kanti! Take the ones you need—if I've got them, you can take them."

Kanti glanced at the cupboard that Ravi had pointed at, but just kept standing there.

Seeing Kanti so ill at ease, Ravi took a hint and went inside.

When he came back out, Kanti was waiting around, having placed an economics book on the table and closed the cupboard door.

"You need only one book?"

"Only this one..." Kanti said softly. "Namaskar."

"You're leaving already?"

Trying very hard to smile a little, Kanti finally said, "I have to go."

As Ravi looked on, Kanti, draped in a black shawl, climbed down the stairs and disappeared from view.

Ravi took the following day off to go to the court. This was the day the court was likely to settle the case launched by the Tukvar Tea Estate.

Ravi arrived at exactly ten o'clock, as though the verdict were going to come right on time, but neither the sun nor the babus had shown up at the court by ten. Hari and Bhudev arrived at eleven, clutching files under their arms. After talking to Hari awhile, Bhudev went to the Bar Association's library, then slipped away somewhere else.

Ravi had sat in the party office a few days earlier and read through the case carefully:

The previous year, quite a while earlier than this season, the tea bushes were being heavy-pruned. The manager noticed that those who could work fast and prune four lots of twelve square feet each from their allotted areas were going home by noon. A day or two later, a new order was issued: from now on, the measurement of the prunings would not be done until two o'clock, and in Block Number 4 and Block Number 7 (where the tea shrubs were planted sparsely), the daily quota for pruning would now be five lots of twelve square feet each. The allotted areas for those two blocks thus increased, and the workers couldn't go home till two-thirty.

Protest and grumbling started up in the plantation.

The people in the parties also encouraged this dissent.

On Friday, October 21, exactly fourteen days after the order was issued, the manager came by to inspect the plantation. When he went to inspect Block Number 9, about half the workers had already finished pruning and left, while the others were also getting ready to leave, even though it was only noon. Only eight or ten people were working in the allotted area.

"On whose orders are you going home at this hour?"

"No one's—our own!" came the ready reply.

"What did you say?"

"Whose order was it not to measure the prunings till two-thirty? Why should we wait around after finishing our work, as though watching over a dead body?"

Someone else added, "And whose order was it to increase the quota for pruning to five lots?

"That was my order," the manager said, grinding his jaws.

On hearing this, the workers swarmed the manager, surrounding him completely.

"Don't let him go!"

"Don't let him escape, don't let him escape—don't let go of him!"

For this offense, the estate had launched a case against seven of its workers in the session court, citing Section 307/34.

As everyone waited around, the father and elder brother of one of the men who had been arrested, Naldhoj Mukhiya, arrived at the court with the wife of Sirilal Rai and Bhairav's two wives.

"We'll win, we'll definitely win this case!" they kept repeating among themselves.

Tall old Bhaktiman Yakha, and equally tall but dark, skinny Rambahadur Chhetri, also arrived at the court in a show of support for their sons, who were both entangled in the case.

Hari drew Ravi over and introduced him to everyone.

Those coming from the plantation showed up at the court just before noon, filling up the front yard.

An additional hour after that, the police brought the seven accused men straight up from the jail and led them into the court. They didn't so much as glance at the family members who were in the crowd to see them.

Another two or three hours passed as everyone waited—nothing happened. In boredom and hunger, those waiting around began to wander away and wander back. A Tibetan woman wasted on alcohol showed up, wailing—others took hold of her and led her home. A crowd placed garlands on a boy who was released on another case, and left.

Bhaktiman began to express some doubt: "Maybe ours… won't happen today."

After a while, Bhudev and a lawyer emerged from the court. The lawyer hurried away to the Bar Association's library. Bhudev came up and announced, "Our date has moved back again. The judgment will come on the twenty-second."

Having waited all day, Ravi suddenly felt very drained upon learning so little.

The following day, out on the street, Krishnalal smiled and said to Ravi, "I saw you coming just now, and waited for you. So, what happened yesterday?"

"Nothing happened," Ravi said. "The judgment's coming on the twenty-second."

They headed towards the school. On either side of the street were rows of boys and girls on their way to school.

"What does Bhudev say?" Krishnalal asked.

"Who knows…"

"Didn't he say anything yesterday?"

"I came back alone."

"Why?"

"Everyone had left."

Krishnalal was quiet for a moment. Then he said, "Ten years can pass by over cases like this!"

"They should have launched a counter-case against the manager."

"They did! Don't you know? Sirilal launched a case but he lost; nothing came of it."

Ravi didn't know this.

"If Sirilal lost his case, then what will happen in a case brought against Sirilal and the others? It's over the same incident," Krishnalal said, glancing at Ravi.

Hari also arrived as they talked.

"Krishnalal is asking…" Ravi repeated the question to Hari. "If the manager is found innocent in one case, what happens in another case involving the same incident?"

"That line of questioning is itself flawed," Hari replied.

Ravi didn't say anything. Krishnalal also didn't ask anything.

"Four of the seven men will be acquitted. They'll be released. The remaining three will be freed with an ordinary penalty," Hari said with great self-assurance.

Krishnalal still didn't say anything.

Upon seeing Krishnalal so silent, Ravi asked with a laugh, "Have you clamped your teeth together? Are you a turtle being flown on a 'sky-path' by we two ducks? Are you afraid you'll fall if you say something?"

Neither Hari nor Krishnalal laughed.

"Did you see yesterday's news from Tibet?" Hari asked Ravi. "The reds have got up to all sorts of things."

"The yellows, you mean," Ravi said with a laugh.

Krishnalal finally spoke: "Let's assume that all seven men in this case go free, as Hari said. Even then, the manager can form a court of inquiry to harass them with indiscipline cases..."

"And when that happens, will we party members just sit around weeding the cabbage patch?" Hari asked.

That afternoon, after stopping by at home to eat, Ravi had gone to the school in Larki to teach history to Class 9. The guard knocked on the door and told him that he was being summoned to the office.

Divya was in the office when he got there. She stood up, and before Ravi could ask, said, "Something's happened to Buwa. Aama said to fetch you immediately..." Unable to continue talking, she started to sob.

Ravi obtained the headmaster's permission to go home with Divya. On the way he asked several times about what had happened before Divya could finally explain.

After Ravi left home, Janak had also been about to go out when he'd felt a sharp pain in his chest... He couldn't get up from the chair, and a heat rose up from somewhere inside his chest. He was sweating from the neck, the ears...

"Did you call the doctor?"

"The doctor's probably there now."

The doctor had indeed arrived by the time they got home. Ravi went and stood by the bedside. Sita was sitting to one side of the bed; Divya went to the kitchen to start a fire. Janak lay supine in bed. His face had yellowed so quickly. Babuni was helping Divya.

After a protracted examination, the doctor didn't even name the illness; all he said was, "I'll give him some medicine." He took Ravi out with him.

"It was so sudden, in just an instance—I don't know what happened," Janak said feebly, trying to smile.

Watching him trying to smile, Divya felt at a loss for words and began to sob again.

The doctor came every day; the following day and the day after that. For the most part Janak was fine, but from time to time he'd experience a sudden pain. During the rest of the time, he was worn out waiting for that pain to return.

During Janak's illness, someone they'd all forgotten came to the house one night.

It was past nine o'clock. Hearing the murmuring of voices at the door and the sound of a hesitant knock, Ravi opened one flap of the door and peered out. Outside, he saw the electric lights and dark roofs under the yellow light of the moon and, standing next to the door, two men and a girl.

"Who is it? Who are you looking for?"

A dark, skinny man in a white cap, traditional daura-sural and canvas shoes shaded his face from the house lights, which were glaring in his eyes, and said, "Isn't this Janak-babu's home? I'm Birman…"

"Birman who?"

Birman got confused. "The master will recognize me. The mistress too. Are they in this house, or have they moved somewhere else?"

Ravi couldn't figure him out. But once he called Sita over, she immediately recognized Birman.

They all piled into one room. Janak was delighted. Ravi and Divya were delighted as well. Sita wanted to scold Birman—"You said you'd be gone for a month—what happened?"—but didn't get a chance to amid all the commotion.

Janak was soon asking Birman: "After you left, did you ever reach home?"

"I got there. I got there later on," Birman said, answering in his old style.

"Whose daughter is this…yours?"

"My own daughter. I call her Sani," he said, looking fondly at his daughter. "Sani! Offer a namaskar. To the mistress too, and here and here too."

Sita, and beside her Ravi, who was seven inches taller, watched on. The dark little girl had her hair parted in the Tibetan style, and was wearing a colourful chaubandi blouse, with flat red bangles all over her plump arms. Sani was sitting on top of a bundled-up woollen rug. From her bag she brought out a wooden jar that must have contained more than two kilos of ghee and offered it as a gift to Sita.

"What a beautiful jar!" Divya cried.

Even Janak exclaimed in praise, "It's made of false-nettle wood, how beautiful."

Sita laughed gaily, her nostrils narrowing and her face sharpening, and said, "Then all of you who like the jar can take that, and I'll take the ghee."

Birman and the others laughed at Sita's words. Her success made Sita feel so restless that… she took Sani into the inner room for no reason at all.

"And who is this?" Ravi asked, pointing at the other man.

"Me?" said the man with a smile. He was dressed in a black Nepali cap and a black waistcoat. "I'm your Bahun."

"My Bahun?" Ravi said, making fun of him.

"My your name is Khagprasad Brahman." Having introduced himself, Khagprasad smiled, displaying his protruding teeth; when smiling, the sparse hairs on his upper lip curled up in a moon shape. Ravi found his way of smiling odd, because he came right up to his face and then retreated. His laughter was very intimate, and the expression in his eyes astonished; so when he laughed it seemed to mean, "My name is Khagprasad Brahman, isn't that ridiculous?" Khagprasad scrawled out "Bramna," as he wrote his surname, but he was in the habit of writing with the paper resting on his knees, the way people did in the courts, and he joined all the words together, leaving no space in between them, so they resembled tendrils of soot dangling from the ceiling above a fireplace, or dried black bananas tied on ropes at the market. All Ravi could make of his "Bramna" was "Trapna".

"I married a woman from Khagprasad's village," Birman said. "Sani's fourteen years old now. Her mother never recovered from giving birth, and gradually, every day, got sicker and sicker; she passed away last year, in the month of Magh. She was so virtuous…" Birman's voice suddenly broke, and he began to cry.

"She was your goddess Lakshmi," Khagprasad said.

Janak chided Birman: "Don't cry, don't cry. What's the good in crying now?"

Khagprasad also said, "Yes, what's the good in your crying?" and picked up Birman's cap, which had fallen to the floor, putting it back on him.

Birman told Janak all of his stories, about how, after marriage, his days had passed in hardship working in a tea plantation in Ilam, and about how his elderly father-in-law hadn't allowed him to come back here.

Birman's daughter was the pillar of his life now. Birman lived only for her. At night he would return home exhausted from the tea plantation's storehouse. It would be daylight before he could even fall asleep. Sani always told Birman not to grieve. But Birman couldn't stop grieving; his grief had aged him prematurely.

Sani would take out her mother's bangles and bead necklaces and clothes, which she had stored carefully in a suitcase, and show them to her father, saying, "Babu, we have all of these mementos of Aama." She'd show him a small box inside the suitcase and say, "We also have this memento of Aama."

Birman would stay silent. He knew that his dying wife had left him a memento that gave him more joy than any of these objects; that memento was their daughter.

"What a tragic story," Divya said playfully.

"Have it written up in a newspaper," Ravi quipped.

Birman listened to this. Receiving a whiff of consolation, he sniffled and said, "Write it down, Babu, write down my story. Write it down and have it printed. I'll tell you everything. Write a book. I'm living this life in her memory. I'll live in her memory without crying or dying. The life of a dead man. As long as I have a fistful of breath, I'll keep her in my heart. Write down my story, Babu: My actual home is in Mulpani. My in-laws are from Sakhejung..."

It was one o'clock by the time they all ate and went to

bed. Spreading out some woollen rugs, Birman remarked, "You haven't changed at all!"

With some sadness, Janak remembered his poor health. "The things you say..." he said. "How could anyone not age after all these years?"

"You really haven't," Khagprasad said, grinning and watching him expectantly, as though waiting for Janak to laugh.

Early the following morning, Birman said, "Let me take leave now. I'll come back."

"Where are you going that you need to take leave?" Sita asked.

Birman answered with a single word: "Assam."

In the outer room, Khagprasad was telling Janak about his own troubles.

"After that, I left your Kathmandu. It's hard to even defecate in Kathmandu. I have your children, and a wife too, in Ilam. For two years I was in pain, Sir, for two years. All your hair on my head fell off. Half of my your body hurt so badly, as if bruised. It hurt just to move. The only time it didn't hurt was when I'd tell myself 'I'm dead,' and not move or even breathe. Then I got your fever, and then here comes your tea..."

"Here comes what?"

"The tea is here." Divya was standing behind them with teacups.

Sita and the others also came in as Divya placed the cups on the table.

Janak asked, "When will you return from Assam, Birman?"

"I can't say, Hajoor. How can a bird flying away with a broken heart ever know when it'll return?"

"Don't say that. What, is your life over?"

"It's over, Hajoor, it's over. I'll blow away my remaining breath in her memory," Birman said, and began to cry again.

The three of them departed after bidding farewell. Sita stuffed five rupees into Sani's hands just as she left.

MK had had the same dream for several nights in a row.

In the dream, MK's knees hurt very badly. The pain in his knees was so acute that he couldn't walk; he had to strain to drag himself forward. He had to endure his own mental agitation and physical agony to get even a short distance ahead. When he did finally drag himself five paces forward, MK would wake up from the dream, his heart racing. As he awoke he'd find that both his kneecaps were in searing pain. He couldn't tell which was more real, the dream or the waking state.

The closer the day of his departure came, the more his agitation and agony at leaving home hollowed him out. Hollowness.

Having bought a lottery ticket, he was convinced that he'd win for sure; he would fantasize that he'd buy the flat, narrow plot of land that he could see from his window, and build a house and plant pompon, chrysanthemum and camellia plants all around it... MK spied a few boys who had put up a net in that plot, who were playing and hollering there, and grew enraged that they should trespass on his property without permission. So deeply was MK convinced by his daydreams, he would sometimes babble in their grip.

On the other side of the house, infirm Janak had recuperated enough to get out of bed and walk around a little. His life still revolved around waiting to feel that pain return. He'd felt it twice yesterday. Today there had been one attack so far.

His days passed in conversation with Sita. They got through talking about his old school and old friends and teachers—all of that. Vines of laughter crept densely over all of the branches of their conversations. The memories of the textbooks he'd studied in the lower classes at school, as well as the lessons they had contained, revived Janak's childhood curiosity. He, whose mind had wearied from the arduousness of life, enjoyed simple tales with all his heart—tales of the devoted dog, the foolish fox, the turtle and the duck. Stories about people depressed him. Every night, he'd ask Sita to tell him an old tale that she knew. He experienced an unsurpassable relaxation in the mind and a deep peace in the heart when Sita recounted those simple tales in the words of the storybooks...

Though his body was worn out, Janak's face and eyes looked clearer and brighter than ever, as though his illness and his fear of illness had cleansed him.

Yesterday, he ran his hands along a row of his old books. He opened each book, leafing through old memories. In one book he found a folded-up sheet of paper that must have been there for years, on which he'd copied down quotations from Keats, Byron, Shakespeare and others, like a collection of ideals. His ideals about life were all old and toothless now. Janak tore up the sheet of paper and threw it away. He also found a Romain Rolland quote inside a copy of *Ramakrishna Kathamrita*.

"I must have suffered from a sickness about collecting quotations back then," Janak thought to himself.

"The duration of your life is short, so offer what you intend to offer us soon; for if you happen to have to depart today, the void that the earth will suffer will never again be filled—because no one else can offer exactly what you can."

Janak couldn't throw away this quotation. It felt newer and more valuable today.

To the farmer, any place with the same crops as those in his fields does not feel foreign; the educated man feels similarly about books. This comparison came to Janak out of nowhere.

Confined at home by his illness, Janak found time to gather and collect all of his scattered thoughts, or, let's say, his new ideals which had sprouted from the broken branches of his previous ideals.

Sita stared out of the window, taking in the warm sunlight and brisk breeze, surveying the green hills and dales of Darjeeling that stretched out in front of her, and said to Janak, "Darjeeling is certainly very beautiful, but it's so rugged and craggy. Look at that..."

Janak went over to Sita and, like her, cast his gaze out the window. Truly, Darjeeling contained not a single stretch of proper land, it was all jungles and cliffs and clumps of earth. He laughed in agreement, and said, "Darjeeling is a rock garden that nature put special effort into constructing."

Sita thought of the small rock gardens that the municipality had built on the roadsides and smiled.

"Sita, if you were ever to go to Falelung Sandakaphu one day!" Janak said, pointing at the tall peak of Falelung, which looked like a barrier to block off the frigid winds of the Himalaya. "If you were to go there one day and look beyond, you'd see the fertile lands of Nepal on the other side: all those fields lying there so splendid, so even. I've thought about this a lot. The Treaty of Sugauli gave all of Darjeeling's cliffs and gorges on this side of the Mechi River to the British; in my opinion, Nepal gave away only its unusable cliffs and gorges, and kept all of the good, habitable land for itself. When I examine the matter from the perspective of that era, I don't believe that Nepal was weeping as it let go of beautiful Darjeeling; rather, the British, having barely gained victory, took whatever they could get of these cliffs and gorges, and said nothing, and hid their shame."

Sita listened on patiently.

Becoming impassioned, Janak said, "We, the Nepalis of Darjeeling, are trusted by both India and Nepal, and so both India and Nepal try to win our love and affection; but Darjeeling is ours and we are Darjeeling's. All the houses and shops in the four square miles of the town, the tea plantations beyond that, and all these lands and trees, they may have once belonged to Bardhaman or Cooch Behar, and now they belong to the government, or maybe the Bengalis and Marwaris will buy them and make it theirs; and yet Darjeeling is ours. Since primaeval times, Darjeeling has belonged to those who can plough its grey and red soil and produce food. It can't be anyone else's. Whoever this soil gives to, that place is theirs; the rest can only live here in hope."

Sita wanted to say something, but Janak went on talking. "We, the Nepalis of Darjeeling, have travelled great distances along with the soil of Darjeeling, and like its trees and rivers and springs, we have, in the cradle of history, been part of one peoples after another. If today someone should ask these alder and juniper trees, these swift rivers and trickling springs,

'Where are you from?' the answer will be, 'I'm from the soil that I'm of…"

"The names of those who donated money may be written on Darjeeling's grand town halls, banks, clubs and houses, but countless Nepalis carried loads on their foreheads, broke their backs, fell ill and died during the construction of those buildings. It is they who made Darjeeling…"

Today Janak remembered, once again, the day they brought Ravi home. That night, he had dreamt of the old house that he used to live in when he was small, and he hadn't been able to fall back to sleep after waking up in the middle of the night.

Babuni looked at herself in a hand mirror while preparing to go to the bazaar, and pointing at the spots under her eyes, said to her reflection the mirror, "There's a cream you can get for four rupees to make these spots disappear, I'm going to buy it."

"Buy it, you have to buy it," MK said affectionately, looking at Babuni from bed, where he was curled up; his eyes met Babuni's as she turned her head to pin up her hair, and they both smiled. "What I don't have is the money to build you a Taj Mahal," MK said, "but I have more love for you than Shah Jahan ever felt."

Babuni was embarrassed, and also pleased. She placed a small vermilion teeka on her forehead, and then, returning the teeka box to the case, said, "Repay Sita-didi's thirty rupees soon, all right? It may not embarrass you, but…I've put up with so much trouble over the years: Don't give me any more trouble."

MK didn't reply.

Amrita had also got ready to go to the bazaar with her

mother. She was waiting eagerly at the door, dressed in a red-and-white kurtha that they had tailored for her for the previous Dashain, with sparkling tops on her ears.

"Why don't you not go, and stay home, maybe?" Babuni said.

Her daughter's face crumpled and she slouched at the doorway.

"Take her along! Why are you ashamed to take her along?" MK said suddenly, and shouted: "If you weren't going to take the child, why did you tell her you would? You want to sashay around by yourself, acting young, wearing cream…!"

Babuni stood with her mouth agape. The mention of cream brought tears to her eyes. She found her husband to be the most loveless and unkind person in the world.

MK gritted his teeth, looking at her keenly, as though he had a lot more to say. "Don't go, Amrita, stay with me. Let this one go out all by herself."

Babuni went out, shoving and smacking Amrita, taking her along. "All because of you…all because of you!"

A silence soon spread through the room. MK got out of bed and examined himself in the same hand mirror that Babuni had used, then put it down on the case.

He didn't like how he looked.

He went on to examine the case, the chairs, the curtains and the planks on the wall. Everything looked old and cheap and inferior, and below his standard. I could have made every picture and every object in the room better than this—I really could have, he thought…

Surprisingly, MK no longer felt anger towards Babuni, nor did he feel love. In this terrifying void, he saw himself living as a prisoner in this small room for all these years. How did I endure…?

He looked at the fingers on his hands. They didn't look like his own fingers, and he didn't want them to be his either.

He'd always found the outside world cruel and disorganized, and now he found his home distasteful as well.

That night, Babuni woke up because of the cold at around three or four o'clock in the morning. When she drew the quilt up to her neck, she realized that even the fabric had gone cold. The room was completely dark, but she could tell that it was close to dawn. She'd had a sweet, dreamless sleep, but now found her heart clutched by fear and doubt. Babuni reached out in bed and tried to rid herself of this fear. She felt for her daughter Amrita. Amrita had only recently got under the quilt, so her cheeks and arms and shoulders were still cold. Babuni reached past her daughter to feel for MK. MK wasn't there. He had a way of curling into himself and sleeping alone, off by himself, so Babuni reached quite a ways with her hands. He wasn't there. Babuni told herself that he must have gone out, and tried to fall back to sleep…

He didn't return after a long wait. "Pushpa's father?" Babuni called out once.

Then she tossed off the quilt and got up. The dark night and cold air were streaming into the room from the open door; for some reason, Babuni didn't dare switch on the electric lights. "Pushpa's father?" she called out again.

When the lights flashed on, Babuni raced her eyes over the room in the brightness. Everything was as usual, but there was no sign of MK. Babuni went out to the verandah, her eyes wide with fear. She saw nothing but the red glare of the streetlamps. Not even a shutter quivered needlessly or squeaked eerily. Babuni went back in and turned off the lights.

"Aama, where's Buwa?" Amrita asked, having got up to look at her mother.

"He's not here, he must have gone somewhere."

"Where did he go?" Amrita asked.

A pale grey light began to spread in the distance beyond the door, which remained ajar. Babuni's ears picked up many kinds of sounds from far away and also from nearby.

Babuni was wailing when Janak woke up.

"Pushpa's father..." Ravi hesitated. "Hung himself and died."

"What?" Janak shrieked.

Describing the incident, Ravi pushed it as far back into the past as possible: "He went down to the garage and hung himself last night."

"Why did he have to die, abandoning his wife and children? That sinful bastard...!" Janak cried, infuriated. He got out of bed, dragged his feet into a pair of wooden sandals and went out.

Fakru and his brother Kaseem, who had recently arrived from the mainland, were loitering by the garage, spitting. Pasang-la had come out and was telling them something. Squeezing out of the bottom of the closed paan shop, Lakhanram shook his head and told his brother Pekhar that committing suicide was an enormous sin. A lot of people had spit; the ground was stained with it.

Janak called out, "Bahini! Go away. Amrita too. Don't cry, don't cry: why cry for a jackass like that, how can such a worthless man be a father... Ravi! Take your aunt and Amrita home and keep them there." After issuing these orders, he headed down the stairs.

A driver boy who had come to Pasang-la's shop for a cup of tea early in the morning was shouting, "Just yesterday, he told me he'd go to Teesta in my Land Rover—and now he's gone." He shut up when he saw Janak approaching.

Janak entered the garage and took a look.

A new rope was fastened onto the thick square wooden beam that had been lain above both sides of the brick wall to hold up the upper floor. In a loop on the rope hung a body with one leg slightly lifted, running away from life; the trousers had slipped down to reveal a pale belly, and the fists were half-closed in a gesture of helplessness. All in all, it was a dirty man who hung there in the same unworthy manner in which he'd lived: his premature death seemed to highlight all of his body's inadequacies and grotesqueries, to display it in this condition.

His face was turned up and tilted leftwards, and some tears had trickled out of his eyes and down the bridge of the nose, to the ear. Out of habit, he must have wiped away the rest of his tears with a handkerchief before dying, and now the body's residual self-love, from after the soul departed, had also dried, leaving behind only a glistening trail.

"Among animals, the strongest survive and the rest die. Among humans, everyone survives, but only the most incompetent die—they die before time." Upon saying this much, Janak turned back and headed home.

He climbed up the stairs, then turned around and told those below, "When the police come and ask for the cause of death, tell them he'd lost his mind. You can say whatever you want about men who die in this manner."

Those below concurred: "True, true. People don't die

like this for no reason, they commit suicide after losing their mind."

Another driver called out to the first one, "Better drive carefully today, boy! The ghost of the dead man might roll your vehicle over as you go down the Peshok hill!"

Even the paan-shop owner, who was opening his shop, laughed at this.

"That poor man only had till today," someone remarked.

Someone else added, "Yes, he had only till today, Thursday."

"He'd obviously lost his mind—no wonder he talked to himself!" someone else said.

The hanging body received not a word of love, pity or sympathy from anyone. For two hours it hung in the garage all by itself, with the exception of a few people who came in to look around. Later on, Pasang-la's dog discovered the body and circled it, barking. When the dog lost interest in the game, even it abandoned the body.

In the afternoon, after the police showed up, people gathered around once more. When they saw from Babuni's body that she was expecting a child, everyone deemed the dead man a sissy and a coward. Babuni and Amrita explained that there had been a small quarrel with MK when they'd gone to the bazaar yesterday, but everything had been fine, as if there had been no quarrel, when they'd returned home.

"He had lost his mind," Pasang-la said.

The sub-inspector turned to Pasang-la and began to interrogate him, "This man came to your shop and asked for booze, but you didn't give him any; and you had your servants capture and kill him by hanging him."

Pasang-la was speechless.

"It could also be something like that," the sub-inspector said with a laugh.

Everyone else began giggling.

Amrita looked at all these people laughing so lightheartedly, as though nothing had happened, and felt that it was a show of disrespect and dishonour. Babuni knew that she'd been disgraced in front of society—and the stain of this disgrace would linger on as ignominy, rather than regret, far into the future for her and her daughters. Babuni didn't cry anymore. She wanted to have the body taken away as soon as possible—this was what she wanted most amid her mixed-up feelings of hatred, guilt and retaliation. She listened politely to those who offered consolation and encouragement, but found it hard to bear, and felt restless.

"I'm here, I, your mother, am here…let the one who wanted to die hang himself and die," Babuni said to Amrita.

That afternoon, Ravi called some friends over, and after placing a small bouquet of rhododendron and trumpet flowers on the one who'd killed himself, they carried him away from the house. Pasang-la alone placed a white khada over the corpse.

Amrita looked on at all of this by herself from the verandah above, tears streaming down her face.

Ravi came home exhausted and sat alone in his room, ruminating:

"If he had to die by suicide in the end, he should have committed some great heist before dying, or else he should have dedicated his life to politics and then died. He died for nothing. The difficult part is to stop loving yourself, but once you accomplish that…he should have done something an ordinary man in ordinary circumstances wouldn't dare to do. He died for nothing. Suicide is the biggest failure a man can experience once he's born…"

Ravi asked himself: "Would you ever kill Janak and commit suicide?

"No: he's a much more necessary man than I. He's useful; to punish him in such a manner would be extremely unjust to him.

"So then, would you kill Isabel and commit suicide?"

On this, Ravi was somewhat slower to decide.

"No, never!" In a fright, he told himself: "I might finish myself off by committing suicide, but I'd never so much as touch her."

Ravi got lost in thought, truly lost in thought. Methods of self-destruction, and the liberation of the thereafter, felt both magnetic and terrifying to him.

Two days later, at school, Ravi heard from Hari:

In his ruling, the session judge had acquitted four of the accused men, and given the other three—Naldhoj, Bhaire and Aitraj—hard sentences of five years' imprisonment each.

"Five years each?" Ravi cried.

"But the rest of them were released," Hari said.

A few more months passed amid hassles and nuisances, and then came the season when the rains soaked Darjeeling's hillsides all day and night. Jayabilas chose this time to finally file a lawsuit. Janak took in this outrage and humiliation in silence. The other day, on the day of the municipal elections, he'd left home for the first time after falling ill. Sita and Divya had gone along to vote with Janak, who was carrying a large multi-coloured umbrella to block the sun, which shone like an unexpected fortune. Janak had instructed everyone from home to place one vote directly on the "inkpot-and-pen", which was Yashraj's election symbol, and to give their second vote to whomever they pleased. Indeed, by eveningtime, the "horse" and "inkpot-and-pen" had won in their respective wards; the "scale", "marigold" and "umbrella" had lost. Bhudev, who had run under the "inkpot-and-pen" symbol, lost in the neighbouring ward—by quite a few votes. It never once crossed Janak's mind, through the entire day, that he had been summoned to the court on the eighth.

When Sita cried, "How can you go to the court…?" Janak deflected her question with a joke:

"If I don't go, they'll come and get me." He saw a shadow flitting over Sita's clear, round, flawless face, and tried to reason with her. "How long can he wait, the poor man? Hasn't it been almost ten or twelve years? He's waited all these years out of respect for us…"

"He's also the one who ruined us," Sita said, interrupting him. "He withdrew his share in the middle, which is how all of this happened. If he hadn't withdrawn it…"

"That's true, everything you're saying is true, but we can't keep saying that anymore, can we? You tell me," Janak said. "There are documents, there's my signature, there's everything required to justify our arrest. And it was his brothers who withdrew their share, not him. He lost sixty thousand on potatoes that year. This is what actually happened, I know it. Everyone began quickly withdrawing their deposits after that, because they were also doing a bit of small-time banking. Poor Kesharchandra began to rove around babbling to himself like a madman. Later, in Silgadi, no one ever found out whether he killed himself or was murdered."

"Well, a man who's gone through all this should also consider what others are going through," Sita said. "He's not getting a single paisa! Did we eat up everything that remained? He had to go ahead and file a lawsuit! He won't get a single paisa, he won't!"

Sita slipped out of his embrace and went over to Babuni's place. She was seeing to all of the caretaking, cooking and feeding for Babuni. Janak had told her to take over as much coal, ghee and medicine as required, to not let Pushpa's mother want for anything; and yet, when Sita wasn't around, Babuni would weep in secret. "Why were you born, orphan?" she'd say to the daughter that she'd given birth to. Babuni didn't even want to look at the baby. In her moments of weakness, she would remember MK and sob. Even now, when Sita arrived without warning, there were tears in Babuni's eyes. With Sita present, she found an added excuse and let loose a stream of tears, wailing, "Why did Pushpa's father do this to us, Didi? I feel so wretched, thinking about it." Her little daughter was asleep beside her, her hands, with fine black lines, curled up into tiny fists.

Sita admonished her sternly, "Look at others… Others are even unluckier than you, yet they go on."

Janak was still lost in thought. It seems that society is built on heartlessness and cruelty; it has not learned to forgive; it doesn't dare oppose me as long as I'm strong, it tolerates me then, but in its view it's a crime for anyone to try and progress… "We'll all be locked up together," he murmured to himself.

Sita left the house at nine o'clock the following morning. She who usually, out of love, asked her husband before eating even a slice of mango or betel-nut, didn't seek Janak's permission today. Today her rage was blind and oblivious, swirling and destructive.

Sita reached Jayabilas's store and stood defiantly outside the door.

Jayabilas noticed, but couldn't meet Sita's direct, furious gaze, and so placed his gaze elsewhere, adopting an innocent air. But then his tongue, practised in business, blurted out, "Do come in, what brings you here?"

"Why should I come in? Why?" Sita cried, going into the shop.

Jayabilas couldn't say anything. A black-and-yellow hue arose from within his chubby cheeks. He narrowed his eyes and pretended to not understand.

"You filed a lawsuit, didn't you? You're worried that my husband's going to die, so you filed a lawsuit!" Still standing defiantly, Sita was screaming loudly enough to be heard outside. "Well, my husband's not going to die, he's not going to die just to make you suffer a loss, you understand? And if he actually dies, I'm here to pay you back. It's not money that we cheated from others, lolling around on a white settee all our lives, like you: we earned our wealth with our own hands, you hear! But he's not going to die, my husband. My husband's not going to throw away his life out of fear of falling in debt to a sly Marwari like you, you hear?"

The Marwari trader's blood also boiled. "I have no enmity with your Janak-babu," he said. "This is a business matter, and it's gone on for too many days. Even then, your Janak-babu bands together with the low-born to swindle me…" Seeing Sita hurt by this accusation and unable to respond, he became aggressive. "Why should I stay silent? He doesn't repay me, and doesn't even show his face here, even though he walks down this road all the time. He never comes in. What, is my money roadside gravel that I should let it go? Should I simply say, all right, bastard, I forgive you?"

"My husband's your bastard? Say that again!"

"You came here to quarrel with me?" Seated in the settee with his teeth gritted, Jayabilas looked up and asked, "Shall I call the police? I can launch a trespassing case right away!"

Trembling with rage, Sita cried, "You come to our place and suck our blood, and yet the trespassing case is against me, not you?" A group of six or seven Marwari traders, Darzi tailors, and a few others, had gathered around. She went on, "Who offered loans to your father and grandfather back in the old days, when they didn't have the wherewithal to open a shop? You're a selfish caste! Whose money did you live on when the bank that your grandfather put all his money in failed? It was my father who brought your grandfather a sack full of silver rupees and saved him from bankruptcy. Ask your father about it, that man who went back to the mainland old and grey-haired! You've forgotten all about this, haven't you? And now you're the one to start a lawsuit and police case against me?"

Jayabilas didn't reply, but picked up a black phone to call Janak at home.

Another Marwari trader tried to reason with Sita: "You should repay the loan, just as Jayabilas and his family repaid theirs. It's a matter that calls for trust. It doesn't suit a lady like you, from a good home, to embarrass herself by coming to the shop to quarrel."

Sita scolded this Marwari as well, "Don't lecture me, you're all the same."

Now that the torrent of rage had left her body, she no longer felt afraid, but her legs were tired and sore. She turned back.

Jayabilas hung up the phone after speaking to Janak. The people who had gathered in front of the store dispersed. A man who had been watching the carnival slipped up to sit down on one side of the settee, and said to Jayabilas, "They say Janak has secretly sold off all his vehicles, have you heard?"

"He sold them?"

"That's what I'm asking you," said Krishnalal. "You should have them seized at once through the court. Otherwise he might run away to Nepal…"

"He won't run away, KL-babu, he's just trying to buy time," Jayabilas said.

KL added up a few things in his mind, and then said, laughing, "There was an old man from Kainjale who had nothing. Janak started a lawsuit and nearly evicted him from his house. But now that there's a case against him, he sends his wife over to quarrel!"

Jayabilas didn't approve of such talk, but didn't say anything.

"His son's the same, he runs around from plantation to plantation carrying banners—not that anyone takes him as a politician. The daughter's all right; she's got looks, and manners, and knowledge as well, but she'll turn into a madam sahib later on, they're all the same…"

Before leaving, KL went up to Jayabilas and whispered about a few other matters, to which Jayablias replied, "It's fine, for you it's nothing, go ahead and take it."

The following day was a sunny Saturday. Sita had gone to the bazaar. Divya had returned early from college and was memorizing deductive-logic definitions for an exam on Monday. Ravi was still at school. Janak had decided that he would start going out more from Monday onwards. It was almost three hours since Sita had left. A new postman knocked on the door, delivered a letter and went away. The letter was from Yamuna. She'd written that she had just returned from Jelep-la to Gangtok, and would come to Darjeeling only at Christmas time. Along with the letter she had sent a photograph of herself in goggles, sitting sideways on a rock (probably on the road to Jelep-la). The letter contained no greetings for Sita, nor did it contain news about Namgyal's health. Janak immediately shot off a reply conveying Sita's blessings and inquring after Da' Namgyal's well-being, and put it in the mail on the same day.

Sita returned home with a young coolie boy who was carrying a basketful of rice, dal, oil and vegetables.

"The bazaar is full of cauliflowers," she said gaily, gesticulating with her hands. Her face was flushed and there was perspiration on her brow. "As for this boy, he tells me he has five siblings younger than him, five! They don't have a mother. His father works for daily wages, but can't find work on days when they're in the greatest need. The poor boy can't even carry a small load like this—I had to carry the rice half the way!"

Janak was studying Sita closely.

The boy took his payment of thirty-two paisa and left. Divya took a break from studying to put everything away. Sita was prattling on animatedly about something or the other. She gave Divya a few paper bags full of supplies and some pink flannel for baby clothes to take over to Babuni.

Janak called out to Sita, "Come here."

She came over to him. Joy and beauty radiated effortlessly from her face.

"You can't fool me by talking so gaily and throwing yourself into all your tasks so energetically," Janak said. "You've got up to no good again today: I've already heard about it on the phone."

Sita burst out laughing at Janak's fake interrogation. "How good you are at reading my mind!"

Janak, too, stopped circling Sita to interrogate her, and started to laugh.

Biting into a soft, red, thin-skinned apple that Sita quartered, he went to the window. Frozen and dazzling, Kanchenjunga hung like a picture in the window frame. Any human footsteps on its peak would be erased by fresh snow, the way insults are erased by a higher consciousness.

As Janak watched on, thunderclouds rolled in, either from the Bay of Bengal or the Indian Ocean, and began to dance in the blue of the sky to distract the mountain from its meditation.

Yesterday, Sita had quietly written a short letter to Dharmaprasad—

Respected Father-jyu,

I hope that you and Mother accept the respectful bows of your daughter, son-in-law and grandchildren. If there is well-being in your body over there, we too will feel blessed over here. In the end, your daughter is now turning to you in the midst of a problem that she has not been able to solve. If it suits your convenience, Father, please come, otherwise please send Brother, even if it means that ten tasks at the school must remain unfinished. I am eagerly waiting for you to come and wash up here after having eaten your meal there.

Your fortunate daughter, Sitarani

Sita had taken the letter to the post office before coming home just now.

The following day was the eighth, so Janak went to see a lawyer today.

It had never occurred to him to say that it wasn't a debt; neither had he thought about asking for it to be forgiven. His only dilemma was whether to pay off the entire debt immediately, or to pay it off in some other way.

He thought of the lines: "If you take the earnings from all of your wins and place them on a single wager and lose it all, and then start over without telling anyone that you lost it, the earth will be yours, and you'll be even more of a man, my son!"

"I'll give him the vehicle and the fields right away. That'll end the dispute," Janak said. "From now on, we have to stop wanting to eat rice from our own fields and riding our own vehicle."

The fields that his father had bought for him…

Sita's eyes were dry, but Janak saw them narrowing for some reason.

"At least we've put together a shelter; if that's all we have left, we'll still be happy," Sita said.

"How can we live in that house now?" Janak said. "How can we show our faces in Darjeeling anymore, after what's happened? We'll have to go to Kathmandu, Calcutta, Assam,

Sikkim, somewhere else—we'll have to. We'll start pulling things together somewhere else..."

"You want people to say he drove us out of here?"

"What else are we to do?" Janak said.

Sita fell silent and stared at him blankly.

"I can't shoot a bullet into my brain and die. I'd do it, too, if the debt wouldn't follow the rest of you around. I can't go and spend years in jail either. My reputation and honour are more precious to me than my life, even my family. I'll pay off the loan, even if it turns me into a naked fakir... I won't take anyone's advice on this; and I won't accept anyone's help."

Sita just stood by and listened.

Janak went to the court on the following day. He was flushed and cheerful, as though unburdened of all of his cares. He exchanged glances with Ajoy, and they smiled at each other but didn't talk. Jayabilas hadn't shown up. Janak signed a few documents for the lawyer and headed towards home at around half-past eleven.

Near Malgodam, he saw Khagprasad approaching from the other direction. Khagprasad recognized Janak and rushed over, flashing his protruding teeth as he smiled, and greeting him with a namaskar. He was clasping a new umbrella with a red plastic handle under one arm. "Do you recognize me?" Khagprasad asked with a laugh.

"Where are you coming from? Where's Birman?" Janak asked.

"He's in Assam, in Darrang. I came your yesterday, I'm going to Ilam, to my own your home."

"What's your Birman your doing in your Darrang?"

"He got married."

"He got married?" Janak asked, astonished. "To whom?"

"To his your own niece!" Khagprasad came up to Janak's face and laughed as if to say, "Isn't that ridiculous?"

"But he said he'd never marry for the rest of his life!"

"That was when he couldn't find anyone!" Khagprasad said, and suddenly got into a rush. "It's getting quite late! I have to catch a ride back… I've got my belongings lined up at the door of the pilgrims' resthouse, Hajoor. I'm late; I'm your leaving now, namaskar, namaskar…"

Janak stood there watching as Khagprasad ran towards the Barrick motor stand, his coat flapping behind him.

Janak wanted to stay around to watch Khagprasad catching his ride, but he was tired, and it felt like he was going to break out in a fever, so he staggered home without further delay.

A week later, after the school let off for a half-day break on Saturday, Ravi and Hari went down to Tukvar without first stopping by at home. They walked the entire way. Clouds of dust were rising. People transporting baskets of chillies, eggs and guavas were on their way to Darjeeling for the following day's market, drenched in sweat on their uphill climb and panting hot air through their mouths. A few had placed their loads down on load-bearing sticks and were watching the two of them.

The tea plantation had set up a court of inquiry and charged all seven men involved in the incident with "indiscipline" and "insubordination". All seven households had received notice. The head clerk, Sirilal, had taken the notice that he received up to the party office to inform them about it.

Just below the large ground, Ravi and Hari reached

Sirilal's house and asked for some drinking water. The head clerk had gone to the bazaar, but his younger brothers were at home. Ravi and Hari stayed on, and Hari asked someone to fetch Sirilal.

Sirilal came over with Bhaktiman Yakha. Bhaktiman had also received the same kind of notice.

"Why did *you* get a notice?" Ravi asked.

"I don't know why. Look, here it is," Bhaktiman said, showing it to Ravi.

"It looks like the same letter went out to everyone," Ravi said after looking it over.

CB Rai and Manprasad, who had been acquitted in the case, also arrived shortly.

Hari teased them, asking, "How did it feel to spend a few days in there?"

"I quite liked it!" Manprasad said. He was a short, thickset boy with a flat face and muscular arms.

"They're trying to send you back in!" Ravi said.

"The most that'll happen this time is that you'll lose your jobs," Hari said. "Although these people won't be able to achieve even that much."

Tall old Bhaktiman boomed out, "What are we supposed to do now? We got to this point by beating up the managers, by having them beaten up. Now everyone's received this paper. We don't know what we're meant to do with it."

"You all know about the incident of October 21," Hari replied. "This notice is related to that incident. They've levelled false charges of indiscipline, which means refusing to work properly, and insubordination, which means the same thing—refusing to do what the higher-ups want—against those who tried to beat up the manager... And they've asked that you prove your innocence and provide some clarification..."

Bhaktiman got angry. "My Aitraj is already in jail on a five-year sentence. How is he supposed to respond to this?"

"That's what we have to figure out," Hari said. "If the accused are judged guilty in this matter, the estate will have the four men who were acquitted in the last case kicked out of their jobs, and they'll never be able to get those jobs back. And when the jailed men come out, they won't be able to find work either."

"Oh..." Bhaktiman nodded. "Now I get it, I understand: Each person receives two sentences."

"They're trying to get you from both sides," Ravi explained with a laugh.

Much discussion ensued. Looking around, Sirilal said, "Neither Bindra nor Lwangphool, Bhaire's wives, are present. I told them to come..."

"I saw both the elder and younger wife going to sell firewood." CB Rai said.

Both Ravi and Hari found this news disagreeable.

"All of you"—Ravi used the polite form of address now—"have been asked to respond by the thirty-first, but when you do so, you should give a uniform reply. You mustn't give different replies, that'll just make things easier for the estate," he said. "It would be better still if everyone were to write and sign the same letter."

"Yes, it would be better if everyone were to sign the same reply," Hari repeated. Then, looking at Bhaktiman, he said, "Even though the notice isn't in your name, it would be good if you were to sign it too; or actually, the estate was just fulfilling a formality, so you don't really need to do that."

Sirilal turned to Hari. "Why don't you just write whatever it is we need to write?"

"All right, I'll write it and type it up and send it over, or you can send someone up to get it."

"One of us will come."

"I'll come myself."

When the discussion ended, some of them headed up to the large ground, and others to the shops. Manprasad had already reached home and started to play the harmonium.

"We should go by Bhaire-daju's house down the way," Hari said to Ravi. "Let's go."

Bhairavprasad Khawas's house was on the far end of the village, but they took it as their responsibility to go there, and headed out.

They took a path lined with yellow blossoms on a moist ridge that was densely blanketed with smooth cardamom leaves, passing a few scattered houses painted with red earth. After crossing a trail covered over by fallen bamboo leaves, they finally saw Bhaire's house.

There was a large mimosa tree in the courtyard, and in its sparse shade, a troupe of children was playing with tyres, and crying and creating a commotion. Some were still hairless while others were grown up: They ran around, chasing each other, going quite a ways away. A few were off to one side, climbing a pile of firewood and playing at being Tenzing.

"Look at how nice this is. I love scruffy children," Ravi said.

The children fell silent and stared at the two of them as they entered the courtyard.

"Children, where are your mothers?"

They didn't say anything.

Ravi repeated the question, and a little girl dressed in a coverall left the troupe and ran into the house.

The house was large. It was painted on all sides with white earth. They had made additions to the building that the tea plantation had given them, making it very liveable, even beautiful. Out front, below the courtyard, was a shed in which cows were lowing, demanding their feed of flour-water and oil cake. Some goats had climbed onto the feeding trough and were trampling all over the bamboo. There were shelves on either side of the door, with budding chrysanthemums, lifeplants and camellias in tin flowerpots. Marigold seeds had fallen from the shelves and were sprouting on the ground underneath. Large butterfly bushes and sheep's ears shrubs leaned towards the drain on top of the house.

When the sound of corn being popped ceased in the house, Lwangphool came out, asking, "Where are they, where are they?" She recognized Hari and greeted him with a namaskar, then greeted Ravi too.

"We looked for you back there, but you didn't come, so we came out to meet you," Hari said.

"We've stopped going out anymore, the two of us just can't manage," she said. "The younger wife has been transporting firewood all morning with Maili from over there. And when Monday comes around, we can't not go to work at the plantation."

"It'll be like that now, you'll have to work hard for a while to support your family," Hari said sympathetically.

Lwangphool's friends had given her her nickname—clove flower—back when she, lithe and fetching, had still been youthful. She was now the mother of one daughter and four sons.

She said, "I hear that they didn't even let him stay on for his first monthly court appearance, and took him away to Calcutta."

Bindra arrived with Maili, loaded down with firewood. Her tender, flushed face became visible only after she went to their store of firewood behind the house, putting down the bundle that was bound tightly with vines, and releasing the strap from her forehead.

"Those who egged them on are themselves safe. While those who never missed a day of work got embroiled," the Khawas woman said. "What am I going to feed the children over the next five years, what am I going to clothe them with, how will I raise them? Where should I send them to study, what should I do and not do, what had we been dreaming of—when I think about all of this, I can't even breathe..." Then she said, "Let me make you some tea."

Ravi spoke about many things, trying to encourage and console them.

"Let's go by the bungalows on our way back," Hari said after they had gone a little ways.

"It's already three-thirty," Ravi said.

"It's only just three-thirty. Let's go to the assistant manager's, that's Prem Krishna-daju, he's really fun. I'll introduce you to him."

"I'm not going to visit any managers or assistant managers."

"Let's just head in that direction, he may not even be in his bungalow."

Past the village, they walked along the tea gardens, which were leafing out with green shoots. When they got close to one bungalow, they saw Prem Krishna-babu occupied with some task in his garden. He saw Hari and called out, "Hello, Bhai!" and came to open his gate.

Ravi had to go in, if only for the sake of politeness.

"Where are you coming from? Did you come to cause more trouble? And who's this? Janak-babu's son! Well, well, I've listened to your lectures. Come and sit."

They all sat on a bench in the garden.

"What would you like to eat?" Prem Krishna-babu asked.

"I'll have an egg," Hari said.

"And Ravi-bhai?"

Ravi wondered what kind of a man this was, and said, "I don't need anything, Sir."

"Why don't you need anything, Sir?" Prem Krishna said as though offended, and then laughed.

"Don't ask, just have something made for him," Hari said, taking off his coat and leaning back on the bench. "If he doesn't eat it, I will."

"Why should I feed you? I feed you, then you go and cause me more trouble."

Even Ravi laughed at this.

"You've planted lots of flowers this year, Daju," Hari said, looking around. "Those asters are really pretty."

When Hari said this, Prem Krishna got up, pulling along Hari and Ravi. "Look at the lily amaryllis you sent me," he said to Hari. "See there, there are small red dots on the white flower. I want you to find me some completely white ones: where can you find those?"

Prem Krishna-babu led them through several rounds of his garden, showing off his flowers. He put an arm around

Ravi, and Ravi became keenly conscious of his large, impressive torso, covered by only a shirt, and his pudgy fingers.

Trying to talk about a flower he knew, Ravi said, "Those geraniums are so large."

"Those aren't geraniums," Hari said. "They're called pelargonium."

"Look at my gladioli, look at how well they've grown," Prem Krishna-babu said, with great pride.

"I don't recognize flowers," Ravi said. "I just know marigolds and chrysanthemums, I know dahlias…"

"There's no fun in looking at a flower without knowing its name," Prem Krishna declared. "The more botanical names you know, the better." Taking some examples, he said, "*Thea synensis* is what tea is called in botany; wormwood is *Artemisia vulgaris*; *Polygonum molle* is knotweed; *Curculigo recurvata* is the name of palm grass; *barberry* is called *Mahonia acanthifolia*; glory flower is called *Tibouchina*, or something like that…"

Hari said, "Those bunched-up blue flowers climbing the wall over there, they're called *Wisteria chinensis*."

"You seem to know quite a lot yourself."

"If you're a man, you ought to know everything."

"I'd like to learn as well," Ravi said. "Those flowers that resemble geraniums—what are they called? I've already forgotten."

"Pelargonium."

"Pelargonium."

The butler came out and announced, "It's ready, Hajoor."

Ravi went along with them now, without any hesitation.

When they were seated at a table inside the bungalow, Ravi asked, "You're not married?"

Prem Krishna laughed. "I'm past the age, why bother now?"

"We'll have to find someone for Daju," Hari said.

Prem Krishna laughed again, and asked, "Do you have any PKs in mind?"

Hari said, "There's one girl, Daju, if you're really serious."

"You said PK," Ravi said. "What's a PK?"

"Patali Kamariya."

Ravi burst out laughing, almost choking on a mouthful of tea. What kind of man was this, joking around about slender-waisted girls: and who had made him an assistant manager?

"What am I to do?" Prem Krishna-babu went on. "All you younger boys got married early and made things more difficult for me. By now I have so many relatives that even when a girl takes a liking to me…I turn out to be her maternal or paternal uncle! And all the women of my own age are mothers; they're taking care of their own families. Only I, Hanuman, am single."

"You sit around and plant flowers," Hari said.

Ravi was laughing very hard at all of this.

"I don't even have enough money. I'm always high and dry at the end of the month…"

"You must earn a good salary; how could that not be enough?" Ravi said. "Why isn't that enough?"

"Your pockets must leak," Hari said.

They got up from eating, and Prem Krishna took them to see his private glasshouse by the bungalow. It contained a profusion of orchids. "I've got twenty-five or thirty flowerpots of *Cypripedium insignia*. The *Vanda roxburghii* finally bloomed this year," Prem Krishna said, looking fondly at an orchid with a protruding white tongue on a stalk with light green leaves on either side. Another plant looked completely dessicated, like a chain tangled up on a stem. He pointed at another plant with a few white orchid blossoms. "This is *Dendrobium falconeri*," he said. "This plant of mine is also in bloom. I'm going to take it to the flower show."

"All orchids look the same to me," Ravi said. He plucked one and put it in the lapel of his coat.

Prem Krishna didn't say anything about this, but an odd expression came over his face. "I'm also going to the bazaar, let's go together," he said.

They went to the garage, and Ravi and Hari soon reached the bazaar with Prem Krishna driving his Jeep.

They made the same kind of small talk along the way, mostly repeating their earlier conversation.

In the bazaar, Prem Krishna took Ravi and Hari to a Chinese restaurant.

After they had some food and came out, Prem Krishna asked, "Is Janak-babu at home right now?"

"Yes. Why?" Ravi asked.

"I came here in order to meet him."

Someone dressed in a nurse's white uniform was coming down as the three of them climbed up the stairs. Ravi recognized her only when she was right beside them: it was Babuni. "Where are you going?" he asked, surprised.

"To the hospital, to work."

"When did you start?"

"I started yesterday." Babuni looked morosely at all of them—Ravi, Hari and Prem Krishna.

Ravi sat Hari and Prem Krishna in the outer room and went in to call his father.

It looked like rain. Hari got up and closed the window behind himself.

The tea arrived before Janak. "It's a service to the nation to drink as much tea as possible," Hari was saying just as Janak came in.

After exchanging greetings, they began to chat.

"I've run out here just to meet you," Prem Krishna said. "It's about the estate again. You must already know..."

"I've heard a litte here and there, but I don't really know the whole story, Prem Krishna-babu; I don't know what's actually happening, or what's going to happen," Janak said, glancing at Hari.

"There's not a lot to know," Prem Krishna said, and went over recent events: "It's the same old case, the one about our estate manager getting beaten up—you know the one. The judgment the other day gave five years' imprisonment to three men, and acquitted four other men."

"And then what happened?"

"The estate has now formed a court of inquiry to try all seven men for indiscipline and insubordination."

On hearing this, Janak fell silent.

"Why are they doing this?" Hari asked.

"I told you," Prem Krishna said. "On charges of indiscipline and insubordination."

"No, no; what I mean is, doesn't this amount to victimization?" he said, saying the latter term in English.

"I can't speak to that."

"You can't say it out loud because you're the estate's assistant manager, but you must feel in your heart that it's victimization," Hari said sharply.

"I'm not going to debate this with you."

Janak adopted another tack to question him: "The session judge found four of the men innocent and released them?"

"He released them."

"And the court of inquiry will investigate the same four men again?"

"It will."

"So the court of inquiry will ignore the session judge's verdict when it sits; it will defy his judgement. Can it do so?" Janak asked.

"It can. According to the Standing Order Act, Section Thirteen (C), it can do so," Prem Krishna said. "It was a police case with the session judge—the seven men had to testify as to whether or not they surrounded the manager and beat him up, trying to kill him. The court of inquiry will conduct an internal investigation as to whether their conduct amounted to indiscipline and insubordination. The session court's verdict won't act as 'res judicata.'

"What does 'res judicata' mean?" Hari asked.

"You're tired, you should just listen without saying anything," Prem Krishna told Hari with a smile.

Hari didn't smile back.

"What I want tell you, and Hari too," Prem Krishna said, turning his impressive torso around to look Janak in the eye, "is that nobody knows what's going to happen in the court of inquiry but, either way, it'll be our own people who suffer. Don't let that happen. They could be found guilty in the inquiry—and as far as I can tell, for many reasons, the four men will be found guilty; and they'll be removed from their jobs. Why let this happen? Bhudev-babu has sent people in to escalate the issue. He's not satisfied having sent three men to jail. He's telling all the accused men not to provide the estate the evidence that it's demanding…"

"He hasn't said that," Hari said, challenging him.

"Apparently he's even telling people not to serve as eyewitnesses in the inquiry. He doesn't care about the legal implications of this."

"What do you think they should do?" Hari asked rapidly.

"Don't let the dispute escalate—that's what I say, what else can I say?" Prem Krishna said, irritably. "You need to talk to Bhudev, or to whomever else, and prevent the dispute from escalating."

"The estate is itself escalating the dispute by forming this court of inquiry," Janak said. "Who's going to restrain them?"

"That's exactly why I came here," Prem Krishna said. "Let those four men give a small written statement saying—we'll work properly, as ordered, from now on. That'll suffice. I'll shut down the court of inquiry."

Neither Janak nor Hari said anything.

"Otherwise the dispute will escalate. Those four men will lose their jobs," Prem Krishna continued, "and that's not all; three out of four of these men are primary workmen. When you remove a primary workman from his job, everyone else in this family has to quit too. So Sirilal's wife, two of Manprasad's brothers and one of his sisters-in-law, and CB Rai's wife and daughter will all lose their jobs as well."

From where did you bring in this rule, Assistant Manager Sahib?"

"It's not a rule I brought in, Hari-bhai; this is the way it's always been," Prem Krishna said. "All of the coolies hired by the estate were hired because of their spouses, on a family basis." He used the English term, "family basis".

For some reason, Janak corrected him, using the Nepali term, "Paariwaarik aadhaar…"

"Yes, since it's on a family basis, when the head of the family, or the primary workman, is let go, he has to move out of plantation housing, and all of the secondary workmen also have to leave with him."

Hari frowned on hearing all this, and asked, "Have you read Reggi's report, *Conditions of Labour Plantations in India*?"

"I haven't read it."

"Read it; it must be in the library at the Planters' Club. Nowhere in the world will you find the custom of the wife and children being forced to leave a plantation when a man loses his job. Where does this rule come from, saying the whole family loses their jobs if the father is found guilty?"

"This is what goes on in the plantations of Darjeeling."

"In three plantations in Assam—Budhla, Rangamati and another one—there was such an uproar over this issue, the case even went to the tribunal. The company lost all three of those cases," Hari said, offering his final outlook.

Prem Krishna laughed and said, slowly, "Why go all the way to Assam? Assam may not have this practice, but Darjeeling does. I know about this. The tribunal upheld the practice in a case here, in Takdah, and it did so in the Patabung case as well. In a case in the plantation in Barnesbeg, a husband lost his job because his wife stole tea leaves. And so?"

"True, true, these things have happened. I know about the Takdah case," Janak said.

Gaining confidence, Prem Krishna splayed his fingers, showing his open palms to Janak and Hari, and said, "Don't let our people get into trouble, that's all I have to say. Think about this for yourselves."

Janak drew in a long breath and said, "Well, I've already sent in my resignation. I'm going to put my own affairs in order now. Bhudev doesn't listen to me anyway, so that's the first thing. Talk to Hari. It's their turn now. I'm worn out, Prem Krishna-babu, what can I possibly do…"

"I don't get along with Bhudev. But I did come all the way here, to you. Think over all this in your own time. All I want is that the dispute not escalate and our people not suffer. I should get going now."

It still wasn't nighttime outside. The evening was only just setting in. It was raining to one side, but the sky was blue on the other side, and the clouds there were clean and white. The rainwater on the roof sloshed down the gutters, gushing over a broken corner and splashing over the garage's cement wall.

"The fog will end in a couple of days," Ravi said, having listened to the debate silently, from the side. "When it's gone, the settlements on the far hills will look like they're right nearby."

Prem Krishna left. From inside, Hari, Janak and Ravi soon heard the rumble of his Jeep leaving.

"He's an estate employee, and an assistant manager at that—how can we possibly trust him?" Hari said, shaking his head.

"Bhudev won't even listen to this kind of talk," Ravi said.

"What's it to him?" Hari said. "All he'll have to do is say, 'No.' Those of us doing fieldwork in the area, we'll have a rough time of it. Has Bhudev ever gone out to do any fieldwork? That's why he was defeated in the elections this time around."

Janak expanded on the topic. "He should do something if only out of fear of the other parties…it would look bad to reach a poor settlement."

"To look bad, or to be triumphant, both seem pointless in the end, meaningless. We all know the inside story about the hollow victory parade that Bhudev staged at the Rahani Tea Estate. He did the same thing at the Pasitang Tea Estate; he even raised money in the name of someone or the other during the case at the Ambek Tea Estate…I just don't trust anyone anymore."

"There are people in the party's committee who sell all its secrets to the Intelligence Bureau," Ravi said. "And if we were to start a movement one day, we already have an agent provocateur in our midst."

A familiar face flashed before all of their eyes when Ravi said this. Hari felt disgusted. He lowered his head and glared at the table in revulsion.

"Don't think about all those things," Janak counselled them. "You must be of a strong character and shut out all these foul thoughts from your mind; only those of weak character run around talking about these things, demoralizing people even more, and worrying them." Finally, he said, "I'll meet Bhudev tomorrow and talk to him. It's better for everyone if we settle this. He should agree. He probably will."

Two days later, Ravi ran into Prem Krishna again in the hospital. They had both come, by coincidence, to visit the same man—CB Rai. That morning, after roll call, as CB Rai went to start the day's work, he and Karne had exchanged words, and Karne had stabbed him with a gardening fork. Even though he'd tried to shield himself, he had sustained quite a few injuries to the head and left arm.

"Is Karne the same Karnabir from the other day? The one acquitted in his case?" Ravi asked.

"That's the one. He's fair, plump, short…" Prem Krishna said.

"What was the reason for the fight?" Ravi asked in a low voice.

Prem Krishna looked at CB Rai lying on the iron-frame bed, and at his wife and daughters, who were standing by the bedside.

"Surely it wasn't about a personal matter?" Ravi asked.

"What's personal and what's impersonal—it's all the same. We'll find out when we hear CB Rai's testimony," Prem Krishna said, determined not to let anything slip out.

The two went out together.

Bhudev came rushing along just then, and passed by, glancing in all directions before going in.

"Didn't he see you?" Ravi asked Prem Krishna.

"Who knows." After a pause, he said, "He probably did see me."

They were going out of the main door when Babuni came in, wearing a black woollen sweater over her white uniform. She was carrying a flat, empty bottle in one hand, and a bouquet of orchids in the other. She smiled when she saw Ravi.

Ravi greeted her with a namaskar.

Then it occurred to him that a namaskar wasn't called for. Flustered by this muddle, he made everyone stop and said,

"Let me introduce you... This is my aunt from next door... And this is Prem Krishna-babu, the assistant manager of the Tukvar Tea Estate."

"Namaskar." Babuni looked at Prem Krishna with her morose eyes, her attractive face like a fine black line drawing on clean sheet of paper.

"Namaskar. Where did you get those orchids? Those are *Dendrobium nobile*," Prem Krishna said. "And they're white, too." He explained to Ravi, "Blue and purple ones are easy to find, but white orchids of this species are extremely rare." Again, he asked Babuni, "Where did you get them?"

Blushing a little, Babuni looked down at the bouquet of orchids and said, "They're from my own verandah, they bloom every year."

"I'll come by and get some!" Prem Krishna said.

Ravi intervened. "You can't take such rare orchids for free," he said. "They'll cost you a hundred rupees."

"I'll pay that."

"So—it would have fetched an even higher price!"

Prem Krishna pretended to get angry at Ravi. "You have no shame," he said in jest. "And if you do, you have only a little bit."

At this, Babuni smiled silently.

She told Prem Krishna, "I've already plucked all the flowers. You can take some when they bloom next year."

"I can recognize them from the leaves, from the stem," Prem Krishna-babu said. "Don't be led astray by Ravi. I'll come over to get it today, or I'll go there right now... I'll leave the full amount of however much money you want with Ravi."

Babuni just stood there, laughing.

The other two went out onto the street, their arms around each other.

"You have a real passion for flowers," Ravi said, outside.

Prem Krishna gave Ravi a hug. "All my friends are married, so when they go home from work at night, their children surround them, and their wives come up to them. How nice! I only have flowers waiting for me. Red lilies look exactly like women to me."

He said this so candidly, it moved Ravi.

"One night," Prem Krishna said, "three or four years ago, I came home a little drunk. And in the moonlight, I saw—magnolia petals had fallen all over the yard, and even on the roof, and everything was white. At that moment, I felt: arre, I too have a home, I too am a man. I'll never forget that…"

"No, no, you should get married now," Ravi said.

"I told you earlier: Find me someone."

Further down the road, Ravi asked, "Are you really going to pay a hundred rupees?"

"The full one-zero-zero. I'll put one rupee in one hand, and two zeros in the other."

"You know, those orchids might be ours, since they're on our verandah," Ravi joked.

"I won't pay for them if they're yours. I'll just uproot them and take them, but tell me one thing: who was that nurse…?"

Prem Krishna asked about Babuni repeatedly, so as they walked down the street, Ravi gave him a summary of her story.

"Ah. And was there a reason husband died in that manner?" Prem Krishna asked.

"Lord knows."

"The dead man must have taken out an insurance policy—or had he not made any preparations?"

"He'd bought a lottery ticket."

They reached the bazaar.

"I want some paan," Prem Krishna said.

A dark woman selling paan, who had black African eyes in bright eyewhites, asked, "What kind of paan?"

"Plain," Prem Krishna said, quietly adding, "One stitch knit and one stitch purl."

Then the two parted ways. As they separated, Prem Krishna called out to tell Ravi that he'd come by for the orchids tomorrow, and he'd also bring the money. He set out towards the police station. Ravi lingered around for a while, then ambled home.

Janak was stepping out, carrying both an umbrella and a raincoat in his left hand. He called out to Ravi and said, "Tell Hari to send word that I spoke to Bhudev about what Prem Krishna-babu proposed. Bhudev didn't agree to it."

It was Sunday.

Demonstrations from four plantations were winding their way up the hill, chanting and gathering momentum, reaching the steep road by Singmari College before it was even ten o'clock.

A demonstration from the Som Tea Estate, which had set out at the same time, had reached the far hill, and was probably somewhere close by.

An incomprehensible clamour and cacophonous uproar drifted up from end to end of the procession; every now and then, the chanting of slogans bubbled up like boiling water from the crowd.

Leading the way at the front was Sanamati, with a white

shawl draped snugly around her head, and a banner on a bamboo pole in her hands.

"Stop, stop. Let's rest awhile. Wait!" Ravi shouted, walking down the centre of the procession.

"He says stop! Everyone rest! Stop!" Harke repeated.

"Hold on, hold on… Don't shove, stop!"

The procession halted slowly, like a train made out of live people. Some people stepped aside for a rest, flopping down on the muddy roadside; others began to tuck the mud off their shoes. Bindra and Jetha Waiba's wife went to a nearby teashop to ask for some drinking water. Krishna lifted a handful of water from the large cement tub meant for horses to drink from, and washed his red, sweaty face. Several boys joined him; some dipped their faces in the tub, others poured water over their heads. Someone climbed onto the tub and began to spray water over everyone…

"Let's go, let's go. Let's go now, call everyone back."

"They're saying come, everyone come. Form a line! Form a line!"

"Ey, Chitre, get in line."

The demonstration started up again.

The slogans were more forceful than before:

"Close the—!"

"Court of inquiry!"

"End all—!"

"Injustice!"

"End all—!"

"Injustice!"

"Long live workers' unity!"

"Long live the revolution!"

"End all..."

Mothers shouted as they marched with sleeping children strapped to their backs with shawls. Husbands and fathers lifted their strong, rough hands as they chanted. Even children who had come to look around the bazaar marched in a row to one side...

Onlookers gawking by the road saw many cardboard posters, big and small, tacked onto bamboo poles. After reading a few, their eyes fell on the women, who were outdoing each other with their sloganeering. The procession was so long that as they gawked on, they felt embarrassed, and also nervous, to be standing apart from the crowd...

Cries of "Stop for a while; wait", arose once again.

"It's here, it's here! The demonstration from Som has arrived." Waves of joy erupted from start to finish of the procession.

"The people of the plantations—unite!"

"Long live workers' unity!"

Once Som joined in, the demonstration grew even longer, surging forward in waves.

It passed Thute bazaar, shouting and marching on, and arrived below Government College. There, a khaki-coloured army truck the size of a house came barrelling down from the other side.

The truck slowed down, most likely because of the length of the procession. Then, turning away from the side that the demonstration was on, it drove slowly down the other side.

Taking this as a victory, the workers began to chant even more vigorously, eyeing the truck. The army drivers inside only laughed.

"What are you laughing at? Your teeth…" someone in the demonstration rebuked them.

Similar questions and expressions of anger arose from all sides.

Ravi rushed up and got the procession to move forward. Chanting started up once again, with double the enthusiasm:

"End all—!"

"Injustice!"

"End all—!"

"Injustice!"

"End all—!"

"Injustice!"

This slogan kept repeating over and over.

It was one slogan, but the pitches, high and low, of all the voices turned it into a thousand slogans. There was only one chant, but within it, as in the call of a cuckoo, both the listeners and speakers heard and expressed a thousand subtle meanings, questions, resolutions, ideals and commitments, along with innumerable other unknowable workings of the mind. The language of the slogan was like that of a beast which, unable to talk, makes exactly the same sound to convey many different feelings.

After passing the office of the forest department, the front part of the procession had reached a spot right above the court.

There, the procession stalled.

Even after sending people to the front to look around, no one could figure out why it had stalled.

"Go on, go on! Why are you stopping? Go on, keep moving."

"It's getting late! Don't dawdle, keep moving!"

Many impatient and angry voices arose from the crowd.

The demonstration simply stalled. It didn't move forward at all.

Ravi ran up to the front to see what was going on. "What, why, who's stopping us? Why are we stopping?"

It turned out that the leather in Sanamati's new sandals had rubbed her heels raw and made them bleed, and having asked for a handkerchief, she was padding her heel.

Ravi shouted, "The rest can keep walking," and the procession moved again, leaving Sanamati crouched over her task.

Some drivers brought word that demonstrations from the plantations in Ging, Pandam, Patabung, Badamtam and Fupsiring had already reached the bazaar, and were waiting there.

All of these demonstrations coiled around the town, as though tiny Darjeeling were under attack from the plantations. The head of one procession climbed up past MP Road and reached the top of Chowrasta. An exhausted procession from the Dali Tea Estate, and those who'd marched all the way from Chungthung, mingled in at this point and were suddenly reinvigorated.

People of all caste and kind had shown up at the verandahs, stairs and shuttered windows of the houses to watch the carnival from above. The beautiful women and men crowding around the curtained windows to peer down in disdain, pity, curiosity and delight at the women and girls and boys and elderly men chanting with all their might: They also seemed like a part of the carnival.

The slogans from the demonstration echoed through the

grand quarters and buildings near Chowrasta, and through their many empty rooms. The reflection of the demonstration marched across the large shop windows. All of the goods in the shops shook from the impact of a thousand footsteps.

The demonstration proceeded from the junction of Gandhi Street and Nehru Street, down to Ladenla Street.

Standing high, the Town Hall looked out like a four-eyed demon at the interminable procession of the raucous demonstration…

For a good twenty minutes, the demonstration disrupted the Sunday quietude of the row with the municipal office, bank and post office…

The tail end of the demonstration had yet to pass the Rink Cinema House when Bhudev began speaking over a mic, instructing the crowd as to how to position itself.

As the demonstration circled the Bhaloo Building, Ravi caught a brief glimpse of Prem Krishna's Jeep speeding by. Prem Krishna was driving, and beside him was a woman in a white shawl. Ravi didn't recognize her, but he did recognize Amrita as one of the passengers at the back. Amrita kept turning around to stare at the demonstration.

They're probably going to Sinchel: this was the thought that came to Ravi. He thought nothing more of it.

In just a flash, the crowd had left Ravi behind.

A row of policemen in black uniforms had climbed up to the post office at the centre of the bazaar, and were standing there with rifles poised by their feet.

The head of the procession proceeded towards Daroga bazaar in search of an open spot, and Kainya Line and Darzi Line were soon swarmed, even as everyone looked on. People were converging in this area from all four directions, from roads wide and narrow, like droplets of water mingling together to flood this bazaar which once, long ago, used to be a lake. As the ceaseless cascade of the procession flowed down from the storage house into this lake, the bottoms of all the shops were submerged, and lost from view. The lake spread out as far as the Currency Exchange Line and the fire brigade. People began to clamber uphill in search of higher ground.

The mic, which had been blaring, suddenly switched off.

The people on a rooftop, who had been using the mic, stared at each other and asked questions, and some of them began to scurry around…

"They must have cut off the electricity!"

The mic didn't come back on…

"The police probably cut off the electricity."

"The police don't cut lines. Electricity belongs to the municipality."

Rumours immediately began to circulate.

"The municipality cut it off, the municipality!"

"But if it had cut it off, the lights would be off everywhere. It's still on over there, in the teashop."

"That's true!"

New chants started up in a flood of outrage. The slogans swept rapidly through the bazaar:

"They must give us—an electrical connection!"

"They must give us—an electrical connection!"

"We demand—the right to make speeches!"

"We demand—our fundamental rights!"

"We demand—our fundamental rights!"

"An electrical connection…"

The demonstrators had turned to face the black row of policemen, to scream at them. To scoff and gesticulate at them…

Someone in the crowd grabbed Ravi by the shoulders, yanking him from behind.

It was tall, skinny Krishnalal. "You're no longer coming to the school these days…?" he said.

"I don't know," Ravi said irritably, and moved on.

Krishnalal watched everything from afar.

Ravi heard the chants echoing out once again. Every now and then the crowd outside the post office would shout, "Police-foolish-foolish!"

The mic still wasn't working.

The Marwari shops had packed up their new clothes and the Tibetan shops their secondhand clothes. Small-time vegetable vendors were still at loose ends.

Into this crowd waded a man in dark glasses trailed by a coolie carrying a large old cupboard on his back. The man admonished the first few people and moved forward, but then, as the number of people scolding him grew, he reined in his anger. It was soon impossible to turn back, and just as impossible to press on. The coolie got upset at having to stand around sweating, bearing the weight of the cupboard. The man allowed the coolie to lay down his load at the post-office stairs. Some bickering broke out when the coolie promptly demanded his payment. When the coolie left with sixteen paisa, a few people began to inquire about how much the man had paid for the cupboard.

Soon enough, a small crowd of chanting people had turned the cupboard on its side to sit on.

Just then, from somewhere not too high up, came the sound of something like an airplane. People turned up to look at the sky. Several huge, khaki-coloured three-ton trucks were making their way gradually through the bazaar's main road, and this terrified everyone. There were men standing at the back, carrying rods, and they sneered at the crowd as they passed by.

That sight alone felt, to both onlookers and demonstrators, like a dare or a challenge. The entire bazaar began to rise up, chanting slogans even more ferociously as banners fluttered around everywhere.

"We need—citizens' rights! We need it!"

"End all—injustice! End it!"

"We need—fundamental rights!"

"End all…!"

Everyone started to jump up and down, chanting these slogans. Some were shoved onto, and others deliberately jumped up on, the post-office stairs. Jayabahadur began leaping around like a shaman. Those nearby even pleaded with him, "All right, lord, tell us definitively: when will we attain the rule of the poor?" Spurred on, Jayabahadur leaped even higher… Soon, the shaman's ritual calls, "Sai-sai," and "Bambo, sai-sai," peaked, along with the sound of laughter. The entire crowd turned in this direction to gawk…

Bhudev began to speak into the mic: "We've halted all trucks, Jeeps and cars. The people of Ghoom Pahad have barricaded the road. We can't be responsible if someone decides to use a car and has it burned for warmth in a bonfire at Ghoom…" The mic stopped working and switched off again.

A few people had gone up to the policemen and were

chanting slogans right beside them, and even shoving them around. Seeing the policemen suffering in silence on the orders of the inspector emboldened them. Someone hurled a rock, and it flew by the inspector's ear, shattering a post-office window.

In the mayhem of that moment, a round black police cap with red tassels tumbled down the stairs, into the crowd.

The bald policeman stared at the crowd below like a man who had lost his honour. The inspector demanded the cap back, but the crowd below only chanted more loudly, neither returning the cap nor responding to him.

An officer rounded up Jayabahadur, Bikram and a Tibetan man, and ordered some policemen to take them to the police station.

A voice called out from the crowd, "Stop, stop; don't let them take those men away!"

"Run, run. Ey, Bikram—run!"

"You must—release our people!"

"Put an end to—police repression!"

"Long live—the revolution!"

"Stop them, stop them, grab them and help them escape!"

"Run, run!"

The inspector grew sombre and issued an order: "Get ready!"

All the rifles flew up all at once. The rifle barrels glinted in the sun. Then they vanished, and the soles of the policemen's boots stamped down the cement stairs.

The crowd, which had surged forward the way an ocean wave defies a king's orders, now suddenly retreated. Everyone there saw each of those rifle muzzles as the snout of some unknown beast facing towards them.

A voice from the far side of the crowd called out, "Let's

go to the governor! Nothing will come of staying here. We have to go to the governor."

A few others quickly chimed in, "Lets go, let's go, let's go to the governor!" and the crowd set off.

"Where are you going?" Hari ran over. "What are you going to do there? Turn back, turn back; there's no point in going there."

"Didn't we see what happened in Chowkbazaar? Nothing will happen here. We have to go to the governor."

Hari held back the surging crowd with the sheer strength of his body, and cried, "Nothing will come of going to the governor! Everyone, turn back. Everyone, please turn back."

"You'll never see unity like this again, Hari-daju!" a tender young boy shouted. "They're coming into our homes and kicking us out." He started weeping on the spot. "Hari-daju! I'm going to die!"

With great difficulty, Hari finally steered the crowd back…

At this point, a wave of laughter rippled out from the other side. The police cap from before was jiggling on top of a bamboo pole.

"Now his coat, now his coat!"

"Grab the officers!"

"His trousers, grab his trousers!"

Those at the front pushed up against the inspector, either from being shoved, or because they really did want to grab at him.

"Grab it, grab his too."

The inspector stepped forward and bellowed out so that everyone could hear him: "I'm warning you all to back up. If you don't back up, I'll issue shooting orders. Everyone needs to back up by the time I count to ten—one!"

Everyone remained just where they were, staring at each other.

There was no space to move, because everyone from all the processions had piled up here.

"Two!"

"Child, I'll carry you!" called out a boy who was blind in one eye, quoting a popular rhyme.

Many of the people who overheard him began to laugh. Then everyone shifted aside a little, pointing the boy out to each other. The chattering increased.

"Three!"

Everyone shouted in unison, "Set the gecko free!"

Then someone beat the inspector to it and yelled out, "Four!" By the time the inspector said four, five and six, everyone was joking around. A debate broke out at six. Even one of the policemen was smiling. Perhaps he also wanted to say something.

"Seven!"

Sanamati showed up at this point and climbed up the stairs, going right up to the inspector. "What are you doing, counting four, five! If you're the son of a father, then shoot me in the chest. What, are you trying to scare us? Cowardly bastard! I'll take off my gunyu and wrap it around your head like a turban!" Her sandals were slung over her shoulders. She reached over, drew a rifle towards her and stuck the muzzle to her chest. "There, shoot me in the chest!" she screamed.

The inspector neither looked at Sanamati nor paid her any attention. He said, "Eight!"

People were getting alarmed. Yet leaving would amount to a humiliation. The pushing and shoving from behind had decreased somewhat, but there was still no passage out. "They won't shoot, they won't shoot!" some voices cried out from behind.

"Nine!"

"Move back, move back, everyone move back, everyone move back," Ravi shouted, jostling up to the front of the crowd, but before he could reach the front, someone yanked him forcefully by the trousers. Trying to free himself, he kept telling everyone to move back…

A familiar voice called out to Ravi, "You traitor, you coward!"

"Ten…! Fire…!"

Bang-bang-bang-bang…

Ravi saw three or four people falling. He realized, and immediately forgot, that there were flecks of blood on his face. Sanamati had collapsed by a pool of blood. He rushed over to her…

"Fire!" came another order.

Ravi felt a searing pain somewhere, then felt nothing.

People were loitering everywhere on the road to the hospital. Section 144 had been imposed in town following yesterday's events. Filing by in pairs, the policemen told those who were talking in huddled groups by the railing not to stand around, but they nevertheless huddled together to talk.

There was no confirmation of the number of people who'd died from bullet wounds. Everyone was anxious to read today's newspaper. Ravi was still unconscious. One person had died earlier this morning.

Sita was sitting at Ravi's bedside, crying…

Divya and Kanti were waiting outside on the verandah.

Divya went back in to Ravi and called out, "Daju."

Prem Krishna-babu and Babuni also came by in the morning.

As for Bhudev, he phoned Janak at home. "It's your turn now. Are you going to move forward or turn back?" he asked Janak.

"You're still not satisfied?" Janak said.

"I'm not going to discuss this with you, we do our work underground. You have to give a speech tomorrow, defying Section 144. You'll be arrested. That's precisely what's required. Because everyone's eyes are on you now. If you have to go to jail..."

"I'm unwell in both body and mind. I won't do this. I don't have the courage."

"We don't care about whether or not you have the courage, though you really ought to think for yourself about whether or not there's a need to show some courage right now," Bhudev raged.

"What can I do if I don't have the courage?"

"If you don't have the courage, then you must act as though you do."

The line went dead before Janak could reply.

Janak wiped away the tears from his eyes with the palms of his hands. "As it is, life is disorganized, and man makes it even more disorganized with his own hands." He'd been saying this to himself since earlier. He looked down, now, at his hands.

The bazaar was swarming with even more people today. There wasn't even a tiny opening anywhere on the streets. Police vehicles drove back and forth on the same road, with men filed at the back. One or two planks from the demolished cupboard were still lying around in front of the post office. Even the most withdrawn person could find something to talk about today.

The tip of the tall electric pole reached for the blue of the sky; the small police station at its base was lost in a throng of people.

A sea of voices spread everywhere.

Janak left the flat road, and slowly climbed up the stairs…

The commotion in the bazaar only doubled.

Halfway up the stairs, Janak had to pause for a rest. The crowd went all the way up to the police station, and policemen dressed in black were visible everywhere. Thousands of heads and eyes and faces were staring out from the crowd.

When he completed his speech, Janak would be arrested in front of this very crowd.

He climbed the rest of the stairs and went up to the mic.

The huge crowd suddenly hushed…

Janak reached for the mic, his hands trembling from infirmity and exhiliration, and looked down, took in a long breath, put his mouth to the mic and said, "Today's meeting will now commence."

IN THIS TRANSLATION

"Someone really ought to have written a novel about the old Darjeeling," Janak says at one point in *There's a Carnival Today,* reminiscing about times past. Indra Bahadur Rai is that someone, and *There's a Carnival Today* is the novel he wrote. It is, at its most intimate, the story of Janak, but at its most panoramic it is the story of post-Independence Darjeeling as it falls under the influence of the two political movements that have shaped its fate: the Naxalite or communist labour union movement in the tea plantations, and the formation of a "Gorkha" identity and the rise of the demand for a Gorkhaland state in India.

Previously the homeland of animist and Tibetan Buddhist Lepcha, Limbu and Bhotia communities, "Dorje-lyang"—the land of the thunderbolt—has transformed rapidly, and is still in a churn. It was ruled by Sikkim and Bhutan before Nepal won it in 1789 in an expansionist drive across the Himalaya. In 1816, following the Sugauli Treaty, Nepal ceded it, as well as all of the territory between the Mechi and Teesta Rivers, to the British East India Company. The British East India Company passed it on to Sikkim, but then, upon

George Alymer Lloyd and J.W. Grant's 1829 "discovery" of "Dorjeeling", wrested back the right to develop it as a hill station, complete with road and railway access. They brought in labourers from impoverished Nepal to do so.

From its seat of government in Calcutta, British India came to prize this rugged area at the foothills of Mount Kanchenjunga for its beauty, its cool, misty summers, and its lucrative, rapidly expanding tea plantations. Darjeeling district, which first took shape in 1865, included the Dooars plains as well as the hill town of Kalimpong, east of the Teesta River. This became a major site of recruitment for the Gorkha regiment to the British Indian army, as well as a place to settle retired Gorkhas. It also became an important centre of learning as Christian missionaries set up convent schools and colleges that attracted students from all over India and abroad.

Over time, the diverse community of settlers from Nepal, who built Darjeeling's physical infrastructure, also gave shape to its society. The majority, who used Nepali as a lingua franca and adhered to Hinduism, began to forge a common identity in India, as Gorkhas. The area's other local residents included the indigenous Lepchas, Limbus and Bhotias, and Bengali administrators and tea-plantation owners, as well as Bihari and Marwari traders. Darjeeling had always had a cosmopolitan air due to its British ties. During the Second World War it became a centre of R&R for British, Australian and American soldiers who infused the area with Western culture, including popular films and music, including the Goan Jazz that Indra Bahadur Rai mentions in this novel. This is the social commingling of *There's a Carnival Today*. In 1947, with India's Independence, when Darjeeling joined the state of West Bengal, it was home to some 30,000 people. This is when Janak's story begins.

There's a Carnival Today is Indra Bahadur Rai's only novel. Following its publication in 1964, he went on to write fourteen more books in a variety of genres: short fiction, literary criticism, memoir and drama. *There's a Carnival Today* is part of his early work, and realistic in style. His later oeuvre veers into experimental writing. Together with two prominent modern poets from Nepal, Tilbikram Nembang (better known by the penname Bairagi Kainla) and Ishwor Ballav, Indra Bahadur Rai founded the abstract "Tesro Aayam", or the Third Dimension, school of writing, introducing an abstract modernist aesthetics to Nepali-language literature. Later, Indra Bahadur Rai invented an exuberant and lyrical deconstructionist aesthetic that he called "Leela lekhan", which perhaps best translates as "play-writing". Much of his later work reads as prose poetry, with a non-narrative structure that can be daunting to the lay reader.

By contrast, *There's a Carnival Today* is entirely approachable. As the author mentions in his 1958 introduction, his observations of "life and the land" have informed this novel. So has his erudition: versed in world literature and critical theory, he brings a keen intelligence to the art of storytelling.

Born in the Balasan Tea Estate below Kurseong on February 3, 1927, Indra Bahadur Rai studied at St. Robert's School and St. Joseph's College in Darjeeling, and obtained a Master's in Arts in English Literature from North Bengal University in 1968. By that time he was already teaching. After a stint as an

English teacher at St. Robert's, he went across the border, to Ilam district in Nepal, to work as the principal of the Karfok Vidya Mandir. He returned to Darjeeling after a few years to teach English at Turnbull High School, and then worked at St. Joseph's College as a professor of English. He has lived in Darjeeling and Siliguri all his life.

His involvement in Darjeeling's larger community life eventually took him away from teaching. Those involvements are writ large in *There's a Carnival Today.* In 1956, Indra Bahadur Rai was elected as a commissioner in Darjeeling municipality, and he served as the deputy chairperson of the municipality from 1965 to 1970. In between, along with Ganeshlal Subba, he led a movement that, in 1961, obliged the West Bengal government to allow Nepali to be used as an official language in the hill regions of Darjeeling district.

His was the generation to reimagine a common identity for India's Nepali-origin majority (who are referred to as "Nepali", rather than as the interchangeable "Gorkha", in *There's a Carnival Today).* The foundations for this reimagining had been laid by previous generations of intellectuals going back to before the start of the twentieth century. Biographer Surya Bikram Gyawali, poet Dharanidhar Koirala and editor and publisher Parasmani Pradhan, who were known collectively as Su-Dha-Pa, founded Nepali Sahitya Sammelan (or Nepali Literary Gathering) in the 1920s to promote the world of Nepali language and literature in India.

Indra Bahadur Rai both developed out of and helped to develop this milieu. Today, Nepali is the mother tongue of some three million Indian citizens, and it is in wider use as a lingua franca. Indra Bahadur Rai was part of a heroic collective struggle for the promotion of this language. The Akhil Bharatiya Nepali Bhasa Samiti (or All-India Nepali Language Committee), which he chaired from 1978-79, ultimately succeeded, in 1992, in obtaining official recognition for Nepali and making it one of the twenty-two languages included in the Eighth Schedule of the Indian Constitution.

In 1976, Indra Bahadur Rai became the first Nepali-language writer to win the Sahitya Akademi Award for a book of literary criticism on Nepali literature, *Nepali Sahityaka Adhaarharu.* He also served as a member of the Akademi's Executive Committee, as well as the convener of the Advisory Board for Nepali, from 1978 to 1988.

Despite gaining national recognition by his peers, Indra Bahadur Rai has not been read as widely as he ought to be in India, entirely because the Nepali language is not widely read outside of the Northeast. Some of his stories have been translated into English and a variety of other languages, and are available for those who seek them out. My own hope, of course, is that this translation of *Aaja Ramita Chha* will allow Indian readers to discover one of the finest writers of their country, and to immerse themselves in his thoughtful, loving and occasionally anguished view into Darjeeling.

While working on this translation, I travelled from Toronto to Darjeeling via Kathmandu to meet Indra Bahadur Rai. This was in April 2017. More than fifteen years had passed since he had launched my first novel in Kathmandu in 2001. I had never been to Darjeeling. I was determined to see all the landmarks—or those that still stood—from *There's a Carnival Today.* I also wanted to ask IB-daju, as I had come to call him, for his help in resolving some of the thornier problems of translation, starting with the novel's title.

There's a Carnival Today does not capture the wry tone of *Aaja Ramita Chha,* which deploys the word "ramita"—a combination of a fair, a show, a spectacle or some fun—ironically. It is a well-known truism that much is lost in translation. Translation is, as Gayatri Chakravorty Spivak has pointed out, bound to fail. The task often comes down to choosing which failure to accept and which to refuse. Though the word "carnival" seemed to most echo the tone of the original, I was dissatisfied with its crudeness.

IB-daju gave it his blessing. He also identified a labour unionist whose name, Reggi, I could not place, as well as Milovan Djilas, the author of *The New Class*, which is mentioned in the novel. He confirmed that Janak is quoting the title of a story by the Nepali writer Bhawani Bhikchhu when he remarks, referring to his long-lost servant boy Birman, "Will he ever come back?" IB-daju also explained the terms "sam" and "pacha", which derive from Rai family relations, which were unfamiliar to me: they indicate the father's and mother's lineages respectively.

At ninety, IB-daju was sharp of mind but frail of body. We spent an hour together at his son Despath's home below the Barrick motor stand. He was deeply engaged and gracious while discussing the translation, and visibly pleased to see the first draft. My mother had accompanied me from Kathmandu. Later, one of IB-daju's daughters, Keval, with whom he lives in Siliguri in the wintertime, walked us through Lloyd's Botanical Garden to the jailhouse, so that I could see where the characters in *There's a Carnival Today* had been detained.

Darjeeling has always loomed large in the Nepali-language imagination: it has played a vital role in developing the cultural life of Nepal, where I was born and where I have spent half my life. I found it very helpful and also quite moving to see the Capital—rebuilt after a fire—as well as Chowkbazaar, the police station, the train station, Chowrasta and the Mahakal temple. I knew, of course, that much had changed since 1958, when this novel was written. Only two months prior to my visit, the West Bengal government had done some redistricting, turning Kalimpong into a separate district. Darjeeling district's population was now close to 200,000. New homes and buildings—and traffic—crowded the town, making it difficult, at times, to see its past.

And the communist movement in the tea plantations, as well as the Gorkhaland movement for statehood, had come into much greater articulation since 1958, though they were both going on during the writing of this novel. In 1955, police had fired at Margaret's Hope Tea Garden during a protest by unionized tea plantation workers. Demands for greater recognition—by making Darjeeling a union territory or a separate state, or by joining it to Assam—had also already been put to Jawaharlal Nehru when Indra Bahadur Rai wrote this novel. Darjeeling's Gorkha population already felt alienated from West Bengal's power centre in Calcutta at that time.

There's a Carnival Today reflects both of these movements, and intimates the future arc that Darjeeling was to follow. West Bengal was led by a communist government till 2011; and Naxalbari, only sixty-five kilometres down the way from Darjeeling, inspired a Maoist uprising that continues through large tracts of rural India today. In Darjeeling in particular, the communist movement's impacts were also felt in the early call for a "Gorkhasthan".

The movement for statehood simmered till the 1980s, with the formation of the Pranta Parishad, who put forward its demand to Indira Gandhi. 1981 saw police firing in Darjeeling's Chowkbazaar, followed by a long period of conflict. The Gorkha National Liberation Front set up in 1986 under the leadership of Subhash Ghising, and through the violence that claimed more than 1,200 lives over the years, it kept up the demand for statehood till the formation of the Darjeeling Gorkha Hill Council in 1988. Subhash Ghising went on to govern over the Darjeeling Gorkha Hill Council, where, in his final years, began to look past the common Gorkha identity in favour of the diverse national identities that comprise it.

The call for a Gorkhaland state did not, however, abate. It was renewed by the Gorkha Janamukti Morcha, formed by Bimal Gurung in 2007. A year later, the Darjeeling Gorkha Hill Council was replaced by the Gorkhaland Territorial Administration, invested with greater power. The demand for statehood continues today, and clashes erupt from time to time, as it did a few months after my visit, when, in mid-2017, the government of West Bengal made the Bengali language compulsory in Darjeeling's schools. The order was almost immediately rescinded, but it sparked outrage.

In between these eruptions, Darjeeling has been the site of low-lying conflict and ill governance. What had once been the vibrant centre of the Nepali-speaking world had diminished into a quiescent backwater by the time I visited. As an outsider I held no views about Darjeeling's politics. Yet in casual conversations and passing comments I could feel the regrets, frustrations and longings of those for whom it is home.

None of these contemporary political events come directly into *There's a Carnival Today*, although knowing about them does add depth to its reading. They also explain some of the racial tensions in the novel, particularly the use of pejorative terms such as "Kainya", for Bihari and Marwari traders and "Madhise" for those from the plains, or the Madhes, who should properly be called Madhesi. (A subtle but important distinction.) Indra Bahadur Rai signals these chauvinisms throughout the novel, though, because of his use of the third-person limited point of view, it can seem that he is also replicating them. To offer clarity to the reader, in my translation I use the pejorative only when a characters uses it, and otherwise opt for neutral terms such as "Marwari trader" and "Madhesi". This is a liberty that I've taken, but one that I believe is true to the author's intention to signal, but not to replicate, chauvinism.

A second issue, also related to identity, concerns the terms "jaat", which recurs throughout the novel. Indra Bahadur Rai uses the term "jaat", or caste, adopting a liberal, specifically Darjeeling usage, to refer to all kinds of communities, including those that in more orthodox Nepal would be classified as indigenous nationalities or ethnic groups or other language- or region-based communities. In his usage, Marwaris are a caste, as are Bengalis and Rais and Newars. By contrast, he uses "jaati", to refer to a peoples, such as the Nepali peoples. I have translated "jaat" interchangeably as "caste" and "caste and kind" to signal this specifically Darjeeling usage.

In addition, for the sake of clarity, I have taken liberty

with the novel's tense changes. As is the case in much Nepali fiction, the original text of *There's a Carnival Today* switches from the past to the present with an inconsistency that can confuse the English reader. I have retained the present tense in passages offering the thoughts and observations of the novel's characters, but have otherwise placed the story in the past tense. I believe this makes for a more enjoyable experience for the reader.

For the reader's enjoyment is, in the end, my goal. I enjoyed reading this novel in its original, and I've enjoyed translating it into English. It is a novel that can be read without any background in Darjeeling at all. It is not, after all, a novel about today's Darjeeling. It is a novel about the old Darjeeling, the one that its protagonist wishes someone would write. How fortunate for us all that Indra Bahadur Rai stepped up to do so.

Toronto MANJUSHREE THAPA

7 September 2017

ACKNOWLEDGEMENTS

Thank you to IB-daju, Indra Bahadur Rai, for trusting me to translate this novel. I have loved *Aaja Ramita Chha* from before the publication of my first novel, which IB-daju launched in Kathmandu in 2001. It is my great good fortune to now translate his work so that a global readership might come to love it too.

Thank you to Ravi Singh for his abiding interest in stories from the Nepali-language world. I owe much to him for all the nurturing he has done for my writing. An especial thank you to Anurag Basnet, himself a translator, for bringing his intimate knowledge of his hometown, Darjeeling, into the editing of this translation. The rare combination of his meticulousness as an editor and poetic flair as a translator made our collaboration truly rewarding. I am also grateful to writer, editor and publisher Basanta Thapa for helping to seek out the meanings of several particularly obscure terms and turns of phrase. He took the trouble to consult Man Bahadur Mukhiya, an eminent playwright of Darjeeling origin, to do so. I could not have completed this translation without his help. A very heartfelt thank you also to Gorakh Regmi for facilitating so much during the entire process of this translation: his help has been invaluable to me.

Thank you to the Banff International Literary Translation Centre for the BILTC 2016 residency, where I completed the first draft of this translation. I learned much from fellow translators there, and was particularly glad for Hugh Hazelton and Katie Silver's guidance, and for Devyani Saltzman's large-hearted vision of the arts in Canada.

I am also grateful to PEN America for a PEN/Heim Translation Grant in 2017. The support of PEN America has made this translation possible.

I would like to acknowledge many, many individuals who directly and indirectly helped this translation, starting with the poet Manjul for starting me down the path of translation more than fifteen years ago in Kathmandu, when we were all young and full of poetry. A gift from him—Parasmani Pradhan's dictionary, *Thulo Nepali-Nepali-Angreji Kosh*—proved invaluable as I worked on this translation. Mark Turin also shared digitized copies of Nepali dictionaries with me, which proved eminently practical in my itinerant life. Thomas J Mathew, himself in the middle of a work of translation, helped me understand the tense changes in Indra Bahadur Rai's original text as an imprint of the oral tradition. Thank you for that. Thank you to Dewan Rai for explaining Rai family terms to me. And a very heartfelt thank you to Sara Shneiderman for helping me think through the translation of the term "jaat", or caste, which Indra Bahadur Rai deploys with a usage that is specific to Darjeeling. I found her paper, "Reframing Ethnicity: Academic Tropes, Recognition beyond Politics, and Ritualized Action between Nepal and India", particularly helpful. I also found

Pratyoush Onta's paper "Creating a Brave Nepali Nation in British India: The Rhetoric of *Jati* Improvement, Rediscovery of Bhanubhakta and the Writing of *Bir* History" to be clarifying on the term "jaati", or peoples.

An important part of a translator's work is to understand the larger context out of which a text arises. Writer Peter J Karthak, of Darjeeling origin, kindly recommended Rajnarayan Pradhan's writing on Darjeeling's literary world; and Pradhan's *Kehi Kriti, Kehi Smriti* and *Darjeeling ka Katha ra Kathakar* proved helpful to understanding the literary community surrounding Indra Bahadur Rai. Sara Shneiderman again helped me grasp the nuances of the political upheavals in Darjeeling during Indra Bahadur Rai's life and times. I learned much from a number of texts that she recommended, including her and Townsend Middleton's introduction in their forthcoming book, *Reconsidering Darjeeling: Histories, Politics, Environments,* as well as these academic papers: "Anxious Belongings: Anxiety and the Politics of Belonging in Subnationalist Darjeeling", by Townsend Middleton; "The Land in Gorkhaland: On the Edges of Belonging in Darjeeling, India", by Sarah Besky; "India's Stabilizing Segment States", by Bethany Lacina; and "Challenging the State by Reproducing its Principles: The Demand for 'Gorkhaland' between Regional Autonomy and the National Belonging", by Miriam Wenner; and "Class Struggle, the Maoists and the Indigenous Question in Nepal and India" by Feyzi Ismail and Alpa Shah. At the Oxford and Shyam Brothers bookstores in Darjeeling, I found *Shree Indra Bahadur Rai: Abhinandan Grantha,* edited by Dr Gokul Sinha and Chandra Sinha, as well as Basant B Lama's *The Story of Darjeeling*, both very informative. I also learned from writings on the Internet, in particular "A Short History of Gorkhaland", by RAIOT and the Sahitya Akademi's 2004 introduction, "Meet the Author: Indra Bahadur Rai". In addition, I was glad to reread Prem Poddar and Anmole Prasad's *Gorkhas Imagined: Indra Bahadur Rai in Translation* as I worked on my own translation.

Many others offered me help during my visit to Darjeeling. I am very grateful to Birendra Basnet for his help in getting me there, and to Sujeev Shakya, Bikash Rauniyar, Sarala Khaling and Surya Rai for their advice. Thank you also to my mother Rita Thapa for accompanying me to Darjeeling, replicating a trip she made with her mother forty years before, and making our days there particularly memorable.

I owe a final thank you, always, to my friends and family. I am very fortunate to have a supportive community around me. It truly sustains me.

MANJUSHREE THAPA